Return To Eden
by
Barbara Michel

This is a work of fiction. Locations are real places, but all characters have been created from the author's imagination. Names of characters or any resemblance to real persons, living or dead, is purely coincidental.

Copyright© 1995
BARBARA MICHEL

Son-Rise Publications
143 Greenfield Road
New Wilmington, PA 16142
1-800-358-0777
ISBN 0-936369-65-5
Printed in the USA

Introduction

In the EDEN series, the Amish and Mennonite people are portrayed as they believe, peaceful, moral, ethical, compassionate, and Biblically sound followers of Jesus Christ who have remained separate from what they classify worldliness. Their strict discipline has aroused curiosity; and the uniqueness and charm of their life-style has kindled considerable appeal. The EDEN series captures this quaintness and allure, combines it with humor and realistic action and offers inspiration to the reader.

This book is dedicated to the memory of my daughter Elizabeth Yvonne Michel who went to glory at the age of 13, and to my husband Gerald who is my research, my travel companion and my Barnabas, my encourager.

Thanks to my Mennonite cousins, Eli and Lizzie Wenger and Ella Wenger, for their hospitality, for answering numerous questions and translating English phrases into Pennsylvania Dutch. I greatly appreciate their escorting me to Mennonite and Amish places, among them a mill where Amish grind their grain, and Groffdale Mennonite-Amish school. Thanks to the many Mennonite and Amish students who wrote to me afterwards.

Thanks to Mr. and Mrs. James Kaikis, and to Florence Biros of Son-Rise, who made possible the publishing of this book.

My appreciation goes to Patricia Dunn for the cover design used in this book.

My appreciation also is extended to Donna Jackson for the typesetting and layout of this book.

Title Page

Chapter 1	page 7
Chapter 2	page 21
Chapter 3	page 31
Chapter 4	page 41
Chapter 5	page 49
Chapter 6	page 57
Chapter 7	page 67
Chapter 8	page 79
Chapter 9	page 93
Chapter 10	page 105
Chapter 11	page 119
Chapter 12	page 131
Chapter 13	page 143
Chapter 14	page 155
Chapter 15	page 167
Chapter 16	page 177
Chapter 17	page 187
Chapter 18	page 199
Chapter 19	page 211
Chapter 20	page 223

1

Lancaster County, Pennsylvania

The August sun beat relentlessly on the gray carriage roof as Elizabeth Beiler Stoltzfus turned Xerxes into the dirt lane that led to her parents' farm. Puffs of dust drifted upward from the horse's clipping hooves. The breeze produced by the moving vehicle did little to relieve Elizabeth's discomfort. Swiping a hand across her moist brow, she sighed. Even the leaves of the majestic oak at the corner of the cornfield seemed to droop.

Oh, Elam, she thought, blinking to erase the image of his smiling face. He would be going back to Mercer County soon. Seeing him again after eight years had been wonderful, but his three-week visit to Lancaster County had invaded her loneliness, created joyous visions, and encouraged foolish dreams.

The sooner he leaves, the better. The thought made her flinch. She must get Elam Miller out of her mind. "For Moses' sake," she whispered, wondering if her attraction to another man desecrated the memory of her late husband.

Straightening her lavender skirt, she glanced into the basket on the back seat. Six-month-old Priscilla slept, although the heat made her fretful. Moisture caused the golden curls that formed a halo around the baby's sweet face to glisten.

Xerxes shook his mane and blew as he stopped at Beiler's front gate. Elizabeth slid the carriage door open, lifted the basket gently, not to waken Priscilla, and stepped from the conveyance. Picturing the container of lemonade her mother usually kept in the refrigerator, she sighed with anticipation.

Eli, her twenty-year-old brother, bolted from the house, letting the screen door slam. Pausing for a second on the top step, he crunched his straw hat onto his tousled blond hair and raced down the path toward her. "John fell. I'll have to hitch up our buggy, unless I borrow yours." He spoke in Pennsylvania Dutch, a German dialect always spoken in Amish homes.

"Take it." A tremor sent a chill through her as she pictured her blond, blue-eyed three-year-old brother. "Is he hurt badly?"

"I don't know." Eli rushed past her and climbed into the driver's seat.

Esther, their mother, hurried from the house, the limp form of the little boy cradled in her arms. Her hazel eyes brimmed with tears of concern. Apparently she'd been baking, for a smudge of flour on her skirt contrasted sharply with the dark-blue material.

"Mama, is he . . ." Gripping the handle of her baby's basket, she swallowed.

"He's unconscious. Eli will drive me to the doctor's. From there. . .I don't know."

Elizabeth figured that would be the quickest way to get her brother help. By the time they got to the phone shack, they might as well go on to the doctor's. She set her basket by the gate to help her mother into the carriage. Jedidiah, Beiler's black dog, stood as though guarding the baby, anxiety shimmering in his eyes. Elizabeth's lower lip caught between her even teeth, as she watched the carriage rumble down the lane. The conveyance disappeared around a bend, but she stood transfixed until she could no longer hear the metal wheels on the stones or the horse's hoofbeats. Wakened by the hubbub, Priscilla began to whimper. Thankful she'd decided to visit, Elizabeth picked up the basket, shooshed the baby, and headed for the house.

"*Vea-gaits* (hello), Elizabeth."

Sarah, her eighteen-year-old sister, opened the screen and stepped aside, concern furrowing her smooth brow. Sarah's tall, slender form was similar to Elizabeth's, although her eyes were light-blue and her hair blond, differing greatly from Elizabeth's brown eyes and reddish-chestnut hair. Both young women had a pretty oval face.

Twelve-year-old Ruth, their plump, rosy cheeked sister, stood in the center of the kitchen, her brown eyes brimming with tears, her expression unusually solemn. Flour whitened her clasped hands. Five-year-old Reuben sat in a wooden rocker in the corner, nursing his straw hat and staring at the floor.

Helplessness settled over Elizabeth, but she groped for the faith that had always sustained her. "Little John is going to be fine." She prayed her words sounded more convincing than they felt. Time would pass more quickly if they kept busy. "Wash your hands, Ruth, and take care of Priscilla." Setting the basket on the bench by the door, she lifted the baby. "Reuben, Jedidiah needs to be brushed."

Silently, Ruth and Reuben obeyed.

Elizabeth moved across the beige-and-white vinyl, skirted the large oak table, and motioned Sarah aside. "What happened?"

"Mama was baking bread while Ruth rolled out noodles. I'd turned to get the bread pans from the cabinet. Little John pushed a kitchen chair to the counter to watch Mama. Instead of standing there as before, he climbed to the counter and slipped on a smudge of shortening. Before Mama could get her hands out of the bread dough to grab him, he toppled to the floor." She chewed her lower lip and wrung her hands. "He struck his head."

"We must pray that he'll be all right."

Sarah opened her mouth to speak, but her voice caught. Nodding, she headed for the pan of bread dough. "I must finish the baking."

Elizabeth grappled in a drawer for a knife. "I'll cut the noodles." Keeping her siblings occupied seemed easy, but she was failing to hold her own worry at bay.

Sighing, Sarah gave the bread dough a punch.

The Lord brought Isaiah 26:3 to Elizabeth's mind, and she felt His reassurance. "Thou wilt keep him in perfect peace, whose mind is stayed on thee: because he trusteth in thee."

"*Ja.*" Sarah looked at her older sister.

Elizabeth smiled. "We'll trust God with little John."

Three hours later, Xerxes trotted up Beiler's lane. Before the carriage stopped, Elizabeth was at the front gate. Relief filled her when she saw little John sitting on her mother's knee. He seemed stunned, but blinked his blue eyes and grinned. Never had a set of dimples brought such joy.

Esther stepped to the ground with her son in her arms. "He has a slight concussion, so we'll have to watch him closely, but he's going to be fine."

"*Danka Got.*" Cradling Priscilla, Elizabeth straightened the baby's pink skirt and strolled to the apple tree. The searing August sun seemed to smother the Beiler farm. Swiping at the excess moisture on her forehead, she sat on a bench that her brother had placed in the shade, spread the pink baby blanket on the grass by her feet, and placed her daughter on it.

Priscilla kicked and cooed, bringing a smile to Elizabeth's lips. Sighing, she straightened her skirt, then, hoping for a slight breeze to caress her neck, she untied the straps of her prayer cap. Her eyes slowly traveled over the farm where she'd grown up. Heat waves radiated from the rooftops of the outbuildings. The leaves of the corn hung lower than usual — as though the stalks were about to pant. Even the rich soil seemed to look toward heaven as though in search of moisture. The ducks floated quietly in the small pond, and not a cackle issued from the hen house.

Jedidiah, usually frisky and coaxing someone to play, meandered to the shade. Flopping to the grass to the right of the bench, he stretched out and sighed. He swished his tail twice, then blinked and lowered his head to his paws.

Elizabeth reached to pet him. "It's too hot for you, too, isn't it Jed?"

He yawned, but didn't bother to glance up.

Elizabeth's eyes traveled to the silo, and her heart lurched as she focused on the top, the last place she'd seen her husband alive.

"It's been almost a year since your papa fell," she said to Priscilla. Besides her memories, the baby's blond ringlets and deep-blue eyes were all she had left of Moses.

A gray buggy, drawn by Jacob Zook's carriage horse, rumbled up the lane. The animal stopped by the gate, blew and pranced. Elizabeth drew a quick little breath when the driver stepped to the ground. *Elam!* ricochetted through her brain and lodged in her heart. The man had been visiting his sister Emma, who was now Jacob Zook's wife.

Spotting Elizabeth, Elam headed in her direction. He carried his six-foot-one frame straight and his broad shoulders squared as though he were impervious to the heat. His golden-brown eyes sparkled over his light-brown beard.

Warmth spread through Elizabeth as she returned his smile. *It's too soon*, she thought, fighting her rekindled attraction to him.

"*Vea-gaits.*" Pausing a few feet from the end of the bench, Elam removed his straw hat. His black broadfalls had slight extensions at the sides where they buttoned to his blue shirt, unlike the Amishmen in Lancaster County who wore suspenders.

"*Vea-gaits*, Elam." She glanced at the three buttons on his shirt front. All her life she'd wondered why men were permitted to use buttons to close some of their garments while women had to use straight pins. *Will the ease and comfort of buttons ever be permitted for Amish ladies?* she wondered. Men even had the luxury of hooks and eyes on their Sunday frock coats.

Elam stood, his fingers playing a rhythm on his hat brim.

"Papa's at the barn with Eli." She lowered her gaze to the grass by his feet.

"*Ja, vell*, I didn't *cume* to see Isaac."

"Oh." She battled the blush she knew stained her cheeks. She felt at twenty-five she was too old to blush over a gentleman's attention.

He cleared his throat. "May I join you?"

Elizabeth slid over to make room for him. He took a seat, and as he placed his hat between them, his fingers brushed hers. The nerves in her arm tingled and a familiar warmth encompassed her. She jerked her hand back, reprimanding herself for being affected by his nearness.

He seemed puzzled. "*Es spied mich* (I'm sorry)." He looked pensive. "Emma would like you to *cume* to her place for supper."

"I'd love to." She felt foolish. Elam's sister had been her close friend for years. Why had she assumed the man had come to call on her? Endeavoring to fight her attraction, she thought about Elam's deceased wife and his two little boys. "It must have been difficult to leave your sons in Mercer County when you came to visit your sister."

"*Ja.* Emma would've liked to have seen the boys."

"Why didn't you bring them?"

"Emma has quite a brood of her own. Two more probably wouldn't make much difference, but Leah felt it would be better if I left them at home," he said, referring to his youngest sister. "Leah's been taking care of them since Mary died."

The sound of his wife's name jolted Elizabeth. *I'm being silly*, she thought, vowing to govern her effusive emotions and act as her Amish family expected her to. *What do they expect?* She pondered how her younger sisters, Sarah and Ruth, seemed to create situations that placed her in Elam's presence. Even Eli prompted situations that threw the two of them together.

She envisioned Moses' smiling face and prayed to retain a clear memory of him. Since Amish don't believe in taking photographs, all she had was the picture of him in her mind. Would it fade if she permitted her heart to embrace another man? The fear of it made her inch farther from Elam. To her distress, her heart reached toward him, ignoring the space she'd created.

Priscilla whimpered. Smiling, Elam bent to scoop her into his arms. "What's the matter, Priscilla?" he asked softly. "You getting lonely 'way down there on your blanket?"

The baby seized Elam's beard with both hands and cooed. He chuckled. The sound of it vibrated cords deep within Elizabeth. "You have a knack with babies."

"*Ja, vell*, having two sons gave me a lot of practice."

"Especially having to raise them alone."

"The responsibility was mine, but Leah and mother helped me a lot." His brow furrowed. "That is until last year when my father took ill and mother had a stroke."

"*Danka Got* your older brother takes most of the responsibility of the farm."

"*Ja.* Jonathan does most of the chores, but with my house on the property, it's convenient for me to help after I get home from work." A faraway look crept into his eyes. "If only Samuel would stay home and do his share," he said, referring to his twenty-year-old brother. He rocked Priscilla in his muscular arms, making her gurgle happily. "Lately, Jonathan has been tiring more easily, so he doesn't do as much as he used to."

Elizabeth wondered why, since the man was barely thirty. "Do you intend to keep your job with the construction company?"

"*Ja.*"

Elizabeth watched him, her smile generous. "Since the Bishop of your district is more strict than the ones here, I'm surprised he allows you to work for a non-Amishman ."

"I'm thankful for the job, for there were hospital bills from my parents' illnesses that my brother couldn't have paid."

"The community would've helped."

He grinned. "*Ja*, but I preferred to do what I could."

As Elam cuddled baby Priscilla, he watched Elizabeth out of the corner of his eye. He was glad he'd made the trip to visit his sister. He hadn't seen Elizabeth for several years. She was even more lovely than he'd remembered. A breeze blew back the corner of her loosened prayer cap, giving him a glimpse of her chestnut-colored hair and invoking the stirring memory of the first time he'd become astoundingly aware of her. Had eight years passed so quickly?

He'd been eighteen the Saturday he'd accompanied his father to visit Isaac Beiler. Esther had been in the yard helping her daughters wash their hair. Ruth, then a four-year-old, had been sitting on the grass, pulling a daisy apart. Sarah, who was ten, was flipping her long blond hair to aid its drying. Elizabeth, seventeen, had been sitting on a stump. As Esther combed Elizabeth's waist-length tresses, the sun had caressed the long rich-brown waves, bringing out gold and deep-red highlights.

"Whoa," Jonah, Elam's father, had said, pulling on the reins to stop the carriage near the farmhouse gate. "*Vea-gaits*, Esther," he called. "Is Isaac about?"

She smiled. "*Vea-gaits*. He's in the barn."

Jonah clucked to the horse and the carriage rumbled toward the outbuildings. Elizabeth had turned and smiled, her velvety-brown eyes sparkling with gold flecks. Elam's heart had lurched, then begun to pound. He figured he would ask for permission to call on her. After all, they'd been friends in school.

Before a deep relationship could develop, Elam's family had moved to Mercer County, leaving behind Elizabeth and what they might have shared. A year later, he'd met Mary and . . .

A familiar warm feeling crept across the leg of Elam's broadfalls, shocking him from his reverie. Sweeping the baby from his lap, he peered at the wet spot.

"*Ach*!" Jumping up, Elizabeth took Priscilla. "*Es spied mich* (I'm sorry)!"

"Don't worry." Elam stood to shake the dampened material that clung to his leg and grinned. "This isn't the first time I've been initiated."

A spontaneous giggle bubbled from Elizabeth. She covered

her mouth with her fingers as though to camouflage her amusement, but laughter danced in her velvety-brown eyes. "I'll take her inside to change her."

"I'll wait here for you." Watching her retreat, Elam held his smile. He'd planned to spend a few days with Emma, but three weeks had passed. Once he'd renewed his friendship with Elizabeth, it had been easy for Emma to convince him to stay longer. He missed his sons, though, and planned to leave soon so he could spend the last few days of his vacation with them.

Pinching his lower lip between his thumb and forefinger, he thought about Mary. *She's been gone for over two years.* Leah was a wonderful aunt to his sons, but Daniel and Jesse Mark needed a mother. He hadn't considered marriage until he'd glimpsed Elizabeth again. The old feeling had instantly gripped his heart, then had mushroomed until he could think of nothing but this lovely woman. So far, he'd been unable even to hold her hand. She acted evasive. *Ferwass* (Why)? Did she still love Moses? Would she ever be able to love again?

"I must give her time," he murmured. His heart raced as he thought about taking her in his arms. Would he ever get the chance? *Is time my friend or my enemy?*

Elizabeth swept into the kitchen.

Ruth stood by the sink, munching a bite of cookie. The twelve-year-old's brown eyes sparkled with mischief and her cheeks, nearly as pink as her dress, dimpled. "What'd Elam want?"

"Emma sent him over to invite me for supper."

"*Ja?* And will Elam be there?"

Elizabeth headed for the downstairs bedroom with the squirming baby. "*Ja.* He's staying at his sister's home, Ruth."

The younger girl rolled her eyes. "That's handy, *ja?*"

Sarah came from the living room. Her light-blue dress matched her eyes. She peered at Priscilla. "She need changed?"

"*Ja.*" Elizabeth sighed. "She wet on Elam."

Ruth giggled.

Esther poked a graying strand of hair back under her prayer cap and swiped a hand across her apron as she came from the *granddawdy* house. "Elizabeth, I heard you say you're going to Emma Zook's for supper. Will Elam drive you home afterwards or will you be returning here?"

"Vell . . . I'll be driving home from here, Mama, so Elam will have to pick me up at my place."

Ruth giggled. "He'll want to drive her home so he can steal a kiss."

Elizabeth peered at her youngest sister. "Ruth, stop being silly."

"*Ja?* If you don't want a kiss, why's your face red?"

Turning away, Elizabeth moved to a window. Elam strolled back-and-forth in the shade of the apple tree. Jedidiah didn't move, but his eyes rolled as they followed the man. Elam's straw hat still lay on the bench. She studied his handsome features, noted his furrowed brow, and wondered what was troubling him. Envisioning the kiss Ruth had mentioned, she felt her cheeks grow warmer. *I can't let that happen*, she thought. If he didn't care deeply for her, she would be hurt. If he did, he probably would want her to return to Mercer County with him. *I can't leave my family!*

Tearing her eyes from Elam, she stared at the chipping paint on the windowsill, remembering that Eli had been asked to paint it. He would, if he gave up on *Rumspringa* (running around years), but Amish boys must be permitted a taste of freedom before they are asked to settle down. Elizabeth's thoughts shifted to Moses. She'd visited his grave twice a week, even through the winter. Leaving the area would be like deserting him. She shook her head. "I can't!"

After Elam left, Elizabeth returned to her home. Why did it seem so difficult to choose between wearing her light-blue dress or her green one? Would Elam even notice? Chiding herself for making a fuss over such a triviality, she donned the light-blue dress and put a matching one on Priscilla.

Elizabeth peered at Jacob John and Emma Zook's frame

house as Elam stopped the buggy near the front gate. Emma stepped onto the porch and waved a plump arm. Three children ranging from four years of age to an eighteen-month-old toddler bounced around her like healthy chicks. Two boys, about five and six years old, romped in the yard with a golden retriever. Eight-year-old twin girls peered out through the screen door.

Elam chuckled. "They're going to have another one shortly after Christmas."

"They have a lovely family," Elizabeth said, but wondered what it would be like to handle such a brood. As young as Emma and Jacob were, and the Amish not believing in birth control, they would undoubtedly have a very large family.

Elizabeth grasped the box of freshly-baked cookies she'd brought. Clutching Priscilla, she climbed from the carriage and headed up the path.

"I'll take the carriage to the shed," Elam said, clucking to the horse.

Emma's smile brightened her round face, and gold flecks sparkled in her hazel eyes. "I'm so glad you could *cume* on such a short notice, Elizabeth."

"*Danka dich* for inviting me."

Emma chuckled. "It was Elam's idea, but I'm glad. It's been too long since you've visited us."

Elizabeth proffered the cookies.

"May I have one, Mama?" the four-year-old asked.

"It's close to supper time, Anna May." The little girl looked disappointed, apparently softening her mother. "But, you may each have a sample." Retrieving one cookie, Emma broke it into pieces and handed the closest children a portion. Within seconds, the two little boys were on the porch, peering at their mother with expectancy. She divided another treat, then turned to offer the twins another as they joined the crowd on the porch. Emma winked at Elizabeth. "I remember Mama slipping me treats." Her grin broadened. "It's a pleasant memory." She waved a hand. "*Cume onn* in and visit while I finish preparing supper."

"I'll help."

Emma bounced across the kitchen, her chuckle infectious. The plain white walls made the room seem cool, and the blue in the vinyl floor covering seemed to emanate friendliness. She pulled a large cardboard box from the corner. "This has a quilt in the bottom of it and will serve as a safe place for Priscilla."

Emma peeled potatoes while Elizabeth helped the twins set the table. She had to watch her every step, for the youngest children played on the floor like a litter of frolicking puppies.

Emma glanced over her shoulder. "Elam's a good man."

Quirking one brow, Elizabeth peered at her friend.

"You agree, *ja*?" Yellow flecks shimmered in Emma's green-brown eyes and her rounded cheeks were rosy.

"I've never doubted Elam's worth, Emma. We were friends before your family moved away."

"*Ja, vell*, I'm not talking about a cordial relationship." Her grin broadened. "You know that, *ja*?"

Elizabeth's cheeks burned as she strode to the round, maple table to place silverware at each place. "Elam will probably leave for Mercer County soon."

"He needs a woman! And his boys need a mama." Emma chuckled. "You're my choice."

"Elam's doing very well, and Leah is taking excellent care of his sons."

"*Ach*! Elam's a lost puppy, and according to Leah's letters, she's letting those *kinder* get away with too much. When they get older, they'll be difficult to control. They need a mama like you."

Elizabeth laughed. "You and Ruth must have been fashioned from the same mold."

"*Ja, vell*..." Emma dumped a measure of flour into a bowl for biscuits. "Your little sister is a smart girl." She tossed in a pinch of salt and measured the baking powder.
"Sarah agrees with me, too!"

Elizabeth's lips parted. "You've spoken to them concerning Elam and me?"

She shrugged. "*Ja.* Everyone thinks you two would make each other happy."

Happy? Elizabeth hadn't questioned that, but happiness wasn't the only emotion at stake.

The screen door banged as Dan and Andy chased the retriever through the kitchen. The twins, Malinda and Amanda, who were trying to fill water glasses, shrieked.

Anna chased three-year-old Elmer around a kitchen chair, then seized the back of his shirt. He fell, bumped his chin on the floor and began to wail. Baby Katy made a puddle on the vinyl and splashed through it. The fracas upset Priscilla, and her cry joined the fray.

Emma turned to survey the kitchen. Chuckling, she lovingly rested her hands on her pregnant abdomen and rolled her eyes.

Things were under control by the time the two men washed and came in for supper. Jacob John, apparently assuming his action wouldn't be perceived, gave Emma a pat on her backside.

She turned to eye him, a grin illuminating her face and deepening her rosy glow. "Take your place, husband," she said around a chuckle.

Sweeping the smallest two of the children into his arms, he headed for the table.

"Me, too, Papa," Anna cried, clutching a leg of his broadfalls.

He grinned. "*Ja, vell*, you'll get your turn."

Elizabeth weighed Elam's reaction. He'd watched with amusement, apparently not missing the adoring swat Jacob John had delivered as he passed his wife. When the man collected his squirming brood, Elam smiled. After watching the joyous family find their seats around the table, his lustrous eyes moved to meet Elizabeth's. Her heart lurched. She hoped her gasp had been undetectable. Her pulse quickened and warmth spreading upward threatened to consume her. What was Elam thinking? What could she do to discourage his growing interest? Did she want to? Taking her place at the table, she discovered that Emma had placed her next to Elam.

As the meal progressed, Elizabeth's dismay grew. Every

time she moved, her elbow touched Elam. When he passed a platter or bowl of food, his fingers invariably caressed hers, and his eyes sparkled, making her heart flutter.

This is ridiculous! She was a widow with a baby, not a silly schoolgirl.

The twins sat across from Elizabeth, their hazel eyes brimming with questions as they looked from her to Elam.

Priscilla whimpered. Elam was sitting closest to the box where the baby had been sleeping. Getting up, he lifted the little girl, then took his seat, propping her up with his left arm.

"I can hold her," Elizabeth said.

Elam chuckled. "So can I, and she seems happy about it."

Little Elmer's brown eyes grew large. "Uncle Elam, are you gonna be Prissy-cilla's papa?"

Elizabeth felt her cheeks grow hot as everyone's eyes focused on her.

2

Elam's chuckle created warmth within Elizabeth. Hoping Emma wouldn't interpret her feelings, she lowered her eyes to her skirt. Forcing her effusive heart into submission, she smiled and faced Emma's littlest boy. "Elmer, I think it's too soon for me to think about getting Priscilla a new papa."

The twin girls bounced on their chairs as though they were both connected to the same string. Then Malinda looked at Priscilla, her hazel eyes sparkling.

Amanda studied Elam. "Is it too soon, Uncle Elam?"

"*Vell* . . ." Elam's light-brown beard camouflaged the deepening hue on his cheeks, but didn't completely hide it. Clearing his throat, he peered at the baby in his arms. "What do you think, Priscilla?"

Seizing a handful of his beard, she tugged and blew a bubble.

Emma laughed. "She agrees with us!"

Elizabeth's heart fluttered. Taking a deep breath, she pushed her chair away from the table and stood. "I'll serve dessert." Since she and Emma had been friends for a long time, she felt at home in this kitchen. Holding a smile, she hurried to open the cupboard and began counting small plates.

"Will you be cutting your last crop of hay soon, Jacob?" Elam asked.

"*Ja*. Next week."

Bless you Elam, Elizabeth thought, relieved that he'd changed the topic.

Amanda joined Elizabeth at the counter. Taking the first two plates of pie, she served her father and Elam. Malinda hovered, waiting for Elizabeth to slice two more pieces.

"*Ach!*" Emma got up and headed for the downstairs bedroom. "You received a letter from Leah, Elam. I nearly forgot."

Elizabeth pictured Jacob and Emma's younger sister. Leah's turquoise eyes sparkled from a pretty, round face. Her honey-colored hair seemed kissed with gold, although no one saw much of it, except when she shampooed and dried it in the sun. The remembrance of the girl's soft bubbly laughter echoed through Elizabeth's recall. *Leah would be eighteen*, she thought, pondering how the girl could have changed over the past eight years since the family had left the Lancaster area.

Elam smiled as he considered hearing from home, but when his older sister returned and proffered the envelope, his heart beat quickened. He'd been away for three weeks. Could something have happened to one of his boys? Had his mother had another seizure or stroke?

Surrendering Priscilla to Emma, he ripped open the envelope, struggled to unfold the paper, and read hungrily.

"Dear Elam,

The boys are doing fine, although they miss you. Daniel's anxious for school to start. We hope you're home to drive him his first day. Jesse Mark says he's going to school, too. I told him he had to wait two or three years, but he doesn't agree.

It's been so warm. When Cousin Joas stopped by, he made us laugh when he said that he gets so hot his artificial leg perspires.

The corn is doing well, but we need rain. Daniel has sold nearly all of his sweet corn and tomatoes. He did a good job for his first effort in growing a crop to sell. He says he's glad to make his papa happy.

Mama's doing fine, as long as she takes her medication, although she seems to be tiring more easily. Keeping up with the regular housework is difficult for me with the boys underfoot. Jonathan brought home seven bushels of peaches. I got them canned, but Mama helped with the peeling.

Jonathan had pain in his chest again. He went to the doctor and discovered a slight problem. At least that's how he describes it. He takes medication, but hasn't slowed down. I think the work is too much for him to handle alone.

I promised Jesse Mark I'd take him for a walk. He's strongly reminding me, so I'll close for now.

*Love,
Leah*

PS When are you coming home? Is there some interest other than our sister and her family keeping you in Bird-in-Hand?"

"Is all well with your family, Elam?" Elizabeth set her pie at her place and took her seat.

"*Ja.* Just about." Considering the reason he'd delayed his departure, he lifted his eyes, met Elizabeth's quizzical gaze, and his heart lurched. Smiling, he proffered the letter, then picked up his fork and attacked his slice of fresh peach pie.

After reading Leah's letter, Elizabeth thought about Jonathan. If he was taking medication, was his heart trouble more serious than he was letting on? In the past, he'd usually made light of his ills. Folding the letter, she placed it on the table. Elam would probably be returning to Mercer County soon. A twinge wriggled on her insides, then her heart struggled to reach him, making it impossible to ignore her feelings.

After supper, Jacob John and Elam went to the barn to check on a sick calf. Elizabeth and Emma cleaned up the kitchen.

"It's time to start bathing this brood," Emma said with a sigh. "*Danka Got* the Bishop permits bathrooms in our district."

"Indoor facilities weren't permitted when we were kids."

"*Ach, ja!*" Emma grunted as she swooped to grasp Katy. "The Bishops in Mercer County don't permit Amish to have indoor bathrooms." She giggled. "When Elam bought his house, it had indoor plumbing. He let his boys take a few baths in the tub. His Bishop heard about it and gave him orders to rip out the pipes before the next meeting Sunday."

Elizabeth followed Emma to the downstairs bathroom and eyed the tub. "It would be difficult to give this up. Do Amish in Mercer County have no indoor plumbing at all?"

"*Ja.* In the kitchen. They use pressure pumps. Elam was used to an outside toilet. That's all we had — until recently."

The toddler riding on Emma's pregnant belly wiggled. "Down, Mama."

"*Ja*, down, but not until I have the water drawn."

The kitchen door banged. "Mama!" Andy burst into the room.

Six-year-old Dan followed. "Uncle Elam says he's ready to take Elizabeth home."

Smiling, Elizabeth gave Emma's shoulder a friendly pat. "I'll see you at meeting on Sunday."

"*Ja.*" Emma looked up and smiled, but remained on her knees in front of the tub. Katy splashed, regaining her mother's attention.

Malinda sat in a rocking chair in the corner of the kitchen with Priscilla. Amanda knelt on the floor and secured the baby's bonnet, then helped her twin wrap the blanket around the infant. Priscilla kicked and gurgled as though she enjoyed giving them a difficult time.

With the baby in her arms, Elizabeth went to the porch. Her heart fluttered as she watched Elam's approach.

"*Cume onn.* I have Jacob's buggy hitched." Gold flecks made his brown eyes lustrous, making her wonder what all he had on his mind.

The sun was setting as the buggy rumbled from Bird-in-Hand. The air had cooled, making the ride pleasant. Elizabeth stole quick glances at Elam, discovering that he was doing the same to her. She held Priscilla in the crook of her right arm, which left her other hand free. Endeavoring to keep it busy, she fumbled with the hem of the baby's blanket.

Elam reached for her hand. When his fingers closed over hers, she felt as though she should jerk away. Instead, she permitted her fingers to entwine with his. The warm feeling that had begun earlier spread like the petals of a morning glory in the first rays of sun until it filled her with a joy that had been absent for a long time. She suddenly realized that the loneliness she'd been suffering was gone. When had it departed?

"I'm glad you live close to Emma," Elam said. "You've been so alone, and my sister loves you like one of the family."

She shrugged with her left shoulder. "Most Amish treat each other like family."

"*Ja*, but there's something special between you and Emma."

Elizabeth smiled. "It would be difficult not to love Emma."

He laughed. "I can remember a few times when I was a boy that I might not have agreed. Leah and I had a few rough times as well."

"I miss her, Elam. Is she the same now as when we were kids?"

"*Ja.*" His gaze intensified. "Will you come to Mercer County to visit?"

"*Ach*, that's so far!" His fingers tightened on hers and she felt his arm stiffen.

"It isn't so far by car. John Zimmerman would drive you. I'd be glad to pay the expenses."

"I could manage, Elam, but . . ."

"*Ja?*" His steady gaze made her uncomfortable.

"Priscilla is so little to travel so far."

Elam frowned. Had he seen through her flimsy excuse? Why was she making one? Was it an effort to put her heart in a cage? Would it be easier or more difficult to subdue her effusive emotions in Elam's territory?

He turned the horse into the lane that led to the Stoltzfus farm. Moses, having been the second son of Abraham Stoltzfus, had built a house on the corner of the farm. Elizabeth now had twenty acres of land, along with some outbuildings. After losing her husband, she cut the livestock to two draft horses, one carriage horse, one cow, a rooster, two dozen hens, and six ducks. As they rounded the last bend in the lane, Elizabeth noticed Minerva, her calico cat, sitting on the nearest fence post, licking a paw, and swishing her long tail. However, her brown-and-white terrier strutted nervously back-and-forth on the porch.

Elizabeth frowned. "What's the matter with Vashti?"

"She's probably anxious for your return." Elam chuckled. "Why did you name her Vashti?"

Elizabeth laughed. "I named her after Queen Vashti, because when I first got her, she refused to come when I called."

He laughed. "So she ignored your summons as the queen did King Xerxes?"

"*Ja.*"

"Why did you name your carriage horse Xerxes?"

"Because he likes to chew on any leafy branches he can reach."

Elam's eyes traveled lazily to Elizabeth's kitchen door. He straightened, his expression sobering. "*Ferwass* (why) is your door standing ajar?"

She gasped. "I always lock it when I leave."

Elam stopped the carriage. "I'll go inside first to make sure everything's all right."

She was thankful she hadn't returned alone, as she often

had since Moses' death.

Climbing down, Elam headed for the house. Elizabeth waited a moment, then clutching the baby, she followed. Stepping cautiously into the kitchen, she looked around. Two chairs had been moved.

They searched the downstairs. Nothing else seemed out of place. Elizabeth put Priscilla in the crib and went upstairs with Elam. The first bedroom was in order. She'd set up the quilting frames in the second. They hadn't been disturbed. Entering the guest room, Elizabeth stared at the bed and cried out.

Elam rushed to her side. "What is it?"

She dropped her face into her hands. Her heart faltered, and she squeezed her eyelids shut, struggling to hold back tears. "There were five quilts on the bed, Elam. They represented hundreds of hours of work. I stitched long into the night all winter to make extraordinary quilts to sell." She sniffed as tears forced their way forward. "Taxes are high in Lancaster County, and I was counting on the money from my quilts to pay them."

"How much were your quilts worth?"

"Three or four hundred dollars a piece." Tears spilled over and ran down her cheeks. Elam took her in his arms. This time, she didn't pull away. Comfort ebbed from him and wound her in a warm and safe cocoon.

"I'll help you, Elizabeth, in whatever way I can."

"I would've been all right! I was making it on my own!" She pressed the side of her face against his blue cotton shirt. Her arms went around his neck.

His embrace tightened. "None of us can make it on our own. We shouldn't try. God has put us on earth to help each other. When we need His help, He is ever present."

"I know. *Es spied mich* (I'm sorry)." She sniffed. "It's natural to be dismayed over losing the income those quilts represented, but I must have faith that God will show me a way." She began to relax within the circle of Elam's arms. "Romans eight, twenty-eight tells us that 'All things work together for good for those who love the Lord and are called according to His purpose.' I must rely on my faith at times like this."

Elam smiled. "*Ja.* God blesses His children, sometimes in ways we don't expect."

His hands moved slowly up her back, his nearness replacing her dismay with contentment. His warm lips rested on her forehead, creating ripples of pleasure that surged through her being. They shouldn't be alone in an upstairs bedroom. She should push away. Placing her hands on his chest, she looked up. Instead of pulling free, she gazed into his lustrous brown eyes.

Slowly, his head lowered. Knowing what was going to happen, Elizabeth figured she should call a halt to her galloping emotions, but had no desire to. When Elam's mouth touched hers, her lips parted to invite his kiss. Her arms encircled him and his embrace tightened. As their kiss intensified, Elizabeth felt her grasp on her reserve slipping. Then, it jerked itself free, tumbled over the edge of resistance and vanished into a sea of yearning.

Their first kiss ended at the beginning of another. It had been so long since Elizabeth had thrilled over a man's caresses. Not just any man would do. It had to be Elam. Her anxious heart swelled, filling her with joy. The affection and adoration she'd kept imprisoned burst its bonds and exploded in shards of electrified particles that penetrated every portion of her body. She'd thought she'd never find love again, but God was repeating the miracle, and she could no longer deny her adoration for Elam.

She rested her head on his chest, enraptured over the wild pounding of his heart. Was it her pulse or his that throbbed in her temples?

"Oh, Elizabeth. I love you."

"I love you, too, Elam." She murmured the words against his shirt, not intending for him to hear them clearly, although the truth of the phrase vibrated to her core. Her heart ached over her divided loyalties. Her life was here with her family. How could she make a commitment when Elam would soon leave for Mercer County?

"Beth, it seems fitting that . . ."

She pushed slightly away. "Is something wrong?"

"Just the opposite. This is right." He took a deep breath. "Will you marry me?"

Although she'd expected his confession of love, his proposal took her by surprise. "Oh, Elam, I . . ."

"I love you, and I need a wife. My boys need a mother. Some men would've married before this, but I insisted on waiting for the woman God had chosen for me."

"I'm . . . not sure . . ."

"About what? We love each other, Beth. Besides, Priscilla should have a papa."

Elizabeth gasped and tore herself from his arms, ignoring his expression of surprise. "There's been a thief in my house and I left my baby in the downstairs bedroom." Her skirt swished as she ran from the room and down the hall. Descending the stairs swiftly, she raced to the bedroom, Elam on her heels. She clutched the top rail of the crib, her eyes wide. "My baby!"

3

"Where's my baby?" Elizabeth wailed.

Elam grabbed her hand. "*Cume onn.* They couldn't have gone far."

As they reached the kitchen door, it swung inward. Elam bumped into Abraham Stoltzfus, knocking the old man's straw hat to the floor and causing him to teeter. Grabbing his upper arms, Elam hung on until the old man regained his balance. "*Es spied mich.*"

Abraham scratched his gray head as his dark-gray eyes surveyed Elam. "Where are you going in such a hurry?"

Elizabeth pushed past him and hurried across the porch. "Someone took my baby!"

Elam rushed outside after her.

"Wait!" Abraham called. "Mama Nancy has Priscilla."

Elizabeth whirled to face him, "Where is she?"

"Searching for you. We knew you had to be close, with the horse hitched n' all."

Nancy May rounded the house with Priscilla in her arms. The woman smiled, her blue-gray eyes sparkling. "Prissy was whimpering so I picked her up."

Elizabeth rushed forward, her fingers trembling as she flipped the blanket back to reveal the infant's face. "Oh, Nan." Her voice was tremulous. "*Danka dich* (thank you)." She clasped her hands. *Thank you, God, for protecting my bab* she prayed. She thanked the Lord for Elam's love, too. T] picturing the quilts, she quickly calculated the amount of her loss. Anguish threatened to rip the peace from her chest. How would she pay her taxes?

A Scripture verse floated into her mind. "Fear not for I am with thee and will bless thee."

She recalled the Scripture verse from Isaiah God had given her yesterday. "Thou wilt keep him in perfect peace, whose mind is stayed on thee: because he trusteth in thee." God had always taken care of her, and she knew He would continue to do so.

Abraham descended the porch steps to join them in the yard. "I have a check for you, Elizabeth."

"Check?" She turned to study his face.

"For your quilts. A young couple read your ad and seemed to want them pretty bad. They weren't coming back this way and they were in a hurry. Mama noticed them and came over. I think you'll be pleased."

Accepting the proffered check, she read the amount and gasped. "It's more than I expected!" Doubt challenged her faith again. "What if this check has no funds to cover it?"

Abraham laughed. "They drove me to the phone shack to contact their bank. The check's good."

Tears flooded Elizabeth's eyes, then spilled over, yet she couldn't help smiling. "God is so faithful. I'll have more than enough to pay my taxes." She felt Elam's hand in hers. Should she jerk free? What would Abe and Nan think of her love for another man less than a year after their son's death?

Nancy May peered curiously at their clasped hands, then she smiled.

Pulling free, Elizabeth moved to kiss the older woman's cheek. "Let's go inside and have a cup of tea." She led the way, wondering if Elam would wait until they were alone and pressure her for an answer. Could she give him one? She rry him, but how could she?

o her cheery kitchen, she crossed the marbleized d beige vinyl. She lit the flame under the tea kettle, h in this district were permitted propane stoves.

Removing the lid from the cow cookie jar, she retrieved a plate and interspersed chocolate chip cookies around the rim with peanut butter ones. In the center, she arranged tiny squares of apple cake.

As she turned, her gaze fell on the wooden rocker in the corner where Moses had always sat to wait for her to serve their meals. She jolted, nearly dropping the plate of goodies. For the first time since his death, she'd entered the room without glancing wistfully at the empty chair. She hadn't even thought of her late husband when she came in. *Is it wicked of me to have forgotten Mose?* She tried to picture him in the rocker. Instead, a vision of Elam clouded her thought. She expected to sense guilt or remorse, but there was only a sweet memory of a life gone on.

Nancy May held the baby in one arm as she got cups and saucers from the cupboard. Running her hand over the beige-and-white marbleized counter, she smiled. "Aaron King did a marvelous job with your cupboards."

"*Ja.* He does good work. Sarah says he's going into business."

Nancy jostled Priscilla. "He has the Bishop's permission?"

"*Vell* . . . no."

The older woman turned to stare at her. "No?"

"Sarah says he bought a van and has no intention of giving it up."

Nancy May's eyes widened. "And suffer *Meidung* (shunning)?"

"He hasn't joined the church."

"No? He must be in his mid-twenties."

"*Ja.*" Elizabeth took the plate of treats to the polished walnut kitchen table. "I suspect there may be trouble."

The older woman strolled across the room, her dark-blue skirt swinging with her ample hips. "I thought a lot of that sweet girl who called herself Martha Kauffman." Nancy May's brow furrowed. "What was her real name?"

"Rebecca Wenger."

"*Ja.* She turned out to be Mennonite instead of Amish. Do you suppose she could've turned our Aaron's head?"

"Sarah says he'd made up his mind before Rebecca came to stay with them."

Nancy pursed her lips. "Sarah's judgment is usually sound. If she thinks Rebecca is blameless, then I'll accept that." She sighed. "But, what about Aaron King?"

"Rebecca told Sarah that he'd spent many months wrestling over his decision to leave the Amish community."

"*Vell*, I should hope he did!" Her frown deepened. "I don't understand how young people can be brought up in our tradition, then go astray."

Elizabeth wrestled with a grin, not wishing to upset her mother-in-law. "Aaron loves God, Nan. He feels he's doing what's right."

"*Vell*, it's not up to me to judge." She nodded as though reaching a conclusion. "I'll pray for him."

Elizabeth served Nan tea, but made coffee for the men. She kept her eyes averted as she filled Elam's cup, but feeling his gaze, her cheeks grew hot.

Abraham studied them with a quizzical expression on his bearded face, then he addressed Elam. "You'll be returning to Mercer County soon?"

"*Vell . . . Ja.*"

Nancy May's right brow quirked. "Alone?"

"My younger brother took a notion to see part of the world. Lately, he hasn't helped on the farm. My older brother has developed a heart condition, so he'll need help with the harvest."

Abraham looked pensive. "I'm sorry to hear that Jonathan isn't well."

"He says his condition isn't serious."

After passing the cookie plate, Elizabeth sipped her tea. Elam hadn't directly answered Nancy May's question. What did it mean? How soon would he be leaving? Did he expect to go home alone? If so, why didn't he affirm it? As she pondered life without Elam, her heart faltered. She wished he would send for his sons and remain in Lancaster County.

Pushing his empty cup away, he stood. "*Danka dich* for the coffee and cookies, Elizabeth. It's time for me to head back to Emma's."

Elizabeth followed him to the door. "*Danka dich* for driving me home." She laughed softly. "Also, I appreciate how you put up with my hysteria over Priscilla's being missing and my shenanigans over the quilts."

Smiling, he grasped her hand and tugged gently. "*Cume* with me to the buggy, please."

Her heart fluttered. Striving to keep a quaver from her voice, she glanced over her shoulder at her in-laws. "I'll be right back."

Nancy May waved a hand. "Don't hurry, dear. We'll visit with Priscilla."

Elizabeth walked beside Elam, trying to slow his stride. With each step, her heart beat quickened. A sliver of moon shimmered in the dark velvety sky. Clouds hid most of the stars, thus the buggy created a deep shadow. Crickets chirped, a night bird called, and an owl hooted from the wood lot.

Guiding Elizabeth around the buggy, Elam pulled her into the cover of shadow and took her in his arms. Apprehension stirred within her, but she gazed up at him, fearing what his kiss might lead to, yet longing to feel his mouth on hers. His warm lips brushed her forehead, feathered kisses down the side of her face, then came to rest on her mouth. His embrace tightened as his kiss intensified. Her worries dissolved, her arms encircled his neck, and she permitted herself to float into a world of bliss.

Pulling away slightly, Elam traced the outside of her cheek with a finger that came to rest under her chin. She could feel the wild beating of his heart as the pace kept rhythm with her own. His smile encompassed her in a cocoon of joy.

"I love you, Beth," he whispered.

She smiled. "You're the only one who ever called me that, and it was so long ago."

He shook his head. "It seems like only yesterday."

"We were kids."

"*Ja.* I called you Beth if no one was near, and I never confessed my indulgence to anyone. Now, I want to shout, telling all how much I love you."

"Shh." She glanced toward the house, but from the far side of the buggy, there was nothing she could see.

Elam chuckled. "If Nan and Abraham heard me, they'd be happy for us."

She bit her lower lip. "Maybe, Elam, but . . ."

His arms tightened, drawing her against him. "There's so much I want to say."

"Not . . . tonight."

"*Ja, vell* . . ."

"I must go into the house. Nan and Abraham might get the wrong idea about us."

"Oh?" He looked hurt, then quickly covered his expression with a generous smile. "I'll see you tomorrow."

"Good night." She stood on tiptoes to kiss his bearded face. "You're a good man, Elam Miller." Afraid her foolish heart would prompt her to say more, she squeezed his fingers, then hurried to the porch. Turning, she waited for his buggy to head down the lane.

The next morning, Vashti followed close on Elizabeth's heels as she pushed open the screen door and stepped onto the porch. The dog looked up, her tail wagging and her dark eyes bright. Elizabeth paused to pet the animal, then moved to the porch post. Her fingers touched the rough wood. The banister needed paint. The floor boards could use a coat, too. Her eyes spanned her small farm. Keeping the buildings in top repair had been difficult since Moses' death.

The sun swaddled her shoulders, it's warmth a friendly companion. The pink-and-scarlet horizon seemed to cast a rosy promise around her. She stood transfixed until golden rays illuminated the sky, then streamed to earth to kiss the dewdrops that lay like jewels on the blossoms in the flower bed.

Breathing deeply, she inhaled the freshness of morning, the scent of damp earth, and the essence released by the flowers at the edge of the porch.

It's Tuesday, she thought. She always visited Moses' grave on Tuesday and Friday. Entering the house, she checked on Priscilla. Assured the baby still slept soundly, she filled a vase with water, set it on the counter, and retrieved the garden scissors. Going outside, she knelt on the moist grass to gather a bouquet. Selecting the most colorful blooms, she snipped the stems. When she had enough, she rose and gathered the vivid array. Minerva mewed and rubbed against her ankle.

Elizabeth smiled. "You'll get your breakfast when I milk Tillie."

Priscilla's crying reached Elizabeth before she stepped onto the porch. Apparently the baby had perceived she was alone, although Elizabeth had been close. In the kitchen, she quickly plopped the flowers into the waiting vase. Water sloshed over the rim, dribbled down the outside, and formed a puddle on the counter. Grabbing a dish towel, she sopped it up, then hurried to her daughter's crib.

"Mama's here." Scooping up the infant, she rocked her in her arms. *Elam would make my little girl a wonderful father.* She pictured Moses, but experienced only a tiny pinprick of nostalgia. "Everything's going to be fine, Priscilla. God will bless us and take care of us."

"Ma-ma."

Tears filled Elizabeth's eyes, and a smile curved her mouth. "That's your first real word." She hugged the baby, pressing her lips against the infant's golden curls. "You're Mama's big girl. I'll get you something to eat, then we must milk Tillie before she complains too loudly."

After eating a hasty breakfast, Elizabeth fastened Priscilla in the infant hiking seat Emma had loaned her, then strapped it to her back. Grateful for the convenience it afforded, she fed the livestock, milked Tillie, then ran the separator in the summer kitchen. As she poured the cream into the almost filled crock, she realized she would have to churn soon.

After cleaning up the kitchen, Elizabeth wrapped her bouquet, took it and Priscilla to the carriage shed, and hitched Xerxes to the buggy. Settling Priscilla in her basket in the back seat, she headed the horse toward the graveyard.

By the time she arrived at the grave site, the baby was napping. She usually took her to the grave, but this morning she was glad to leave her sleeping. Not wishing to ponder what that meant, she grasped the bouquet and headed across the cropped grass. Kneeling beside Moses' grave, she lay her gift at the base of the stone.

"Good morning, Mose. I . . ." Her voice faltered. She'd always told him how much she missed him. She bit her lip as a vision of Elam gripped her mind and heart. How could she tell Moses that she loved another man? Did he somehow know? *If he does, he'll understand and give his blessing.*

"Oh, Mose, I'll never forget you." She touched her lips with trembling fingers. "When you and Elam were boys, you got along so well. If you could choose a father for Priscilla, I know you'd pick Elam." Sensing peace, she smiled. "I'll come back on Friday, Mose."

After several silent moments and numerous conflicting thoughts about Moses and Elam, she rose, gazed at the headstone a moment, then turned and strode quickly to the buggy.

Elam left the barn and headed for the house with Jacob. The golden retriever kept pace, his tail wagging as his eyes traced the flight of a bird from one tree top to another.

Jacob glanced sideways at Elam. "You get anywhere with Elizabeth last night?"

Elam's heart warmed, then tentacles of pleasure stretched to every part of his being. He envisioned their kiss and his heart raced. "*Vell* . . . I can't rush her."

Jacob laughed. "Emma doesn't have a problem with that!"

"Emma's a bit vocal, Jacob."

"*Ja*. She's determined to get you married to Elizabeth."

As they stepped onto the porch, three of the youngest children raced to meet them. Elam swept little Katy into his arms. Jacob picked up Anna May and took Elmer's hand. As Elam opened the door, the mingling aromas of brewed coffee, sliced oranges, and ham sizzling in the skillet wafted out to greet him.

Waving a pancake turner, Emma grinned, flashing her dimples. She had a smudge of flour on one cheek, and a curl had escaped from under her prayer cap. "You hungry?"

"Always. But especially after morning chores." Chuckling, Elam took off his straw hat and hung it on a peg by the door.

"I got a letter from Mama yesterday, Elam. I left it beside your plate."

He supposed he should have left for home days ago. Guilt seemed to wear slippers, but he could still feel it shuffling through him. "Is . . . anything wrong?"

"No."

Picking up the letter, he began to read. One paragraph seemed to stand out. He read it again.

"Jonathan is working hard. I think he's doing too much. He seems more tired lately, and he hasn't been looking well. I've tried to encourage him to slow down a bit, but he insists that he's all right. Last night, I caught him rubbing his chest as though he had pain. When he noticed me watching, he smiled and told me he'd had a muscle spasm. I don't know what to think."

Folding the letter, Elam sighed. "Emma, what do you think about Jonathan?"

"Oh, he's probably been overdoing a bit." She made a face. "I don't suppose living with Mattie helps."

Picturing the taut lips and piercing dark eyes of his haughty sister-in-law, Elam frowned. He wanted to give Elizabeth more time, but he felt pressured to return home. Maybe he would speak with Elizabeth this evening.

"There's the postman, Mama," Amanda said. She pushed open the screen door, let it bang, and dashed toward the mail box.

Her twin followed like a shadow.

Watching, Jacob scratched his head. "What's going on with those two?"

Emma laughed. "Amanda sent for a free catalogue last week, and the girls can't wait for it to come."

Jacob frowned. "What sort of catalogue?"

"*Ach.*" Emma shrugged. "Just a catalogue."

The furrow between Jacob's eyes deepened. "They're only eight!" He shook his head. "The pull of the world is influencing Amish children at a younger and younger age."

Emma clacked the platter of ham onto the table. "I pray every day for my *kinder*, then try to leave them in God's care." Her smile seemed infectious.

Jacob's features relaxed. "*Ja.* Why worry when we can pray?"

When the girls returned, Amanda handed her father some of the envelopes, and Malinda gave the rest to Emma.

"You girls get your breakfast." Emma sorted through the pile of envelopes and laughed. "Here's another letter from Leah. You'd think she had nothing to do but write."

Elam watched his sister as she opened the letter and began to read. Her grin faded. Slowly the color drained from her face and she gripped the back of a kitchen chair.

Jacob got to his feet. "Emma?"

Her mouth moved, but no sound came.

Elam jumped up and headed toward her. "Emma, what's wrong?"

She seemed to sway.

Leaping forward, Jacob grasped her arm. "Emma!"

4

Jacob John gripped Emma's arm as he peered at her pale face. Pulling out a kitchen chair, he guided her into it, worry creasing his brow. "What's wrong?"

The letter trembled in her hand as she proffered it to Elam.

His eyes spanned the sheet, then focused on the third paragraph. Guilt exchanged the slippers it wore for heavy boots and stomped through his stomach. He handed the letter to Jacob. "I have to go home."

"I'll... help you pack." Gripping the edge of the table, Emma started to get up.

Jacob rested a large hand on her shoulder. "You stay put for awhile."

Elam swiped a hand across his forehead. "I have to see Elizabeth before I go, and I'll have to make arrangements with one of the Beachys to drive me to New Wilmington."

"Take my buggy and go to Elizabeth." Jacob headed for the door. "I'll borrow my father's buggy and go to see John Zimmerman about your trip home."

"*Danka dich.*"

The children stood wide-eyed. Malinda moved to her mother's side, Amanda shooshed baby Katy.

Elam headed for the stairs. "I'll get a change of clothes and take a shower. I plan to leave as soon as possible—after I see Elizabeth."

Within minutes he was ready. Jacob had the buggy hitched

and waiting at the front gate. Jumping in, Elam turned the horse and headed down the lane, his fingers tightening on the reins. He tried to maintain calmness, but his heart throbbed in his temples. How could he best confront Elizabeth? How could he return to Mercer County without her? How could he not, if she refused to accompany him?

As he stopped the buggy at her front gate, he noticed Abe Stoltzfus, Elizabeth's brother-in-law, coming from the house. He carried himself erect, appearing tall, although he wasn't quite six foot. His broad shoulders and muscular arms gave him an air of power. Elam figured the man had designs on Elizabeth.

"*Vea-gaits* (hello)," Abe greeted, increasing his pace and extending his right hand.

"*Vea-gaits*." The shimmer in Abe's green eyes underscored Elam's suspicion about the man's intention. "Is Elizabeth all right?"

Abe's grin broadened. "*Ja*."

Elam wanted to ask this man why he'd been visiting Elizabeth this early in the day, but he bridled his tongue, figuring the choice of admirers was up to her.

"*Vell*..." Abe readjusted his straw hat. "I have some chores at the barn." Turning, he strode away.

Taking a deep breath, Elam went to the house. Before he could knock, Elizabeth opened the door. Specks of gold shimmered in her brown eyes. Her smile faded as she studied his face.

"Is something wrong at Emma's?"

"Not at Emma's." Stepping into the kitchen, he took off his straw hat and tossed it to the bench. Catching her hands in his, he gazed into her upturned face. "Jonathan had a heart attack."

"Oh no. Was it serious?"

"He's in the hospital. I have to go home, today."

"Oh. I. . .understand." She blinked and the color drained from her lovely face. "You. . .came to say good-bye?"

"*Cume* with me, Elizabeth. You can live in my parent's home until we're married."

Her soft lips moved, but no words came. Moisture collected on her lower lashes. Slowly, she withdrew her hands and turned away. "I can't leave."

The muscles constricted across Elam's chest, making it difficult to breathe. He was handling this all wrong. Stepping forward, he placed his hands on her shoulders. "I love you, Beth."

"I. . .I. . ." She drew a fragmented breath.

He turned her to face him. Tears spilled over and ran down her cheeks. "Beth," he whispered, pulling her into his arms.

She rested her face against his chest. "I wish you could stay."

"I could've remained another few days, if it weren't for my brother's condition, but because of my sons, I would've had to return home before long."

"I was hoping. . .maybe—"

"Maybe what?"

"When your brother gets well, would you consider moving back here with your boys?"

His heart faltered. "My work is around New Wilmington. Besides, even when Jonathan improves, he'll still have the condition."

"What about Samuel? Can't he take over the farm work?"

Elam sighed. "Samuel is irresponsible. He's lovable, but . . ."

"Maybe he'll become more reliable, now."

"He isn't home. He went to Ohio with a friend a week after I came here. Mother needs looking after as well as my father."

"Leah takes care of the older folks."

"*Ja*, but I feel like I've been taking advantage of her." He tightened his embrace. "I want to marry you, Beth."

"I can't leave Lancaster County. My family is here — as well as the Amish community I grew up in."

"My family would become yours, and being Amish, you would soon become part of my church."

"Oh, Elam, you don't understand." She looked up, her face

tear stained.

Bending, he kissed her cheek. "I'm pressuring you, and I vowed I wouldn't. If you need more time, that's all right. When or if you're ready to come to me, I'll send a car for you and Priscilla. I'll pay your expenses."

"I could manage, but . . ."

Priscilla had been kicking and cooing in the playpen near the window. She began to whimper. Elam moved across the room, bent, and swooped her into his arms. Gurgling, she reached for his nose. "I'm going to miss you, little one," he said.

Elizabeth moved nearer. "When are you leaving?"

"As soon as I can make the arrangements." Just the thought of leaving created loneliness within him. With the baby in one arm, he put the other around Elizabeth and drew her close.

Elizabeth swallowed and battled tears. What she'd most dreaded was happening. If she refused to go to Mercer County with Elam, she would lose him. If she deserted her family and the memories of Moses, guilt might ruin a relationship between herself and Elam. What choice did she have? How could she forsake all she knew — for Priscilla's sake.

"I wish we had had more time, Beth," he whispered, pressing his lips against her forehead.

Footsteps resounded on the porch. Elizabeth moved to the window. "It's Mama Stoltzfus. I promised her she could take Priscilla to her place for a while this morning."

Nancy May opened the door and stepped into the room, her smile bright and her rounded cheeks pink. "I came for Priscilla."

Elam moved forward to proffer the wriggling infant. "I think she's ready for the adventure."

The older woman laughed. "*Ach*, she's nearly always ready to go visiting."

Getting a paper bag, Elizabeth shoved a few clean diapers inside it and handed it to Nancy May. "I'll serve supper at six o'clock, if that's all right with you."

"*Ja*. Abe will be back from auction by then." Accepting the diapers, she smiled. "We're looking forward to spending the evening with you and Priscilla." She glanced at Elam. "Will you be here for supper?"

"No."

She studied his face. "Is something wrong?"

"I'm leaving for New Wilmington shortly."

Nancy May sobered, then seemed flustered. "I'll. . .say good-bye, then." Turning, she headed for the door. "You young people probably have things to talk about."

Elizabeth watched her mother-in-law go, struggling to maintain an outward calmness. When she was alone with Elam, she turned to face him. His expression was pleading, but he said nothing. Overcome, she moved quickly to him, wrapped her arms around his neck, and pressed her face against his shirt.

"Beth . . . Oh, Beth." His voice sounded choked.

Elizabeth lifted her face for his kiss. She clung to him, wanting the moment to last as long as possible.

Elam crushed her against him. "I want you with me."

"I want to be with you Elam, but --"

He feathered kisses across her forehead and down the side of her face. "I'll pray every day for you and Priscilla and that you'll come to me."

"*Ja.*" As she uttered the syllable, she felt the futility of it. Before she was ready to release him, he was on his way to the buggy. She swallowed hard as she watched his retreating back. *I must remain here for Priscilla's sake*, she thought. The only relatives the baby had were nearby, and that was all she had left of Moses. How could she take Priscilla away from both sets of grandparents? Here she would grow up with aunts, uncles and cousins. In Mercer county she would have no one.

Good-bye, Elam, her heart said, painfully. She moved to the porch and stood statuesque until the buggy vanished down the lane, then she stared at the road until the dust particles settled.

Isaiah 26:3 had become one of her favorite verses, especially when her emotions challenged her ability to cope. Her lips moved as she recited it. "Thou wilt keep him in perfect peace, whose mind is stayed on thee: because he trusteth in thee." Elam's love and trust in God would solace him, too.

Her spirit was strengthened, but her heart grieved. With a strangled sob, she whirled and ran back into the house, slumped in the rocker, and reached for her Bible. Opening it at random, she looked at a verse in Isaiah 41. Her lips moved as she read, "Fear thou not; for I am with thee: be not dismayed; for I am thy God: I will strengthen thee: yea, I will help thee: yea, I will uphold thee with the right hand of my righteousness."

Closing her eyes, she rested her head against the back of the rocker and drew a deep breath, trusting God for guidance.

Mercer County

Hues of gold and scarlet stained the western horizon. Brilliant rays slanted across the landscape and tinted the plain white farmhouse a dusty pink. Leah Miller paused at the edge of the porch, broom in hand. Shielding her turquoise eyes, she peered to her left. She noted the lengthening shadow of the barn, then her eyes followed the tree-shaded lane toward the highway, until it vanished behind a stand of pine. A pleasant evening breeze toyed with the loosened ties of her white prayer cap and caused her long dark-blue skirt to whisper against her legs.

"Please come, Elam," she whispered, wondering if her older brother had had time to respond to her letter. Would he leave their sister's place right away? When he arrived, would he stop at his own house first or come to their parent's home? At times, being forbidden a home phone was so frustrating.

"*Vell*," she said to herself, knowing worry wasn't conducive to getting her housework done. She would have to trust Elam's judgment. Sighing, she resumed sweeping, her mind in flux.

Realizing she'd swept the same area of the porch twice, she propped the broom against the house with a resounding clack. Minnie, the gray-and-white cat, sat on the banister licking a paw and washing her face. Her two kittens, Ruffy and Tumbles, romped nearby.

Six-year-old Daniel appeared at the screen door. "Is Papa comin'?"

"Not yet." She smiled to encourage the boy. His slender face, light-brown hair, and hazel eyes were a duplicate of his mother's, although her face had been more filled out.

"Aunt Leah, you said Papa would probably be home today."

Another sigh escaped from deep within her. "*Ja, vell*, I thought he might." She would have to get the boys ready for bed, soon. Why had she told them they could expect their father to come home today? They had been too excited to eat their dinner, and after a long afternoon, they had been too disappointed to eat much supper. Bedtime would be difficult.

A picture of Elizabeth Stoltzfus drifted into her mind, bringing a smile to her lips. If what Emma said about Elizabeth and Elam were true, maybe she would be getting a new sister-in-law soon. She hoped so, not only for Elam's sake, but for his sons. *And mine, too*, she thought. She'd been so occupied with caring for her sickly parents and Elam's boys, not to mention the extra farm work, that she'd had little time for herself. *At this rate, I'm going to be an old maid!* She sighed, feeling more like forty than twenty-one. She reached for the screen door handle, but withdrew her hand when she heard a horse's hoofs and buggy wheels bumping over the stones on the lane.

The door flew open. A bright smile lit up Daniel's countenance as he sprang onto the porch and raced to the banister.

The screen door banged again. Jesse Mark raced by Leah to join his brother at the rail. The three year-old's light-blue eyes sparkled, and dark-blond curls dangled on his forehead. More ringlets caressed his ears and neck. "Is it Papa?"

Daniel leaned farther over the banister to peer down the lane toward the approaching buggy, and his smile faded.

5

Jesse Mark bounced, causing his blond curls to bob. "*Vell*, is it Papa?"

"Nah." Daniel's tone sounded as glum as he looked.

Jesse Mark's blue eyes suddenly shimmered with tears. Letting his hair grow as long as the Amish custom demanded enhanced its beauty. His hair was much like Leah's, although her hair was a shade darker and had to be rolled up under her prayer cap.

Blinking, he peered up at her. "Who's comin', Aunt Leah?"

Squinting, she peered into the buggy. "I think it's your Aunt Susanna." She pictured the pretty younger sister of Elam's late wife. Susanna's curly blond hair and light-blue eyes, as well as her round face and dimpled cheeks, had been duplicated in Jesse Mark. The boy resembled her more than his own mother. Was that why he seemed to be Susanna's favorite?

Tim, the tawny-colored collie, appeared in a barn doorway, yipped, then bounded across the barnyard toward the buggy. He waited patiently, tail wagging, for Susanna to alight. She stepped to the ground, petted him, then retrieved a small round woven basket from the buggy. Slinging the handle into the crook of her left arm, she strolled through the open gate and up the flagstone walk toward the house. Her slender, five-foot-eight figure moved gracefully, and her deep-purple dress contrasted with the pink and yellow blossoms that seemed to peer over the rim of her basket. A small straw-colored curl had escaped from under her prayer cap. She shoved it back into place.

"*Vea-gaits*," Leah said.

Susanna smiled, flashing deep dimples. "*Vea-gaits*." Climbing the porch steps, she scooped the flowers into her hand and proffered them to Leah. Her smile broadened as she gazed at Daniel and Jesse Mark. "How are my favorite boys?"

Grinning, Jesse Mark ran forward to greet her, but Daniel stood at a distance as though pondering her next move. Did he perceive his younger brother's closer position in Susanna's heart?

Reaching into her basket, she withdrew two cookies that were frosted with pink peppermint icing. "I brought you fellows a treat."

"*Danka dich.*" Jesse Mark accepted his cookie, took a big bite, and grinned.

Daniel moved forward to get his. "*Danka dich*, Aunt Susanna." Striding to the banister, he peered longingly down the lane.

Tim trotted to the porch and appeared disappointed. Susanna laughed. "I didn't forget you, Tim. Reaching into her basket, she brought out a dog biscuit and gave it to the canine.

"Papa's comin' home," Jesse Mark said around a mouthful of cookie. He wiped the crumb that had stuck to his chin and licked the pink icing from his upper lip.

Susanna's blue eyes were bright as she faced Leah. "I stopped at Elam's house, but he wasn't there. Has he returned, yet?"

"No."

The woman's smile seemed to fade slightly. "I assumed he'd come home as soon as he heard about Jonathan being in the hospital."

"*Ja.* Maybe tomorrow."

"How's Jonathan?"

Leah sniffed the vivid array of blooms in her hand. "He's improving, but recovery will take a long time."

"*Danka Got* he's as good as he is."

"*Ja.* Will you come in and have a cup of tea?"

"*Danka dich,* but I have another stop to make and I want to get home before it gets late."

"After Elam's back and settled, I'll have you over for supper."

Susanna brightened. "I'd like that." She handed her basket to Leah. "I picked some peppermint tea for your mother. Elam likes my cherry tarts, so I baked several." She left the porch, then hesitated. "I'll see you and the boys soon." Turning, she hurried toward her buggy.

Leah stood watching until the carriage rounded the bend and vanished behind the grove of pine, then she took the basket of tarts and her bouquet inside. After filling a vase, she plunked the stems into the water and set the arrangement on the table.

"Daniel," she called, returning to the porch. "Jesse Mark, it's time for you boys to get ready for bed." She tried not to be affected by their dejection as she herded them toward the door.

The hum of a motor vehicle drew her attention. Turning, she squinted and looked in the direction of the sound. The little boys stopped and whirled simultaneously.

An unfamiliar dark-blue van came up the lane and stopped at the gate. Leah saw a man and woman in the front seat and one passenger in the back. The driver got out. Something about him struck a familiar cord. The side door slid open, and Elam climbed out.

"Papa!" Daniel leaped down the two porch steps and streaked across the lawn. Yipping, Tim joined him.

Jesse Mark followed as fast as his three-year-old legs would allow, his eyes bright. "Papa!"

Elam rushed through the gate. Dropping to one knee, he caught a boy in each arm and hugged them close.

Smiling, Leah moved down the flagstone walk to greet the couple who had brought her brother home. The man wore jeans and a light-blue sport shirt. The young woman wore a pink flowered dress. At first she'd taken them for *Englischers*, then noticed that the woman wore a prayer cap.

Elam stood and greeted Leah, but continued to grip a hand of each of his sons. "Aaron King drove me home, Leah. Remember him?"

Leah gasped. "Now I do!" "*Vea-gaits*, Aaron." A frown toyed with her brow. "You're Amish, yet you drive?"

"*Vell*... that's a story for later." He removed his straw hat. The last rays of the setting sun played on his dark waves. Laughter danced in his dark-brown eyes. "You've changed a little in eight years, Leah." He smiled and motioned to the woman by his side. "I'd like you to meet Rebecca Wenger."

"*Vea-gaits*." Smiling, Rebecca stepped forward. Rosy cheeks set off delicate features in her pretty oval face. Tawny-colored hair showed at the front of her cap, and her amber eyes glistened with gold highlights.

Leah fumbled with the pin in her apron as she surveyed the woman's pink dress. "You're . . . Amish?"

"Mennonite."

"Oh, *Ja*." Leah glanced at the van, then back at her visitors. "*Cume onn* in. You must be hungry after your long trip."

"We stopped for dinner, but that was some time ago." Elam boosted Jesse Mark to his shoulders and took Daniel's hand. "Do you young men want something to eat?"

Daniel grinned up at him. "*Ja*. Now that you're home, I'm hungry."

"There's beef stew left over from supper." Leah pictured the large pot of it she'd prepared, having assumed he and some friends would be there for the evening meal. "I'll warm it up." She led the guests to the living room and waited for them to get settled.

Elam sat on the couch with Jesse Mark on his lap while Daniel crowded close to his side. "I must slip over to the *Granddawdy* house to see Mom and Dad."

"They aren't feeling well, Elam," Leah said. "They're in bed for the night. Can your greeting wait until morning?"

Elam nodded, apparently travel-weary and anxious to relax with his sons.

"I'll have eats ready in a jiffy," Leah said.

Rebecca followed her to the kitchen. "May I help?"

Leah smiled. "*Danka Dich.* You may set the table." She pointed to the cupboard. "You'll find plates and cups behind the second door."

Going to the wood stove, she took the lid from the front burner and shoved in kindling. Stirring up the coals, she soon had the fire blazing. Replacing the cover, she dumped the stew into a pan and set it on to heat. She noticed Rebecca glancing at her and wondered what was on the girl's mind.

When the places were set, Rebecca spoke. "Sarah Beiler said you and she used to be school playmates."

Leah gasped. "You know Sarah?"

"She and I have become very good friends."

"It's easy to be Sarah's friend. I missed her dreadfully after my family moved from Lancaster County."

"She said she missed you, too." Rebecca glanced around as though she were looking for something, then seemed uncomfortable. "I'd . . . like to use your bathroom."

Leah stifled a giggle. "Our Bishop isn't as lenient as the Bishops in Lancaster County. Our bathroom is the little house at the back of the lot."

The peach hue on Rebecca's cheeks deepened, making her even more becoming. She laughed softly. "I'll be back."

Leah watched her make her way down a well-worn path. Dusk turned her pink dress to dusty-rose. It was such a pretty shade. Leah wished her Bishop would permit lighter colors. A flowered print was too much to wish for, though. Was wearing a softly colored dress really that worldly? She figured what was inside a person was more important than the color one wore. She turned from the window. If Rebecca was a friend of Sarah's, she was all right. She set a large dish of applesauce on the table and got out a knife to slice a loaf of bread.

Elam stretched his long legs and shifted Jesse Mark on his lap. Daniel squirmed to get closer. Elam hugged them both.

His heart warmed as his eyes spanned the familiar room. The off-white walls were void of ornaments, as they were in all Amish homes. Elam sat on the worn brown sofa. A small stand set at each end supported oil lamps. Across the room, a flame glimmered in an oil lamp on the stand between a dark-green chair and the wooden rocker where Aaron sat. Braided rugs lay in strategic places on the bare floor.

Twisting to look at his father, Jesse Mark grinned. Then, he flung his arms around Elam's neck.

Aaron smiled as though memory had captured his thoughts. "I'm anxious to visit with Jonathan. It's been a long time since we played ball together during recess."

Elam laughed. "He'll be glad to see you."

"Doesn't he live here?"

"*Ja.*"

"Where's his wife?"

"Aunt Mattie went to the hospital to visit Uncle Jonathan," Daniel said.

The aroma of beef stew wafted into the living room, whipping up Elam's appetite. Leah called them, and they quickly took places at the table. Supper conversation remained light. Everyone ate heartily.

Elam swallowed the last bite of his dessert. "Susanna bakes the best cherry tarts in Mercer County." He glanced at Rebecca. "Susanna is my late wife's younger sister."

"She likes Papa," Daniel said, then shoved another bite of tart into his mouth.

Jesse Mark straightened. "She came to see you, Papa, but you weren't here yet."

Noticing Daniel's frown, Elam wondered what was bothering the boy. If Daniel had been willing to air his troubles in front of company, he would have already done so. Elam made a mental note to inquire, later.

Leah made a fresh pot of tea and refilled their cups. A car came up the lane and stopped. A door slammed, and the vehicle sped away. Within moments, someone jerked the screen door open. Mattie entered the kitchen, stopped with a jolt, and surveyed them with piercing dark eyes. "What's going on, Elam?" Her tone seemed to chill the room.

He introduced Aaron and Rebecca, explaining that Aaron would accompany him home, but that Rebecca would be spending the night here.

Mattie propped a fist on one plump hip and raised her thick right brow. She was in her early thirties, but seemed much older. "You could've let me know so I could have prepared for company, Elam."

"There wasn't time. When I heard about Jonathan's heart attack, I came as soon as I could."

Jerking the strings of her brown bonnet, she swiped it from her head. She poked a stray strand of mousy-brown hair back under her prayer cap and straightened her square shoulders. "The guest room isn't ready."

"Rebecca can use the second bed in my room, Mattie," Leah said.

"*Ja?*" Her face was slender and her nose narrow, giving her a slight bird-like appearance. "They're guests, Leah."

Endeavoring to dispel the shadow that Mattie had cast over them, Elam chuckled. "Aaron isn't a guest. He's a friend." He waved a hand toward Rebecca. "And this is the lovely girl he plans to marry."

Mattie turned to Leah. "I presume you plan to cook breakfast?"

"I usually do."

Mattie swished her brown skirt. "Don't get lippy, girl."

Leah sighed. "You must be tired after your long day at the hospital."

"*Ja*, and I expected to come home and relax."

"Why don't you go to your room, Mattie." Leah's smile seemed a bit crooked. "I'll bring a cup of hot tea in to you."

"Bring one of those cherry tarts, too." She glanced at Aaron, then Rebecca. "It was nice to meet you." They were the right words, but sincerity seemed lacking. Tilting her chin, she eyed Elam. "It's good to have you back — finally."

"I'm glad to be home, Mattie."

Her narrow nose twitched. "Had you been home sooner, Jonathan might not have taken ill."

Leah rested a hand on Mattie's arm. "Jonathan has had a heart condition for some time."

Mattie pulled away and headed for the first-floor bedroom. "That's all the more reason for Elam to accept his share of the responsibilities."

Elam watched her retreat, knowing that being Amish didn't automatically make a woman virtuous. *No wonder my brother had a heart attack.*

"Aunt Maddie's mad," Jesse Mark said.

Daniel shrugged. "She's always mad!"

"*Ja*!" Eyeing him, Jesse Mark giggled.

Elam had considered apologizing for his sister-in-law's inhospitality, but the boys had covered the situation better than he could have. Leah and Rebecca exchanged knowing glances.

"Leah!" Mattie's harsh voice ricochetted through the kitchen, making everyone jump. "Leah!"

6

"Leah!"

Elam closed his eyes and took a deep breath. Mattie's screeching jangled a person's nerves.

Leah placed a cherry tart beside the tea cup, grasped the tray, and glanced apologetically at Aaron and Rebecca. "I'll be back." Her tone was controlled and her words soft.

Elam admired how his younger sister put up with Mattie's raillery without becoming ruffled. Did she ever put the woman in her place when there wasn't an audience?

Entering Mattie's room, Leah pushed the door shut with an elbow.

"There's no call for this!" the woman shrieked.

Elam glanced at Daniel. The boy's face had paled. Was it from apprehension — or guilt?

Jesse Mark squirmed. His chair squeaked as he bent toward his brother. "I guess she found 'em."

"Shh." A red hue flooded Daniel's face as he glanced at his father.

Mattie's angry tones rumbled through the bedroom. Evidently she'd retreated to a far corner, for her words were unclear. Leah's quiet urging did little to dispel the woman's wrath.

Swallowing, Daniel blinked. "Let's go home, Papa."

Reading his son's expressions told him they might have pulled something. "Aaron will be coming home with us, and I don't want to leave Rebecca until your Aunt Leah comes back out."

Jesse Mark looked at him, his eyes light-blue spheres of innocence. "Tim wants to go home, Papa. He's afraid of Aunt Maddie."

"Your dog can take care of himself." Elam scratched his beard. "Did you boys do something that would make your Aunt Mattie angry?"

Jesse Mark giggled.

Daniel peered at his little brother, his hazel eyes beseeching.

Leah returned to the kitchen, her expression unreadable. "It's past the boy's bedtime, Elam. Maybe it would be a good idea to take them home."

"*Ja, vell* . . ."

She smiled convincingly. "Aaron would probably like to get some rest. Rebecca and I will be fine."

"Are you coming home with us, Aunt Leah?" Daniel asked, his voice tremulous.

She glanced at Elam.

"I can manage."

"But, Papa, Aunt Leah will help us with our prayers."

"*Ja?*" He pondered Leah's leniency and Daniel's guilty expression. "Is there a reason why I can't hear your prayers tonight?"

Mattie's shoes clacked on the floorboards as she approached her bedroom door.

Daniel's eyes widened. Sliding from his chair, he headed for the porch. "Let's go, Papa."

Jesse Mark bounced from his perch and ran after his brother. "I wanna ride in Mr. Aaron's car."

Frowning, Elam got to his feet. Should he wait to be confronted by Mattie — or hurry away for the sake of his sons?

Rebecca seemed to understand his dilemma. "You go ahead. Leah's right about the boy's bedtime."

Thankful for her insight, Elam smiled. "We'll see you in the morning." As Mattie's tread approached, Elam and Aaron went outside.

Leah followed them to the porch. "I'll have breakfast ready at six, Elam."

"*Danka dich*," he called over his shoulder as he followed his boys to Aaron's van.

Jesse Mark climbed into the back seat. "Can Tim ride, too?"

"He can follow us." As they rode the four hundred feet to Elam's house, he considered the relieved look on Daniel's face. What had the boy done? He sighed, wishing he could forget accosting him, especially on his first night back.

Giggling, Jesse Mark glanced at his older brother. "Aunt Maddie was really mad!"

"Be quiet!" the older boy whispered.

Elam suppressed a moan. Putting off a confrontation was impossible. When he got the boys into bed . . .

Rebecca followed Leah, but remained inside the screen door. Mattie crossed the kitchen, her stride betraying her disgust. Sniffing, she paused to glare out the window. Rebecca stole a side-glance in time to notice the woman's nose twitch. Being Amish didn't automatically bestow goodness, and Mattie's seemed sorely deficient. Leah waited until the van had pulled away, then entered the kitchen and began collecting the dirty dishes.

Mattie propped tight fists on her ample hips. "I don't suppose you need my help with the clean up."

"I'll take care of it."

Mattie heaved a sigh. "Visiting Jonathan every day takes so much out of me." Turning, she went to the living room, slumped into the rocker, and grappled for the recent copy of *The Budget*. Flipping the paper open, she ran her finger down a column.

Laughing softly, Leah stepped closer to Rebecca. "One thing Mattie always has energy for is searching for gossip. She says that it's because she must know what to pray for."

Rebecca smiled. Gathering up some of the dirty plates, she took them to the sink. She opened the tap, but soon realized that cold water was all that was available.

Leah went to the stove and brought the kettle to the sink. "There's enough hot water left, so we won't have to wait." She dribbled liquid detergent into the dish pan, then emptied the kettle into it.

After cooling the water to a comfortable degree, Rebecca began to wash the dishes. She considered the wood cookstove, then the lack of other conveniences here that were permitted for Amish who lived in Lancaster County. She'd heard that Old Order Amish in Ohio, as well as in other settlements, weren't permitted to be very progressive either.

Leah picked up a clean plate, but before she dried it, she peered out the window above the sink. "Elam just lit a lamp in his living room."

Bending nearer to the glass, Rebecca could see a faint glimmer in the house across the field. "Did the boys do something naughty?"

Leah giggled, then covered her mouth. She peered over her shoulder at Mattie, then stepped closer to Rebecca and lowered her voice. "Last week, they overheard me confess something to Susanna. You'd like her." Leah put away a stack of plates and started to wipe the silverware. After another cautious glance into the living room, she said, "I told her that when I was younger, I picked burrs and hid them under Mattie's sheet."

Laughter bubbled into Rebecca's throat, but she kept her voice low enough that Mattie couldn't eavesdrop. "So the boys decided to repeat your prank?"

"*Ja*, just about. They put them under the pillow cover of her rocker." She grinned. "Mattie sat on them." A sigh escaped. "I pray Elam isn't too harsh with them. Mattie deserved it, the way she's been treating them — especially Daniel."

"She's stern?"

"*Ach*, that's putting it mildly."

"What are you girls whispering about?" Mattie shook the newspaper at them, slapped it to the floor beside the rocker, and stood, her expression foreboding. "We'll have no gossip in this house."

Leah smiled as she faced her sister-in-law. "There's one cherry tart left, Mattie. Would you like it?" Picking up the pastry, she held it toward her sister-in-law.

Mattie glared at the kettle. "Is the water hot for tea?"

"We used it for the dishes."

"Humph! Mama Miller should've trained you better." Seizing the tart, she headed for her room. "Forget the tea. I'll eat my tart in my room where I can enjoy a little peace."

Leah watched her go, a frown betraying her feelings.

"That finishes the dishes." Rebecca dried her hands.

"It will be time to get breakfast before we know it." Leah hung up her towel and headed for the stairway. "*Cume onn*, I'll show you where you're going to sleep."

Retrieving the overnight case Aaron had placed on the bench beside the outer door, Rebecca followed Leah up the stairway.

Elizabeth tossed and turned in her bed. Rolling onto her side, she gazed out the window at the moon. Elam was so far away. Could he sleep? Was he tossing, too, and staring at the same moon?

Priscilla began to fuss. It had been difficult to get her to sleep, and now, after only ten minutes, she was awake again. Sighing, Elizabeth got up, put on a robe, and picked up the baby.

"What's your trouble, baby mine? Do you miss Elam, too?" She figured the question was silly. "You aren't wet, and you ate just minutes ago."

Priscilla cuddled against Elizabeth and quieted. Unable to sleep anyway, she took the baby to the wooden rocker in the dark living room. The chair squeaked as she rocked, the sound seeming to be amplified in the silent house. Vashti trotted in from the kitchen and curled up on the braided rug by her feet.

Having the dog in the house was a comfort, but the animal did nothing to dispel her loneliness.

At dawn, Elizabeth still sat in the rocker. Her left arm was asleep. Gently, she moved Priscilla to her right arm, then rubbed her neck. Feeling stiff and exhausted, she staggered to her feet. Going to the bedroom, she put the baby in the crib and slumped across her bed. Maybe she could sleep until six o'clock.

Yawning, she stretched and covered herself with the sheet. Closing her eyes, the emptiness within her seemed to keep slumber at bay. Fifteen minutes passed. Priscilla began to cry. Elizabeth frowned. It wasn't like Priscilla to fuss. Was she coming down with something?

She chose her light-green dress, but getting dressed was a chore, for the baby continued to whimper every time Elizabeth put her in the crib. Finally, somewhat harried, she tucked the baby in the crook of her left arm and went to the kitchen to get breakfast. She spilled water on the floor and coffee grounds on the counter. Figuring it would be too difficult to stir hot cereal with one hand, she decided to fry herself an egg. Getting a bowl, cracking the egg, and scrambling it was no problem, but as she turned to take it to the stove where the skillet sizzled, Priscilla kicked. The baby's foot struck the bowl, knocking it from Elizabeth's grasp. The bowl crashed on the floor and shattered, splashing yellow egg all over the kitchen floor.

Fighting tears, she went to the summer kitchen for a scrub cloth. Someone knocked on the door. She hesitated, wondering whether to clean up the mess first or to see who was calling.

"Elizabeth?" Abe Stoltzfus called.

She opened the door. "I'm . . . a bit . . . disorganized this morning, Abe, but come on in."

His broad-shouldered frame and muscular arms made him seem taller than his five-foot-eleven. Removing his straw hat, he ran his fingers through his dark-brown hair. When he entered the kitchen, he glanced around, then studied Elizabeth with questioning green eyes. "I came over to milk Tillie for you, but it looks like you could use some help in here, too."

"*Ja.* Priscilla was fussy all night. I haven't been able to put her down to get breakfast."

Reaching out, he took the baby and grinned at her. His handsome features, as well as his cordial expression, were a lot like Moses's although his coloring was much different. His ruddy complexion gave him a healthy glow. He made gurgling sounds to Priscilla. "You giving Mama a hard time?"

Elizabeth wiped up the mess on the floor and cleaned the coffee grounds off of the counter. "Have you had breakfast?"

"Not yet."

"If you entertain Priscilla, I'll cook."

His grin broadened. "Very *vell.*"

While Elizabeth bustled around the kitchen, she could feel Abe's eyes on her, but pretended not to notice. While the potatoes, eggs, and ham fried, she baked raisin muffins and made coffee.

"Breakfast smells good." He handed her the baby and took the place she motioned to.

After silent grace, they filled their plates and began to eat. Priscilla fussed, but as long as Elizabeth held her, she seemed to be somewhat pacified.

Abe ate slowly, as though he had something on his mind. Finally, he said, "I was afraid you might go to Mercer County with Elam Miller."

Elizabeth's heart lurched, and she struggled to keep her features relaxed. "My life is here, Abe. I can't leave my family and the community I'm used to. Besides, I'd feel guilty if I couldn't visit Mose, and put flowers on his grave."

"He's been gone almost a year, Elizabeth. It's time you think about getting on with your life."

She took a swallow of coffee and averted her gaze.

He reached for her hand, but hesitated. "I've been thinking. You need someone around here, Priscilla needs a papa, and I...I—"

"Would you like more coffee?" she interrupted, uneasy of

what he might be about to say.

He disregarded her question. His eyes sparkling, he held her gaze. "Elizabeth, I think we should marry."

"Oh!" She almost choked on a bite of muffin. She supposed she should have seen this coming, but she'd always just thought of Abe as Moses's older brother. "Abe, I think a lot of you, but—"

"That's a good beginning." He finished his eggs and pushed his plate away. "Instead of building a Granddawdy house onto the main place, the older folks could live here, enabling us to take over the homestead."

"Abe. . .this is. . ." She was going to say it was so sudden, but was it? Abe's actions over the past several months flashed before her, and she felt awash with the revelation. Had accepting his help with the farm work led him on? Was he just being practical? Would turning him down hurt him? He would be a good father for her little girl, and he *was* a good man. He would take care of her, and she could remain in her beloved Lancaster County. An image of Elam flooded her mind, and her heart ached.

Priscilla began to kick and whimper, giving Elizabeth the excuse she needed to leave the table. "I pray she isn't getting sick."

Abe looked worried. "If you think she should see a doctor, I'll be glad to drive you."

"*Danka dich*, Abe, but I'll wait and see how she feels later today."

He nodded, got up, and headed for the door. "I'll milk Tillie and take care of your horses." He paused with his hand on the door handle. "While I'm here, I might as well feed the ducks and chickens."

"I'd appreciate that."

Priscilla began to wail.

Abe grinned. "You look after her, I'll take care of everything outside."

She was almost grateful enough to hug him, but after his

proposition, she intended to keep her distance—unless she decided to accept his offer.

"Eat your mush, Daniel," Elam said.
"I hain't hungry."
Leah studied the boy's face, then addressed her brother. "He always eats a good breakfast. What's the matter?"
"We had a discussion last night." He felt like a tyrant, but it was his responsibility to raise the boys right. "There will be no more burrs under pillow covers, and I told him he has to apologize to his Aunt Mattie."
"Elam, do you think —"
"*Ja*, I do."
Jesse Mark munched a slice of bacon, his blue eyes shimmering. "Maybe Aunt Maddie's still sleepin'."
"There's no hurry." Elam ignored Leah's frown. Emma had warned him that Leah was being too lenient. It was a good thing he'd only been away for three weeks. His vacation would soon be up, and Daniel's school would start next Monday. He hoped to spend considerable time with his sons the next few days. He glanced at Aaron. "After breakfast, I'll have to look over the farm. Later, we'll go in to see Jonathan."
"Good. Rebecca and I would like to go to New Wilmington this morning."
Leah refilled his coffee cup. "Will you be back in time for dinner?"
"*Ja*."
At the sound of Mattie's footsteps in the first-floor bedroom, Daniel gripped the edge of the table and swallowed. Elam felt sorry for the boy, but right was right. But when he thought of the burrs pricking haughty Mattie, he had to fight a grin.
The woman entered the kitchen, swishing her dark-blue skirt. Pausing a few feet from the table, she eyed Daniel.

7

Elam watched his eldest son out of the corner of his eye. The boy squirmed and continued to stare at his untouched mush.

Mattie took a step closer to the table. "*Vell*, Daniel?"

Sighing, he met her gaze, his brown-green eyes unwavering. "*Es spied mich*, Aunt Mattie."

Her brows lowered a degree. "Sorry for what?"

Jesse Mark grinned, his dimples deep indentions in his round cheeks. "Fer gittin' caught."

Mattie drew a quick breath. Eyeing Elam, her lips tightened. "*Vell*, if you ask me, I—"

"You've received an apology, Mattie," Elam said.

She took her place at the table. "Some children are permitted too many liberties. If those boys were mine, I'd see that they were brought up properly."

Years ago, when Mattie had failed to conceive, Elam had felt compassion toward her and Jonathan. Now, he decided that God knew what He was doing. Reaching under the table, he grasped Daniel's knee and squeezed affectionately. The boy glanced at him and grinned, then gripping his spoon, he began to shovel mush into his mouth.

Elam smiled. Thank God he didn't have to depend on Mattie to help raise his boys. Leah was wonderful, although she let them get away with too much. *Elizabeth would have the perfect balance between leniency and discipline*, he thought, warming as a vision of her captured his mind. Had it only been yesterday morning that he'd said good-bye to her? Emptiness yawned within him, then yearning rushed in to fill the vacuum. Something akin to an octopus grew in his stomach, then tentacles stretched through him twisting and knotting like wild grapevines. His throat constricted as though the vines were entwined around his neck, making it difficult to swallow.

Rebecca watched. Elam had handled Mattie with firmness without criticizing the woman. She wondered if anyone ever got the urge to slap her, but that ungodly action would only make matters worse. If anything ever unlocked Mattie's heart, love would be the key.

A carriage stopped by the gate. Tim woofed a greeting as he left the porch.

Leah stood. "I'll see who it is."

"*Vea-gaits*, Leah," a pleasant female voice greeted.

"Good morning. *Cume onn* in and have breakfast."

Soft laughter rippled up the path as the visitor approached. "I've already eaten."

"There's fresh coffee."

"*Danka dich*." The woman stepped into the kitchen, seeming to bring sunshine with her. Blond hair shimmered from under the front of her prayer cap, and her light-blue eyes sparkled.

"Rebecca, Aaron," Leah said, "I'd like you to meet Susanna Yoder."

They acknowledged the introductions as Elam stood and turned to face the woman. She stepped quickly forward, and he caught her hands in his. Pink color bathed her cheeks, and her smile broadened, deepening her dimples.

"It's so good to have you home, Elam."

"It's good to be back."

Mattie cleared her throat, got up, and strode away from the table. "Susanna."

Susanna eyed the woman, her smile faded slightly, and her eyes filled with question. Obediently, she followed the older woman to a far corner. Elam frowned. Leah bit her lower lip and moved closer to Mattie as though she were intending to eavesdrop. It wouldn't have been necessary, for Rebecca could hear the woman from across the room.

"You look like a hussy," Mattie said.

Susanna gasped.

"You'd better get a basin of water and scrub that rouge from your cheeks."

"I'm not wearing rouge."

"*Ja?*"

"I've . . . never needed make-up, Mattie."

The older woman sniffed. "Have you never heard that pride goeth before destruction?"

"But . . ." Susanna's cheeks, which had been a soft pink, now blazed fuchsia.

Elam looked disturbed. "Mattie, isn't it time for you to get ready to go to the hospital?"

"*Ja.* I also presume it's my Christian duty to speak with the Bishop about the frivolousness of some of the young ladies in our district." Twitching her nose, she went into her room.

Elam moved to Susanna and grasped her hand. "Don't let Mattie's harshness upset you."

Her smile returned as she rested her other hand on his. "*Danka dich* for your concern, but everyone knows Mattie."

Rebecca surveyed the couple. Was Elam being a protective brother-in-law—or was there more to it? It was plain that Susanna had more than a sisterly interest. What had happened to the budding romance between Elam and Elizabeth Stoltzfus? She'd thought she'd witnessed their growing affection to each other. Had she been wrong?

Releasing Susanna's hand, Elam turned to Aaron. "I'm going to look over the farm."

Aaron nodded. "Rebecca and I will be leaving for New Wilmington shortly."

Daniel slid from his chair and joined his father at the door. "I'm going with you, Papa."

"Me, too!" Jesse Mark bounced across the room.

Elam took a small straw hat and plopped it on the littlest boy's head, handed another one to Daniel, then donned his own. Sweeping Jesse Mark onto his shoulders, he reached for Daniel's hand.

Susanna strode forward. "I might as well tag along." She looked quizzically at Elam, "If it's all right."

He smiled. "We'll be glad to have you."

She grasped Daniel's free hand. The foursome crossed the porch and headed toward the barn. Susanna said something that made Elam laugh.

"Susanna seems to care for Elam," Rebecca said.

"*Ja.* She loves the boys, especially Jesse Mark."

"She shows partiality?"

"She tries to hide it, but he looks so much like her, I can't blame her for taking to him." Leah looked pensive. "Susanna is sweet and would make Elam a good wife."

Rebecca turned to watch out the window. Susanna smiled vibrantly, flashing seductive dimples. Elam didn't seem to mind. What man would? If Elizabeth had designs on Elam, she'd be wise to do something about it soon.

Wiping a hand across her brow, Elizabeth sighed. It was warm again today, and Priscilla refused to take a nap. She thought of her mother. "We'll visit Mammy, Priscilla."

Donning her bonnet, Elizabeth took the baby and went to the carriage shed. She set the baby's basket on the back seat while she hitched up Xerxes. Priscilla wailed until they were headed out the lane. Elizabeth felt almost bleary-eyed from lack of sleep. Maybe her mother would have some advice.

Esther came out onto the porch as Elizabeth drove up. The older woman smiled, but concern shadowed her hazel eyes. "Are you all right?"

"*Ja,* Mama."

Eli, her younger brother, jogged from the barn. His blond hair curled from under his straw hat. He stopped at her carriage door, his blue eyes glistening. "I'll take Xerxes to the stable."

"*Danka Dich.*" Climbing down, she headed for the house. Priscilla had fallen asleep during the ride, but now she was fussing again.

Esther frowned. "You look harried, Elizabeth."

"I'm troubled over what could be bothering Priscilla. She's been so fussy, but she isn't teething, and she doesn't seem to have a fever."

The older woman accepted the baby and touched her lips to the infant's forehead. "She's cool to the touch."

"*Ja.*" Elizabeth sighed.

Sarah appeared at the door. Her smile was warm as always, her pretty oval face emanated affection, and her blue eyes were shining. "The water's hot. I'll have tea in a jiffy."

Twelve-year-old Ruth peered out from behind her sister, her brown eyes questioning. "What's wrong with Priscilla?"

Coming in, Elizabeth crossed the room and sank into the rocker. "She's probably fine."

Esther came to place a hand on her older daughter's forehead. "You aren't running a fever, either, dear."

"She's love sick," Ruth said. "And Priscilla is probably upset because she expected to get a papa." She rolled her brown eyes and flipped her hands. "But, Elizabeth ruined it all."

"Ruth, don't be naughty," Sarah reminded softly.

The younger girl giggled. "Poor Elam's probably mooning around, too." She pointed a finger at her older sister. "Or maybe he's already found someone else."

Elizabeth took a deep breath. "This morning, Abe ask me to marry him."

Ruth's eyes widened. "I thought you loved Elam!"

"I can't tear Priscilla away from Lancaster County." She blinked to disperse the sudden tears in her eyes.

"I'd hate to see you leave," Esther said, "but if you and Elam love each other, it's a precious gift and shouldn't be tossed away."

Priscilla continued to fuss, wanting constant attention. Esther frowned. "I think you should take her to see a doctor. Eli will drive you."

Elizabeth agreed.

Elam paced back-and-forth in his living room. Pausing at the stairway, he glanced up. "Daniel, are you dressed, yet?"

"*Ja*, Papa."

"*Vell*, then, let's go." Elam toyed with his straw hat. It wasn't like him to be apprehensive, but a son didn't start attending school every day. Was this what it was like to be a mother? He sighed.

Jesse Mark bounced down the stairs, grinning. "Can I ride to school with you 'n' Daniel?"

"You have to stay with your Aunt Leah."

The little boy's smile faded. "*Ferwass?*"

"After I drop Daniel off at school, I have to go on to catch my ride to work."

Jesse Mark stared at the oval braided rug by his feet, then tapped it with his toe. "If Aunt Leah followed us in her buggy, she could drive me back home."

Elam realized he was gripping his hat. Sighing, he put it on. "This is Daniel's first day at school, so it's his big day. You stay with Leah, and when I come home, we'll do something special."

"Just you 'n' Me, Papa?"

"*Ja*. Just you and me."

The sparkle returned to the boy's eyes. "I guess it'll be okay, then." He chewed his lower lip. "With Daniel gone, who will I play with?"

"Aunt Leah said she'd do whatever you liked this morning."

Daniel's heels thumped on the stairs as he descended. His hazel eyes showed anxiety, but his grin said everything was all right. "You ready, Papa?"

"*Ja*." Elam wished he felt as confident as Daniel looked.

His stomach felt like the butterflies had donned skates and were engaged in a roller derby. Had his first day of school been such an emotional upheaval? His mind rolled back. He remembered the excitement and enthusiasm. Then, he recalled the look on his mother's face. Had the luster in her eyes been tears? A grin toyed with the corners of his mouth. *Ja.* He blinked, wiped a hand across his eyes, and headed for his buggy. "Let's go, Daniel."

The doctor had found Priscilla in perfect health, but had prescribed a tonic for Elizabeth. Several days had passed, and she felt more harried than ever. Her thoughts were on Elam, except when she was distracted by the baby's fussing.

"*Danka Got* yesterday was an off Sunday," she said. Lately, she'd taken to talking to herself. Shushing Priscilla, she moved to a window and stared out at the drab day. Droplets ran down the glass in tiny rivulets. She supposed they needed rain, but the dark clouds only added to her gloom.

"Let's visit Emma, baby mine. Maybe she'll have a suggestion."

The thought made Elizabeth's heart beat faster. Maybe she would get first-hand information about Elam. She wrapped Priscilla, then tied her own navy-blue bonnet, flipped her cape over her shoulders, and headed for the carriage shed, Vashti on her heels. In her rush to get the baby in out of the drizzle, she slipped into a rut, turned her ankle, and cringed as pain shot up her leg. Hobbling into the shed, she slid open the carriage door.

Priscilla began to cry the instant Elizabeth left her on the seat. Disregarding her fussing, Elizabeth went for the horse. Thunder rumbled. Xerxes stomped, whinnied, and fought the bit. Vashti got excited and circled Elizabeth, tripping her. Gasping, she seized a wooden support beam to keep from sprawling in the fresh manure that Xerxes had inconveniently dropped. A splinter rammed under her fingernail. She cried out and clenched her teeth to keep from buffeting the horse.

Tears streamed down her face.

"What's happening to me?" She'd never struck any of her animals. "God, please help me resolve my quandaries."

Her finger thumping with pain and tears still wet on her cheeks, she hitched the horse to the buggy and headed for Emma's. Lightning flashed, thunder rumbled, and Priscilla wailed even louder. The drizzle turned into a downpour. Xerxes splashed through puddles, his dark coat becoming slick. He shook his drenched mane, but it clung to his neck. Rain drummed on the carriage roof, blocking out all other sounds, except for Priscilla's deafening wail.

As she halted the horse by Zooks' front gate, Jacob raced out to help her. Leaving him in charge of the carriage and animal, she thanked him and ran to the porch, protecting Priscilla with her cape.

Emma opened the door, worry shadowing her face. "Is something wrong?"

"Everything's wrong!" Elizabeth had until then managed to control her distress, but Emma's compassion brought tears.

Emma took the baby. "You get out of that wet cape." Cooing at Priscilla, she unwrapped her. The baby stopped crying and blinked. "What's bothering you on such a pretty, dark rainy day, little one?"

Elizabeth hung her cape and bonnet on a hook by the door, dropped into a kitchen chair, and propped her chin in her hands. The twins came from the living room. Malinda scooped up Priscilla and soon had her laughing.

"Take her in the room with the other <u>kinder</u>, girls," Emma said, then surveyed Elizabeth's face. She set a box of tissues within reach, moved to the stove and lit a flame under the kettle. "I'll make a pot of tea."

Elizabeth dabbed at her eyes with a tissue. "What am I going to do with Priscilla?"

"She's all right. What are you going to do about you?"

"There's nothing wrong with me."

"*Ach*." Emma moved to the table and sat in the nearest

chair. "You've lost weight, you're pale, and there are dark circles under your eyes."

"Because of the way the baby's been acting, I haven't been eating much, and I can't get any sleep."

Emma looked pensive. "Or is it the other way around?"

Confused, Elizabeth peered at her.

"Listen to Priscilla squealing. She's having a good time with my *kinder*."

Alarm seared through Elizabeth. "Am I losing touch with my little girl?"

Emma smiled. "Just the opposite! You've been so high-strung. Lately, you've been jumpy and tense. That betrays your inner turmoil."

"Oh! *Es spied mich*."

"There's nothing to be sorry about, except for not confiding in a friend." She hesitated, then reached for Elizabeth's hand. "Have you heard from Elam since he left?"

New tears welled in Elizabeth's eyes. "No."

"I know you love him. I'm delighted about that, but you let him go away alone. I can read your suffering in your eyes. I know babies, and I'm convinced that Priscilla is feeling your torment. Children know when their mother's are distraught, but they don't understand why. That upsets them, sometimes a lot!"

"If Elam really cares, why doesn't he write?"

"He has a lot to do. He took three weeks off to visit me, then Jonathan had that heart attack. It's harvest time and the work on the farm is running behind schedule. Elam has the boys to take care of, too, and this week he had to go back to work. He promised not to pressure you."

Elizabeth wanted to accept Emma's excuses, still . . .

"Leah wrote last week." Emma frowned. "Susanna Yoder is visiting Miller's nearly every day. She's the younger sister of Elam's late wife. She gets along great with the boys, especially Jesse Mark. He looks so much like her."

"She's . . . a good woman?"

"*Ja*, and pretty, too. Leah knew how Elam felt about you. She says he's quiet and withdrawn some of the time. She thinks his wistful expression comes when he's thinking about you." The furrow between her brows deepened. "Leah says she thinks Elam might turn to Susanna on the rebound."

Pain shot through Elizabeth. "I thought about going for a visit, but until Priscilla straightens up, I can't plan a trip."

"*Ach*! You can't afford not to!" She sighed. "Susanna probably would make Elam a good wife, but I had my heart set on you." She grinned. "How soon can you be ready to leave for Mercer county?"

"*Vell* . . . I'd have to write to Leah and arrange a time."

Emma's grin broadened. "I've already done that. I got a letter from her this morning. She says she has the guest room ready. She even scrubbed up Jesse Mark's crib and freshened the baby sheets."

Elizabeth blinked. "*Vell* . . . maybe I could be ready . . . by Saturday."

"This is only Monday!" Emma laughed. "I'll help you get ready. Sarah will help, too. We'll have you on your way by tomorrow."

"I have to make arrangements for someone to drive me."

"Jacob will go to see John Zimmerman. He's starting a taxi business for us Amish."

Elizabeth pictured the young Beachy Amishman, his curly sandy hair and laughing green eyes. "He's so young."

"He's twenty-one and enterprising. He's already made three trips to Mercer County. Mama Zook says he's cautious but qualified."

"Did John drive Elam home?"

"Aaron King drove him, because Elam had to leave right away, and John was in Philadelphia."

Elizabeth frowned. "Even if John is available, I can't leave tomorrow. Elam won't know I'm coming."

Waving a hand, Emma laughed. "Surprise him."

"I'd have to make arrangements for someone to care for my

livestock."

Emma waved a hand. "Abe's been doing a lot of it. He'll take care of everything for you."

Lightning lit up the sky, then a clap of thunder rattled the windows. Another flash was followed by deep rumbling that shook the foundation of the house. Squealing, the children tumbled over each other to get to the kitchen.

Emma laughed. "All this, and I forgot to make your tea."

The kitchen door flew open and Jacob burst into the house, his eyes wide. His wet clothing clung to his form, and water dripped from the brim of his straw hat. "Lightning struck the carriage shed! It's on fire!"

8

Emma leaped to her feet. "Andy! Sound the alarm!"

The second oldest boy sprang out the door and raced for the bell rope.

Jacob eyed his oldest son. "Dan! Get a bucket! Come with me!" Whirling, he ran outside.

Elizabeth stood gripping her face, then concern over Emma being six months pregnant frightened her. "Amanda, keep Priscilla and the small children in the house!"

Emma was on her way out the door. "Malinda! Run to the barn and get all the buckets you can find."

"Wait, Emma." Elizabeth raced after her. "I'll pump the water."

"The buggy is in the shed!" Emma cried.

Andy continued to yank on the bell rope. The bell clanged, summoning neighbors. Elizabeth prayed the storm wouldn't muffle the sound of the alarm. She raced into the yard. Pelting rain soaked her clothing and stung her face. "Xerxes is tied to the stable fence. I'll get him and hitch him to your buggy!" She ran across the barnyard, slipping and sliding in mud that coated her shoes. Her ankle hurt, but she ignored it. Her horse was excited and kicked as she unfastened him from her carriage. "Don't act up, Xerxes!" She led him to the shed, thankful that the fire was on the far end of the building. Smoke poured out the front door and collected in a cloud. Elizabeth wished she had something to put over her nose. Jacob raced by with two buckets of water. Dan came with his pails halffull, but it was all the six-year-old could carry.

Elizabeth's fingers trembled as she fumbled with the harness. In her haste, she tripped over her sodden dress and nearly fell. Grasping the bridle, she led Xerxes into the barnyard, pulling Zook's carriage away from the burning shed. She tied the animal to a fence and raced back to Emma. "I'll pump for awhile." She grasped the handle and continued to fill buckets.

Emma seized a bucket handle.

"Wait!" She grabbed the handle and pulled it from Emma's grasp. "The shed isn't worth your losing the baby!"

Emma's face paled. She put a hand on her abdomen as though the chaos had made her forget her condition.

Men came running from every direction, a bucket in each hand. An eleven-year-old neighbor boy took over the pumping. Elizabeth seized the filled bucket and ran toward the fire.

"More water on the inside!" Jacob yelled.

After several trips from the pump to the shed, Elizabeth was panting. Her sodden garments weighted her down, her prayer cap was askew, and her dress streaked with mud. She took over the pumping, again, hoping to catch her breath.

When the fire was out, the men began to joke and laugh. Everyone was soaked, so the heavy downpour no longer mattered.

Jacob removed his singed straw hat and combed his hair with his grimy fingers. "We only lost the back of the shed. The heat bubbled the roofing, but it needed replaced anyway."

One of the men slapped him on the back. "We'll come over in a few days and patch up the damage."

"*Ja*!" a wiry little man called. "It'll be an excuse for a get-together."

Elizabeth looked at Emma and grinned. "We'd better go in and make sandwiches for the men."

"*Ja*." Emma laughed. "I think I could stand a cup of tea now, too!"

Elizabeth followed Emma into the house. "I'll slice bread, and you can scurry up something to put between the slices."

"Right." She counted heads, making sure her children were all accounted for. "Amanda, you can put on a pot of coffee."

"I'll make hot chocolate," Malinda said. "It's a good thing we baked cookies this morning." She glanced at Elizabeth and laughed. "You'd better comb your hair and put on one of Mama's caps."

Elizabeth touched her head. Her prayer cap was gone and her hair hung in wet strands down her back. Glancing at the kitchen floor, she gasped. "We're tracking mud!"

"*Ach*, I'll scrub when this fracas is over." She looked at Elizabeth and grinned, her hazel eyes bright. "Malinda's right. You're a mess!"

"You are, too, Mama," Amanda said, laughing as she lit a flame under the coffee pot.

Emma headed for the downstairs bedroom. "*Cume onn*, Elizabeth. We'd better change into dry clothing."

After donning one of Emma's dresses, Elizabeth made it fit better by pinning an apron tighter. She combed her hair, put on a clean cap, and looked around for Priscilla. To her amazement, the baby was sleeping in the box in the corner of the living room. She smiled at Amanda. "Is this what it takes to get her to sleep?"

The girl giggled. "If so, don't plan on it again in a hurry."

Malinda looked out a window. "Three buggies are coming up the lane, Mama."

Emma smoothed her hair, refastened her prayer cap, and went to peer over her daughter's shoulder. "It's the Zimmerman's and the Lapps." Two teen age girls jumped from the first buggy and ran to the porch. Laughing, they stopped to shake the raindrops from their capes. "We came to see if we could help, Emma."

"It was a small fire, and your fathers helped put it out."

The tallest of the girls giggled. "Mama brought a cake and Aunt Lizzy brought a pie. We made some sandwiches, so let's have a party."

The men, sweaty, streaked with mud, and smelling like charred timber, clambered onto the porch. Jacob found chairs and benches for everyone. Malinda passed sandwiches and Amanda arranged cookies on plates for the other girls to offer to the guests. Elizabeth scurried through the kitchen filling coffee cups and making Kool-Aid. All the while, she prayed for guidance and made plans for her trip. Priscilla slept.

The next morning, Elizabeth bustled through her bedroom collecting items she would take with her to Mercer County. She wore a faded dark-blue dress because she had no intention of taking it with her. Smiling, she folded her new pink dress. It seemed fitting that she should wear it the first time for Elam.

Sarah Beiler, her younger sister, arrived to entertain Priscilla. "I think Emma's right, Elizabeth," she called from the living room between coos to the baby. "Priscilla is a perfect dear, unless she's with you."

Gasping, Elizabeth moved to the doorway to study her blond, blue-eyed sister. "How can you say such a thing?"

Sarah glanced up. "Oh, Elizabeth, *es spied mich*. I just meant that — *vell*, since Elam left you've been sort of overwrought. Emma said that the baby was probably aware of your gloom. I was agreeing with her, that's all." Her soft lips curved into an encouraging smile. "Once you see Elam, and your heart feels at home, I think Priscilla will return to her contented self.

"I pray you're right."

"Here comes your mother-in-law. She probably wants to say good-bye, so I'll take Priscilla to the swing."

"*Danka dich.*" Elizabeth smiled as she scurried to the living room to open the door for Nancy May Stoltzfus.

"*Vea-gaits*, dear." The older woman stepped through the doorway, clutching a small box. "I brought raisin-filled cookies for your trip." Not proffering the parcel, she crossed the room, sat on the sofa, and patted the cushion beside her. "I have something to confess, dear."

Elizabeth took a seat beside the woman.

Nancy rested her hands on the box. "Do you remember the *Englischer* that used to visit Mose?"

"Dave Stanton?"

"*Ja.*"

"I haven't seen him since Mose . . ." She cut off her words, for discussing Moses still anguished Nancy May.

"He was a Christian, Mama Nancy. Mose depended on him to drive, if he needed to go somewhere in a car."

"*Ja.* For non-Amish, he's a good man." A slight frown deepened the creases between her eyes. "I think Dave knew we're against taking photographs, but I saw him occasionally with a camera. I figured Mose would tell him what not to take pictures of. After Mose . . ." She blinked at the moisture in her eyes and cleared her throat. Hesitating, she ran a finger along the edge of the sofa.

Elizabeth gently touched the woman's arm. "We don't need to talk about this."

"*Ja*, we must." Nancy May sighed. "After the funeral, I received a card from Dave. He'd enclosed a photograph of Mose, stating that he thought I might want it."

Elizabeth's heart lurched. The lump in her throat prevented her from responding.

"Knowing I should burn it, I went to the stove, lifted the lid, and looked at the smoldering coals that would make quick ash of the picture. Then I looked at my sweet boy's face. He was smiling." Her voice caught. Sniffing, she took a quavering breath. "*Vell*, instead of burning the photograph, I hid it. It was all I had left of him." A tear escaped and trailed a wet ribbon down the woman's face. "I was keeping the picture for Priscilla, since she never knew her Papa. I want you to have it." Lifting the lid of the cookie box, she withdrew a sealed envelope and gave it to Elizabeth.

Her fingers trembled as she accepted the gift. "*Danka dich.*" Her first impulse was to rip the envelope open and look at the photograph, but having second thoughts, she let it rest in her lap. Photographs were forbidden, yet — When she was alone. . . "I'll treasure your gift, Mama Nancy, and make sure Priscilla sees it — when the time is right."

Susanna Yoder shut down the noisy gasoline motor that ran their washing machine and marveled, as always, at the sudden peace. Hoisting the last basket of wet clothes, she headed for the line, her navy-blue dress whispering against her legs. A blue bird sang, its notes corresponding with the melody in her heart. Elam was home. She'd been an eleven-year-old child seven years ago, when her sister had married Elam. *Even then, I idolized him.* Susanna's heart swelled.

Holding three clothespins between her teeth, she adjusted a sheet, then clipped it to the line. "I'll make sure I get him this time," she mumbled.

"Susanna!"

"*Ja*, Mama." She glanced over her shoulder at the older woman who remained bent over the rinse tub on the porch.

"There's one more sheet." Anna Mary sloshed it in the rinse water, cranked it through the hand wringer, then strode across the grass toward her daughter. "Do you plan to go over to see Leah again today, dear?"

"I'd like to." She had no intention of confessing that her trips had been to see Elam, not Leah. She studied her mother's tired features. The woman's hair had turned gray since her husband's death a year ago. Susanna did what she could, but grief had taken its toll. She accepted the wet sheet. "I'll hang all the clothes and empty the wash water before I go."

"All right, Susanna." She heaved a laborious sigh. "Your brother's going into New Wilmington with a friend, and he won't be back for supper."

"I'll be back, Mama, so you won't be alone."

Anna Mary smiled, her features relaxing. "I've always been able to depend on you."

Shaking the sheet, Susanna tossed it over the line. "You can depend on Amos, too." She pictured her handsome older brother. He'd just turned twenty. His eyes were turquoise; his blond hair was darker than hers, and being a man, he was permitted to let it hang to his collar. He adored Leah Miller. She smiled. Leah would make a great sister-in-law. But, Andy was also attracted to Elsie Miller, Leah's cousin, and couldn't make up his mind between the two.

Susanna pictured Elam's smiling face and hummed as she hung the rest of the clothes. She hoped he would be home before she had to leave Miller's place this afternoon. She thought about Mattie and frowned, hoping the woman wouldn't get back from the hospital until after Elam got home from work. She shrugged. Even if the woman accosted her, it would be worth it to be in Elam's company for awhile. Envisioning being near him, her heart raced.

Anna Mary brought a hand wash to the line, pinned it up, then turned to her daughter. "Did Leah say anything to you about Elizabeth Stoltzfus?"

Susanna shrugged. "Who's she?"

"I think she was a Beiler. Elam's mother said the woman's a close friend of Emma's."

"You look worried, Mama. Did Rachel say something about the woman to trouble you?"

Anna Mary's frown deepened. "I think Elam may have feelings for her."

Something tightened within Susanna. She felt as though she were strangling from within. Her stomach felt as though horses were galloping through. She turned away, not wanting her mother to see her distress. Was the monster within her jealousy? Her lips were taut as she clenched her fingers. *I'll not lose Elam*, she vowed. *I won't!*

Leah had rolled out noodles, hung towels over the back of kitchen chairs, then draped the ovals of dough over them to dry. Retrieving the first flattened oval, she spread it on the cutting board on the counter, cut it into two-inch strips, laid the strips on top of each other, then thinly sliced noodles. As she toiled, she pondered her letter from Emma. Would Elizabeth Stoltzfus come for a visit? If she did, and Elam asked her to stay, would she? Leah bit her lip. How would Susanna react to Elam's interest in another woman?

Jesse Mark giggled. Leah frowned. Daniel had been home from school for only a half hour, and both boys sounded like they were having too much fun. Dropping her knife onto the counter, she washed her hands, intending to investigate. A car stopped in front of the house. A shriek informed her that Mattie had come home early. Shuddering, Leah hurried onto the porch, stopped with a jolt, and gasped.

Daniel and Jesse Mark knelt in the yard facing each other, a kitten between them. Daniel had just dipped a brush into a can of bright-red paint and swiped it the length of the feline's back. Ruffy meowed, scrambled, jerked free, and streaked toward the barn. A stripe of brilliant red stained the gray kitten's left ear, traced along her spine, then trailed down her right side.

Mattie stood transfixed, blinking. Regaining her voice, she stormed through the gate. "Why'd you boys paint the cat?"

Jesse Mark turned innocent blue eyes in her direction. "Cause gray wasn't very pretty."

"Humph!" Mattie's dark eyes pierced Leah. "Don't you ever watch these boys?"

Leah descended the porch steps, but paused a few feet from the *kinder* to watch the navy van that cruised up the lane and stopped in front of the house. Mattie straightened as though she intended to appear regal, but her dark-blue dress was drab and her brown bonnet far from a crown. A young woman climbed out of the van with a baby in her arms. Leah rushed forward. Even though eight years had passed since she'd seen Elizabeth Beiler, she would've recognized her anywhere. "I'm so glad you came!"

Elizabeth smiled. "I'm glad I could make the trip."

After hugs, Leah took the baby. "So, this is little Priscilla." Mattie cleared her throat.

"Oh, *Es spied mich*, Mattie. This is Elizabeth Beiler

Stoltzfus. Elizabeth, I'd like you to meet my sister-in-law, Mattie Miller."

The older woman smiled as she extended her hand. Leah wondered how long it had been since Mattie had smiled. It transformed her sour features into something almost affable. Blinking, Leah stared.

"How's Jonathan?" Elizabeth asked.

"He's improving slowly." Mattie drew a deep breath. "I expect him to be released from the hospital in a few days."

"That's wonderful."

Mattie's eyes returned to the boys. They stood at attention, practically quavering in her shadow. Daniel continued to grip the brush handle. A drop of red paint left the end of the bristles and stained a weed by his foot. "Where'd you get that hideous paint?"

Daniel swallowed. "It was just sittin' out by the road."

She leaned to peer into the can. "There's hardly any left." She eyed Jesse Mark. "What else did you paint?"

"Nothin', Aunt Maddie."

The woman seemed to be stifling a huff as she faced Leah. "You'd better get them cleaned up." She stared toward the barn and shook her head.

"As for that kitten . . ."

Leah's gaze met Elizabeth's laughing brown eyes. "These are Elam's sons."

"*Ja.* I assumed so. Is he home?"

"Not yet. Come in and relax. You've had a long trip." She glanced toward the car. "What about the driver? Will he stay for supper?"

"I think he was hoping to be invited."

"Of course he's welcome. Is he going back tonight or staying over?"

"Is there a place he can stay?"

"*Ja.* Elam has an extra bedroom."

"John was hoping for that. It was a long trip." She turned toward the car and motioned for the young man to join them.

Smiling, he ran his fingers through his sandy curls and donned his straw hat. He seemed friendly but less than confident as he joined them in the yard.

A buggy rumbled up the lane, and Leah turned to peer in that direction. "Here comes Susanna Yoder."

Mattie strode quickly into the house. Leah prayed the woman would go to her room and stay until supper. She seemed to be in a better mood than usual, though.

Susanna climbed from her carriage and came up the path, her lively gate making her deep-purple skirt swing. She smiled, but Elizabeth's presence seemed to unusually pique her interest. John moved to the apple tree some distance away as Leah introduced the women. Elizabeth's smile remained constant. Did Susanna's seem to waver?

"This is Elizabeth's baby?" Susanna peered at Priscilla.

Leah proffered the little girl.

Susanna hesitated, then took the wiggling bundle. "*Vea-gaits*, little one." There seemed to be a catch in her voice, and tiny tones of green that Leah hadn't noticed before, shimmered in the woman's blue eyes.

"Can you stay for supper, Susanna?"

"*Danka dich*, Leah, but my brother won't be home for supper tonight, and I promised Mama I'd be back." She handed Priscilla back to Leah and trained her attention on the boys. "You going to paint something red?"

"Nah." Daniel lowered his gaze and dropped the brush into the near empty paint can.

Jesse Mark giggled. "We're done. We painted Ruffy!"

Susanna laughed. "What a lucky kitty!"

Daniel frowned. "Aunt Mattie didn't like it."

"*Ach*, don't worry about Aunt Mattie. I think a red kitty would be very pretty."

"*Danka dich*, Aunt Susanna." Daniel looked pleased.

Leah cringed. She noticed Elizabeth's smile fade as though she considered Susanna's reaction to be unwise. Leah handed the baby back to Elizabeth. "I must get you boys cleaned up before your papa gets home." She looked apologetically at Elizabeth. "I'll make tea as soon as I get things under control."

"I'll make the tea." Susanna smiled. "After all, I'm used to the kitchen." She aimed her gaze at Elizabeth. "This is practically my second home."

"I imagine it is." Elizabeth tone was soft. "Aren't you Elam's sister-in-law?"

"*Ja*." The word came out quickly. Susanna whirled and entered the house.

"*Cume onn* in, Elizabeth." Leah led the way, a boy's wrist clasped in each of her hands. "Don't you boys touch anything until I get the paint off of your fingers." She sighed. "I'm glad neither of you got any on your broadfalls."

Jesse Mark blinked up at her. "You gonna tell Papa?"

Leah grinned. "Not unless I must."

"I hope he doesn't see Ruffy until she cleans off the paint," Daniel said, his frown shadowing his slender face.

"*Ja, vell*, I don't think she'll be able to do that easily."

Daniel looked worried, but Jesse Mark grinned. Leah figured another adventure was already beginning to form in his mind. Daniel, being the oldest, usually got the blame for not stopping the episodes, but she knew that most of the time Jesse Mark had been the instigator. She wondered how long it would take Mattie to prattle this story to Elam.

John Zimmerman followed them into the house. He stood, straw hat in hand, looking self-conscious. His green eyes shimmered with appreciation as he watched Susanna.

Smiling, she motioned to the wall by the door. "Hang your hat on one of the pegs, then make yourself comfortable in the living room." She turned to Elizabeth. "You'll find a rocker in the room."

"*Danka dich*." Elizabeth seemed to suddenly grow uneasy. For a minute, she watched Susanna bustle around the kitchen, her brown eyes quizzical. She caught her lower lip between her teeth, then moved to the living room.

Leah tightened her lips. It was *her* responsibility to make her visitors feel at home, and she wished the boys hadn't made the situation difficult. She frowned. Susanna was acting peculiarly. What had gotten into her?

Susanna took over as though she were the hostess. She made tea and arranged cookies on a plate. As she served John Zimmerman, she smiled, flashing deep dimples. He was instantly besotted. She seemed cordial toward Elizabeth, but Leah perceived a strange reluctance, although it only showed in Susanna's blue eyes.

Leah moved to the rocker and noticed that Priscilla had fallen asleep in Elizabeth's arms. "Let me take her upstairs to your room and put her in the crib."

Smiling, Elizabeth gave her the baby.

Susanna seemed to ponder the situation, then she said, "I'll take tea and cookies to the Granddawdy house for Rachel and Jonah."

Leah nodded. "That would be nice."

Arranging the items on a tray, Susanna then hurried through the living room and swept through the swinging side door which now connected the main dwelling to the Granddawdy house.

Elizabeth watched her go. Emma had told her about Susanna's loveliness, but had underestimated the girl's allure. Had Elam already succumbed to Susanna's charm? Her heart ached. She'd been foolish not to accept Elam's proposal. Had he assumed the problems in their relationship were too complicated to be resolved? Amishmen don't usually wait long to secure a wife. Had Elam already fallen for Susanna? Were they already committed to each other?

As questions tumbled over themselves in Elizabeth's mind, her stomach knotted and her heart pounded. Had she been foolish to come? Would she be returning to Lancaster County with John Zimmerman tomorrow?

She took a cookie from the plate Susanna had set on the stand and took a bite, but the tasty morsel seemed to turn to plaster in her mouth. She swallowed, wishing for Elam to hurry home. Then, dreading the possibly disappointing confrontation, she prayed he would be late. Her throat constricted, making her feel as though she were going to choke. She sipped the sweet tea, but it seemed tasteless, now.

John stood. "I think I'll take a walk around the farm."

"Have a good time." Elizabeth smiled, thankful he was leaving the room. She'd felt his eyes on her and wondered if he'd perceived her discomfort.

Alone in the living room, she surveyed her surroundings. The brown sofa and green chairs were drab and uninteresting, but looked comfortable. The small tables bedecked with oil lamps and the braided scatter rugs made the room cozy. It was similar to all other Amish homes, even her own — except her burgundy and cream decor was more colorful. Emma had warned her that the districts here weren't as progressive as in Lancaster. She wondered what to, or not to, anticipate.

Hearing horse and buggy wheels clattering up the lane, she jumped to her feet, longing to race to greet Elam, but discovered her legs wouldn't move. Leah's footsteps resounded on the stairs as she descended to the kitchen. Elizabeth closed her eyes. Pressing her trembling fingertips against her pulsating temples, she struggled to regain her poise, and drew a deep breath. Maybe the visitor wasn't Elam.

"Papa's home!" Daniel raced through the kitchen and out the screen door.

"I'm comin', too!" Jesse Mark hurried out, letting the screen door bang.

Elizabeth jumped. Her breath came in short gasps. She curled her fingers into fists to try to stop their trembling. Slowly, she moved to the doorway, but paused just out of sight of the kitchen entrance.

Susanna whisked back through the swinging door and scurried through the living room, her skirt swishing. She appeared not to notice Elizabeth as she swept by her. She crossed the kitchen as Elam and the boys entered. "*Vea-gaits*,

Elam." Her tone was soft and her voice melodious.

"Susanna! It's good to see you."

"Do you really mean it, Elam?"

"I don't say things I don't mean."

Elizabeth stepped to the doorway. She knew she was pretty, but how could she hope to measure up to the alluring Susanna? Elam's back was to her. He grasped both of Susanna's hands. The girl smiled up at him, her cheeks rosy and her blue eyes shimmering.

I'm too late, Elizabeth thought, forcing back hot tears that fought to escape.

Leah touched Elam's arm. "We have company."

He chuckled. "Since when is our Susanna company?"

"I'm not referring to Susanna."

"*Vea-gaits*, Elam," Elizabeth said, her voice catching.

Still gripping Susanna's hand, he whirled. His gaze locked with Elizabeth's. His smile dissolved, and his lips parted. Elizabeth stared at the couple. She opened her mouth to tell Elam how happy she was to see him, but the words stuck in her throat. She clasped her hands to still her trembling fingers. Her heart hung suspended between ecstacy and despair as though wondering which way to swing. Suddenly, it seemed difficult to breathe.

9

Elam blinked. He'd envisioned Elizabeth so often. Was this another apparition? He wasn't aware of the firm grip Susanna had on his hand until he tried to free his fingers. He pulled away slowly so as not to seem rude. Half expecting Elizabeth to vanish, he stepped forward. "How's Priscilla?"

"She's . . . fine."

Elizabeth's complexion was a bit wan, and he wondered if she'd been ill. "And you?"

"I'm . . . fine, too."

Elam paused. Their conversation was awkward. He wanted to rush forward and embrace her as he had so often in his dreams, but there were eyes watching as well as too many unanswered questions concerning her reason for being here. Moisture made gold flecks sparkle in her lustrous brown eyes.

"You've been well?" she asked, her voice tremulous.

"*Ja.*" He wanted to tell her he'd been miserable since he'd said goodbye to her in Bird-in-Hand, but he didn't want to air their intimacies in front of Susanna, Leah, or his boys.

Priscilla began to cry. Elizabeth headed for the stairs.

"Wait." Elam grasped her hand. "Is she in the guest room?"

"*Ja.* Leah put her in the crib."

"Let me go for her." At first, she seemed reluctant, then she smiled. He took the stairs two at a time, thankful for a few minutes to collect his senses. Why hadn't Leah told him Elizabeth was coming? Daniel and Jesse Mark scurried up the stairs behind him. He smiled, thankful for the opportunity to introduce them to Priscilla without others witnessing their reactions.

Daniel paused at the bedroom door, doubt shadowing his hazel eyes.

Jesse Mark ran to the crib, grasped the bars, and peered at the crying infant. "What's the matter with it, Papa?"

Elam chuckled. "That's what we're going to find out." As he lifted Priscilla, she looked at him, blinked, and quieted. Crossing the room, he sat in a rocker and rested her in his lap.

Jesse Mark hung over the right arm of the chair, his eyes light-blue spheres of expectancy. Reaching slowly, he touched the baby's booted foot. "It has little feet, Papa."

"She's a girl. Her name is Priscilla." He looked at Daniel. The boy stood gripping the door frame and staring at the floor. "*Cume* here, Son."

Obediently, he moved closer, but let his arms dangle at his sides. Instead of looking at Priscilla, he turned his head to gaze out the window.

Jesse Mark bounced at Elam's right elbow. He touched the baby's hand. She grasped his finger. He giggled. "She likes me!"

The older boy's lack of interest concerned Elam. He actually seemed troubled. "Daniel, isn't Priscilla a pretty baby?"

"*Ja.*" Still, he kept his eyes averted.

Elam stood. "You sit in the rocker." He waited for his oldest son to get comfortable, then he put the baby in the boy's lap. "Put your arms around her so she won't fall on the floor."

He obeyed, but held his arms rigid. Finally, he looked at the baby, but his expression was unreadable. She began to kick and fuss, probably because of the way he held her. "Take her, Papa. It's Jesse Mark's turn."

Bending, Elam lifted Priscilla. Daniel slipped from the rocker and raced from the room. Puzzled, Elam listened to the boy's retreating footsteps.

"My turn, Papa." Jesse Mark scrambled into the rocker and

adjusted the pillows.

Turning back to his youngest son, he smiled at the uplifted chubby arms. Gently, he laid Priscilla in the three-year-old's lap, but was hesitant to withdraw his supporting hands.

"Let go. I wanna do it myself. Daniel did."

Elam moved away, but remained poised in case he would have to catch the little girl.

Jesse Mark grinned down at her. "*Vea-gaits*, baby. I'm glad you came to play with me." He began making clicking and cooing sounds.

"Oh." Blinking up at him, Priscilla reached for the boy's nose.

"She smells pretty."

"That's baby powder."

Jesse Mark gazed up at Elam, silver specks dancing in his blue eyes. He grinned, deepening his dimples more than usual. His round face beamed. "She likes me, Papa!" Lowering his long gold lashes, he peered at the baby. "I like her, too!"

Warmth spread through Elam. If Elizabeth agreed to stay, there would be no problem with Jesse Mark. He fought a frown. However, with Daniel . . .

Elizabeth had watched Elam until he'd vanished at the top of the stairs, then she turned to face the other two women.

Susanna smiled. "I guess he's anxious to see the baby."

"Priscilla adores him." Elizabeth held her smile, but felt uncomfortable under Susanna's scrutiny.

Leah went to the counter and began to swiftly cut noodles. "I should've had this done a long time ago."

"Let me," Susanna said. "You see to the rest of your supper."

Leah surrendered the knife. Grabbing a quilted mit, she opened the oven door to check the roast. "It's nearly done. So are the potatoes."

"Supper smells delicious." Elizabeth stepped forward. "I'll set the table if you show me where the dishes and silverware

are kept."

"The plates are in the second cupboard to your left," Susanna said, before Leah had a chance to. "The silverware is in the first drawer to the right of the sink." She didn't look up, but continued to feverishly slice noodles.

Elizabeth noted her determined expression and wondered why making pasta was such a challenge. She opened the cupboard to get plates. Daniel clomped down the stairs, raced across the kitchen and out the door, letting it bang.

"Daniel Miller!" Leah called. "You come back and close that door properly." She watched him head for the barn, his pace increasing. Sighing, she opened the cupboard and began to collect water glasses.

Clipped footsteps resounded as Mattie joined them. "You're going to let that boy ignore your commands?" She glared at Leah, then crossed the room to peer out a window. Clucking her tongue, she bent to pick up a small rectangular basket. "*Vell*, I see no one gathered the eggs."

Leah balanced a tray of water glasses on one arm and began to place one behind each plate. "I didn't have time, yet, Mattie."

The older woman smiled at Elizabeth. "If she made those boys mind, she'd have more time to do the chores."

Leah's face remained expressionless. "The boys were good today, Mattie."

"*Ja?*" She moved to the door, her brown skirt flipping. "I suppose painting a kitten gaudy-red is being on their best behavior." She sniffed. "Not to mention ignoring your summons."

When Mattie crossed the porch and headed for the henhouse, Elizabeth expected Leah to defend herself, but she remained silent. "How many places shall I set, Leah?"

"Eight," Susanna said, forcefully driving the knife through another layer of noodles.

Leah glanced at her, then looked at Elizabeth. "Counting John Zimmerman, there'll be nine. Mama and Papa eat here — unless they're under the weather more than usual. When that's the case, I take it to the *Dawdy House* and serve them."

Elizabeth reached to the second shelf for cups and saucers. "I haven't seen Rachel and Jonah since they moved away."

"They're anxious to see you."

Elam descended the stairs with Priscilla, Jesse Mark in tow. "They knew Elizabeth was coming?"

"None of us did. Emma said she was working on it. We just hoped."

"Oh." He swung Priscilla in his arms, making her laugh.

Daniel came to the house, but instead of coming in, he sat on the top porch step and gazed toward the cornfield. The collie flopped to the floorboards beside him, panting and wagging his tail as though he expected the boy to play with him. Maintaining a glum expression, Daniel rested his hand on the dog's tawny head.

Susanna finished cutting noodles and tossed them until they separated and lay in small twisted strips that resembled a group of white worms. After washing her hands, she strode to the screen door. "Daniel, would you and Jesse Mark like to come to my house for supper?"

Daniel was ruffing up Tim's tawny coat. His hands stopped and he gazed up at her with serious hazel eyes. "*Danka dich*, Aunt Susanna, but I'll stay here with Papa."

"But he has another baby to play with tonight." She smiled coaxingly at Jesse Mark. "How about you, my little man?"

"Nah." He grinned, his dimples matching hers. "I wanna stay 'n play with Prissy-cilla."

Her smile seemed to wane slightly. "*Ja. . .vell*, some other time, then."

"Do the boys eat with you often?" Elizabeth asked.

The woman turned to Elizabeth, her lips drawn into a seductive bow. "Not as often as I'd like them to." She blinked her long blond lashes. "But. . .maybe some day. . ." Tilting her head at a coy angle, she peered at Elam. He was gazing at Priscilla. Her gurgling laughter drew Susanna's attention. "She's adorable."

Elam glanced her way. "*Ja.* She's just what we need around here." He rocked the baby in wide sweeps, his grin broadening when she laughed and grabbed for his beard.

Susanna drew a long slow breath.

Mattie returned, set her basket of eggs on the bench inside the door, and looked at Elizabeth. "Leah said you might be coming, but we didn't expect you so soon. It's nice you could visit before cold weather sets in."

Elam stopped in mid-swing and turned to look at Mattie, puzzlement stealing his smile. "Visit?" His brown eyes caught and held Elizabeth's.

Turning away, she busied herself setting silverware at each place. Later, she and Elam would talk. Somehow, in front of Susanna, she preferred to remain silent. If she decided to stay, she wanted Elam to be the first to know. Besides, she had to find out how close he was to Susanna before she considered staying for even a brief visit.

Susanna seemed disturbed, although she continued to smile. "I must be going. Mama is expecting me."

"It was nice to meet you, Susanna," Elizabeth said.

"*Ja.* You, too." She pushed open the screen and slowly crossed the porch. "I'll see you tomorrow." She paused to pat Daniel's small shoulder. Bending, she whispered something in his ear. He nodded. She hastened her footsteps as though she'd suddenly remembered an unfinished chore.

Going to the door, Elizabeth watched her leave. *I don't like the buggies here as well as at home*, she thought, studying the orange-brown canvas covering Susanna's conveyance, and comparing them to the gray carriages in Lancaster that had sliding doors and glass windows. If she stayed, there would be a lot of inconveniences she would have to accept and adjust to. *No bathroom*, she thought with a grimace. Her family had had an outhouse when she was small. Had she been so spoiled so quickly? She thought of other inconveniences. How many sacrifices would she have to make?

Oh, God, she prayed, *help me not to be selfish. Give me*

a willing heart. Remembering Susanna, she swallowed. What if the woman had already captured Elam's affection? Her heart drummed as the fear took root. *If that's the case, God, bless them, but give me strength and courage to accept it.*

"Which one of you boys want to go to tell Mammi Rachel and Papa Jonah to come for supper?" Leah glanced first at Daniel. The boy sat transfixed, staring at Susanna's vanishing buggy.

"I'll go!" Jesse Mark scurried through the living room and pushed open the swinging door that connected the main dwelling to the four-room *Dawdy House*.

Mattie surveyed the table. "I'll slice the bread." Moving to the sink she washed her hands.

"Daniel," Leah called. "Come wash your hands for supper."

He rose, entered the kitchen, and turned on the spigot. As he rubbed soap on his fingers, he seemed to study the bubbles with intensity. Elam watched him, a frown furrowing his brow.

Jesse Mark raced back into the living room, letting the swinging door violently flapp behind him.

Mattie whirled, a scowl shadowing her features. She pointed the bread knife that she still clutched. "Young man, you go back through that door and come into this house in a civil manner."

The little boy blinked. His smile vanished and his dimples looked like tiny sad depressions in his chubby cheeks. He turned, walked to the door and vanished to the other side.

"He's just a little boy," Leah said, her tone soft, but firm.

"Humph." Mattie scowled at the spot where he'd last been seen. "*Vell?*" The syllable reverberated through the house and seemed to bounce off the walls.

Elam frowned. He looked as though he were about to speak, but he remained silent, apparently not wishing to aggravate the already tense moment. Slowly, the door swung inward to admit Jesse Mark.

"That's better." With a sniff, Mattie finished slicing bread, put the plate on the table with a clatter, and propped her fists on her ample hips. "Where's John Zimmerman?"

"I'll call him." Leah hurried to the porch.

Daniel moved to his place and stared at the table.

Elam looked at him. "Go to the living room and hold the door for your elders," he said quietly.

"*Ja*, Papa." He strode to the living room as though he had a weight on his small shoulders. Pushing open the adjoining door, he stood holding it.

"*Danka dich*, Daniel," a kindly voice resounded. Leaning on a walker, Rachel slowly made her way through the living room. Jonah maneuvered his wheelchair behind her.

Elizabeth's heart hurt within her. The couple had aged so much in eight years that she hardly recognized them. She moved forward, hoping her smile camouflaged her concern. "*Vea-gaits*, Rachel." She looked at the old man. "To you, too, Jonah."

He laughed, his voice cracking. "*Vell*, if it hain't the lovely Elizabeth!"

"Welcome, dear. We've been anxious for your visit." Rachel's soft-gray eyes and friendly smile hadn't been altered by ill health. She looked at Elam and her smile broadened. "Let's see Elizabeth's baby."

"You sit down, Mama, and he'll let you hold her." Jonah was thin, his face above his gray beard wan, but his sagacious blue eyes still twinkled with expectancy. Grunting, he pulled out a kitchen chair for his wife.

Thanking him, she sat, shoved her walker aside, and reached for Priscilla. Jesse Mark bounced beside the old lady, but Daniel stood on the far side of the room, watching. John Zimmerman came in, scanned the Miller family with his eyes, then smiled at Rachel. Leah lifted the roast and vegetables and Mattie set the food on the table. Jonah took his place as head of the family, although the responsibilities of the farm had been passed on to Jonathan. Everyone took a place and bowed their heads for silent grace.

Leah had placed Elizabeth next to Elam. She let her hands

lay in her lap and closed her eyes. Her heart lurched and began to pound when she felt Elam's fingers cover hers. Since their hands were hidden by the cloth that draped over the edge of the table, she rested her left hand on top of his. Jonah said the amen. Elizabeth opened her eyes to find Elam gazing at her. Had his silent grace been as fragmented as hers had been? Warmth bathed her cheeks. He gently squeezed her hand, then released it.

"Eat your carrots, Daniel," Mattie said.

Stabbing a round slice with a fork, he drew circles through the butter on his plate.

Elam watched him, a frown toying with his lips. "If you eat your vegetables, I'll take you boys fishing Saturday morning."

Mattie's fork clattered to her plate. "Shouldn't you start to cut the corn on Saturday?"

"There'll be time for that." Elam smiled, apparently trying to put her mind at ease. "I was away from the boys for three weeks, and I want to spend a little time with them."

The woman looked annoyed. "If you'd been here to help, maybe Jonathan wouldn't have had a heart attack."

"Now, Mattie." Jonah's tone was corrective, but soft. "We're in God's will, and everything will go according to His plan."

She busied herself cutting her portion of roast. If she was resentful over the slight rebuke, she hid it well.

"Give me the baby, Mama," Leah said, lifting Priscilla from the old woman's lap. "You won't be able to eat with her wriggling."

Rachel looked disappointed. "All right, Leah, but I get to rock her after supper."

Jonah laughed. "If things work out the way I expect them to, you'll have lots of babies to rock."

Elam grinned.

Heat flashed across Elizabeth's cheeks as she envisioned having babies with Elam. Her heart reached out in eager anticipation, but then, picturing Susanna, she felt stricken. Had

Jonah been referring to the lovely young woman who had served them tea and cookies this afternoon? Suddenly the savory bite of roast in her mouth became tasteless. Her throat tightened, and her stomach felt as though the lining had turned to granite. Determined to hide her dismay, she smiled and swallowed, forcing a look of normality.

Elam found it difficult to wait until after supper to get Elizabeth alone. When her plate was empty and her tea cup drained, he stood. "Leah, watch Priscilla and the boys." He gripped Elizabeth's hand. "*Cume onn.*"

Jonah laughed, his voice cracking. "You didn't ask the lady if she was finished eating, Son."

"I've had plenty." Elizabeth got up and accompanied Elam to the porch. The blood pounded in her temples and her knees felt weak. "Shall we sit on the swing, Elam?"

"Let's take a walk. I want to show you the farm."

Her mouth went dry as they crossed the barnyard. She wished he would tell her how he felt. If he procrastinated much longer, she wondered if she would scream.

As they walked, Elam pointed out fields of corn, showed her where they had grown oats and where they would soon plow to plant winter wheat. They walked by his house, but instead of taking her inside to see it, he only waved his hand, telling her that was where he lived. Had he lived there with Mary? What difference did that make? She was gone. It was the thought of him with sweet Susanna that brought moisture to her eyes, blurring her vision.

"Elam . . . can we talk . . . about the future?"

He appeared pensive, and his steps seemed to falter. "There's something you should know right away, Beth."

She swallowed. Trying to meet his gaze failed, so she stared at the side of the barn that screened them from the house. This was what she had asked for. Now she was sorry she'd pressed the issue.

Elam drew a long breath. "It's about. . .Susanna."

Pain shot through Elizabeth, and she felt numb. "You mean you. . .and Susanna?"

"*Vell . . . Ja.*"

Elizabeth wanted to run, maybe all the way back to Lancaster. Why wouldn't her legs move? Why had she come? Blinking, she forbade the tears that threatened.

"For a long time," Elam began, then hesitated. "*Vell*, you see, Susanna . . ." He cleared his throat. "After Mary died, Susanna's parents encouraged us to get together. I want to explain the situation right away, so you'll know what to expect."

Unable to restrain her tears, she turned her head to hide her face from him. This was torture. She wished he would get it over with quickly.

"Beth," he said slowly, his voice brimming with compassion. "Susanna intends to marry me."

Elizabeth gasped.

10

Elam felt Elizabeth's body jerk as though someone had struck her. Gripping her shoulders, he turned her to face him. She lowered her chestnut lashes, but a tear trailed moisture down one cheek. "Beth! Oh, Beth."

She opened her mouth to speak, but no sound came. She tried to pull away.

He tightened his grasp. "Beth, what's wrong?"

She looked up, her velvety-brown eyes shimmering with a dampness that made the gold flecks seem to swim. "You said you loved me! Now, you say you're going to marry Susanna!"

"You misunderstood." He pulled her into his arms. "I love you, dearly. There's no one else for me." He kissed the side of her face and held her close. "I was miserable after I left Lancaster, but there was nothing else I could've done. My job is here. After Jonathan's heart attack, I have the farm work, too. Leah needs help with my ailing parents, and Mattie only complicates matters."

"But, you said Susanna . . ."

"She has some obsession about marrying me. I have no intention of doing so. You're the only woman in my heart, Beth."

"I love you so, Elam," she whispered.

His mouth covered hers and ecstacy seemed to float them into another world. He'd hungered for her kisses, but instead of being satisfied, he craved complete fulfillment. "Stay, Beth. Be my wife."

"*Ja*, Elam. For always."

Daniel rounded the barn, stopped with a jolt, and stared. Apparently Elizabeth had seen him from the corner of her eye, for she pulled away quickly. Whirling, Daniel fled.

"Daniel!" Elam called.

Not slowing, he vanished into the corn field nearest the house.

Elam frowned. "He's been acting strangely this evening. Did something happen to upset him before I got home?"

"*Vell*," she drawled, "not unless the kitten . . ."

"*Ja?*"

She looked pensive, then shrugged. A grin toyed with her soft lips. "*Ach*, it was nothing."

Elam thought about his oldest son's reaction when he'd introduced him to Priscilla. "Daniel's been acting oddly since I got back from Bird-in-Hand."

"It's probably because he missed you."

"*Ja*." He shrugged. "I'll handle him later. I brought you out here to smother you with kisses." But. . .before that, "I feel I must warn you about Susanna."

Elizabeth's eyes widened. "Warn?"

He sighed. "Susanna's sweet and lovely, but who knows what she might do if she's losing something she thinks she wants." His mind rolled back over the past seven years. "When I courted Mary, Susanna was only a child, but she seemed jealous. After I married her sister, she refused to speak to either of us. Once, Susanna might have tried to harm Mary."

"How?"

He felt reluctant to dredge up the shadowy events of the past, but he felt he should. "Susanna could have tripped, but she fell against Mary, nearly shoving her through an opening in the second-story barn floor. If Mary hadn't been quick enough to seize the edge of the chopper, she would've tumbled into the bull pen where she probably would've been trampled or gored by the temperamental animal."

"Oh, Elam."

"Susanna insisted it had been an accident. Afterwards, she seemed to change. Eventually, the differences between her and Mary were resolved and their sisterly relationship resumed."

"Elam, are you saying . . ." Elizabeth spoke in a choked whisper. "Are you afraid she might try something like that again?"

"I don't want to think so, but. . .Susanna seems, *vell*, possessive." He pulled Elizabeth into an embrace, shuddering at the thought of losing her. "I want to love you, make you happy, and keep you safe for always."

Her arms went around his neck, and she rested her head against his chest. "I want to make you a perfect wife and be the best mother ever for your sons."

"My boys will be your sons, and your daughter, my little girl." Love swaddled them in a cocoon of joy that promised a wonderful future together.

Oh, God, Elam prayed, *don't let anything destroy our faith in each other. We are first your servants, oh Lord. Please fulfill our hopes, expectations and dreams.*

Elizabeth stretched and yawned. The scarlet sunrise cast a rosy glow around her bedroom. Sunshine filled her heart, too. *Was it only yesterday that I questioned Elam's love?*

Turning her head, she gazed at the crib. Priscilla had slept soundly all night. Had Emma been right? Had the baby been disturbed because she was sensing Elizabeth's torment? A smile curved her mouth. "Oh, baby dear, everything's going to be wonderful, now," she whispered, envisioning her future with Elam and his sons.

The aroma of brewing coffee and frying bacon mingled with that of muffins baking and wafted up the stairs. Flipping back her quilt, Elizabeth got up. Elam planned to stop in for breakfast, and she intended to be dressed and ready to greet him.

Moving to the wall where her dresses hung on pegs, she looked at her light-green one, then at the light-blue. "The new pink one will do nicely," she said, pondering the twinkle in

Elam's eyes when he gazed at her.

Dressed, she moved to the crib. Bending, she tenderly brushed a blond curl from the sleeping infant's round rosy cheek. She smiled as she tiptoed to the hall and slipped down the stairway, her feet light on the treads.

Mattie stood at the woodstove stirring something in a pan.

Leah had sliced oranges and arranged them on a plate. Their tangy essence added to the tantalizing smells that filled the kitchen. Lifting the plate, Leah turned, noticed Elizabeth, and her eyes widened. Her mouth moved forming soundless words as she waved frantically with her free hand. Elizabeth puzzled over what the girl was trying desperately to tell her.

Evidently the fluttering commotion piqued Mattie's curiosity, for she turned to face Elizabeth. Her eyes widened, and her mouth gaped. Elizabeth stepped backward until the plaster wall stopped her. The way Mattie's dark eyes riveted her to the wall made her feel as naked and helpless as a pinned insect. The woman's piercing stare seemed to hurl bits of sleet against her flesh. As in all Amish homes, one drape hung to the side of each window. Elizabeth wanted to seize the nearest one and wrap it around herself. She wished she could run, hide, or vanish. Instead, she stood as though rooted.

"Pink?" Mattie spit the syllable at her. "And they say you're virtuous?"

Elizabeth felt dizzy. "What's. . .wrong with pink?"

The older woman drew a quick breath. "You look like a harlot!"

"Mattie!" Leah looked horrified. "Amish in Lancaster County wear pastels. Elizabeth doesn't know about our dress code."

"She'd better learn -- and quick!" Mattie waved a spoon that was coated with a thick cream-colored substance. "If any of the ladies in our district see you dressed like that, they'll think you're a hussy." She sniffed. "And the Bishop would go into spasms!"

The knot that had formed in Elizabeth's stomach tightened.

"I'll. . .go up and change."

Mattie turned back to the stove. "You'd better do so immediately."

Leah bit her lip, her features portraying compassion. "Do you have a darker dress?"

"Ja. The medium-blue one I wore yesterday."

Mattie huffed. "That one is too bright, too."

"The medium-blue one's fine," Leah said, finally moving to the table to set down the plate of sliced oranges.

"You'd better get a move on," Mattie said. "This oatmeal is about ready."

Feeling like a recalcitrant school girl, Elizabeth fled up the stairs and into her bedroom. Hot tears stung her eyes, but she refused to let them humiliate her further. She'd suffered enough under Mattie's whip for one day. Slowly, she removed her lovely pink dress and donned the trip-worn blue one. Her eyes spanned the light-green dress, then the light-blue one. What was she going to do? Why hadn't Emma warned her?

"That's unfair," she whispered. Emma had never lived in Mercer County and probably hadn't realized their strict dress code. She ran her fingers over her new dress, admiring the pretty soft-pink shade of the material. Could she get away with wearing it just for Elam?

She descended the stairs less lighthearted than before and studied Mattie's back. So far, Elizabeth had seen her in blackish-green, and earthen-brown. This morning, her dress was a dark reddish-brown color that reminded Elizabeth of an old scab. Did the woman assume that wearing drab colors automatically made her virtuous?

The sound of an approaching buggy made Elizabeth's heart rejoice. She would endure Mattie's darts if it meant being near Elam. Crossing the room, she glanced out a window. "Elam and the boys are here."

Mattie counted bowls and began scooping up gobs of the sticky substance she called oatmeal. Elizabeth hoped she wouldn't be expected to eat a portion. How could Elam handle being served cereal that resembled plaster? Would the boys eat it without complaining?

Leah arranged plates of food on a large tray. "I usually serve Mama and Papa breakfast in their kitchen." Hoisting the laden tray, she headed out through the living room. "I help them wash and dress at about nine o'clock."

Elam opened the screen door. Daniel and Jesse Mark raced into the kitchen, but halted abruptly when they spied Mattie.

The woman looked down her narrow nose. "Take your seats, boys."

They quietly did so. When Mattie placed filled bowls in front of them, they stared at it, looked at each other, and burst into spontaneous laughter.

Mattie whirled to peer at them, her brows raised. Elam seemed to be struggling to control a grin. He took a place and motioned for Elizabeth to sit next to him. He dribbled pancake syrup on his oatmeal and took a cautious bite. Clearing his throat, he reached for his coffee cup.

Daniel sat straight in his chair, eyeing his steaming bowl. "Papa, I'd rather have scrambled eggs with my bacon."

"Me, too!" Jesse Mark continued his bouts of giggling.

Elam took the bowls of oatmeal and set one behind each of the boy's plates, then served his sons a portion of scrambled eggs.

Mattie sniffed. "How long are you and Leah going to continue to spoil those boys?"

"Take your place, Mattie, and eat your oatmeal while it's hot." He glanced at Elizabeth, a sagacious twinkle in his brown eyes.

"Are you going to drive me to school today, Papa?" Daniel asked.

"I have to leave early to catch my ride. You don't have to leave for school for over an hour. You can walk with Joas Yoder."

Mattie served herself, sprinkled brown sugar on her cereal,

stirred it with her spoon, and took a sizable bite. Her expression remained unreadable as she swallowed and took another spoonful. This time she swallowed twice. After the third bite, she left her spoon sticking in the muck and reached for her coffee.

Jesse Mark giggled. "Don't you like it, either, Aunt Maddie?"

Her chin rose slightly. "There isn't a thing wrong with the oatmeal." She spooned another gob into her mouth, held it there a moment, then swallowed hard.

Elam kept his eyes downcast, but a sly grin tugged at his mouth. The boys continued to watch Mattie. With iron determination, and apparently a stomach to match, she continued to eat.

"Are you going into the hospital this morning, Mattie?" Elam asked.

"I can't go in until this afternoon." She glanced at Elizabeth, then back to her bowl. "Leah and I have to dye some clothing today."

Not my pink dress! Elizabeth thought, her stomach feeling as though she'd swallowed a brick, and she hadn't even tasted Mattie's oatmeal.

After breakfast, Elam hugged his sons. "I'll see you boys when I get home. You be good for Aunt Leah."

Daniel nodded.

Mattie picked up her napkin and dabbed her mouth. "And don't get any more bright ideas like yesterday's shenanigans with the kitten."

Jesse Mark's eyes glistened and a spontaneous grin deepened his dimples.

Taking Elizabeth's hand Elam led her to the summer kitchen and closed the door. Smiling, he took her in his arms. "I love you, Beth."

His lips were warm and his kiss tender, and it aroused feelings that Elizabeth had forgotten existed. As his mouth teased hers with fervent caresses, her every nerve tingled. Her heart raced, making her temples throb. His kiss grew more ardent and his embrace tightened, sending waves of pleasure surging through her.

Breathless he pulled away. "If I don't leave right now, I'll miss my ride to work."

Laughing softly, she leaned back in his arms, swept away on waves of heightened passion. She prayed they could be married soon. Most marriages in the Amish community took place in November and this was already the first week in September.

He feathered kisses down the side of her face. "Can we be married this fall, Beth?"

"*Ja*. Oh, *ja*."

After Elam left for his construction job, Elizabeth fed Priscilla. Jesse Mark stayed close by, watching her every move, but Daniel went to the porch, and seemed to be sulking. Leah washed the dishes, and Elizabeth dried them. Mattie had gone upstairs for a time, then bustled through the house and vanished into the summer kitchen. They could hear her banging around, but paid no heed.

"Aunt Susanna's coming," Daniel announced, heading out to meet the woman.

"*Vea-gaits*!" she called, before her carriage horse stopped. Climbing down from the buggy, she hugged Daniel. "How are you this morning, my big little man?"

He grinned up at her. "Fine, now that you're here."

"Here comes Joas. Are you going to walk to school with him?"

"Ja." Seizing his lunch pail, he hurried to meet the older boy.

Susanna swept into the kitchen, her smile bright. "Good morning, ladies." Her blue eyes drifted to the baby. "And to sweet Priscilla."

Mattie bustled into the kitchen and rooted in one of the cabinets. "Ah! Here it is!"

Susanna turned to the older woman. "What's that?"

"Fabric dye." Mattie sniffed. "I must darken Elizabeth's shocking dresses to a more presentable color."

"Oh." Susanna's smile brightened. "I'll be glad to help you."

"*Cume onn* then."

Susanna excused herself and followed Mattie to the summer kitchen. Leah watched them go, her expression pensive. Elizabeth tightened her jaw. She felt she should be the one to dye her own dresses, but she hadn't even been consulted. She was thankful that Susanna had volunteered to help. Her judgment wouldn't be as prudish as Mattie's.

"Elizabeth!" Mattie swept back into the kitchen. "Bring me those disrespectful dresses."

Elizabeth stared at the woman, feeling as though she'd been smacked in the face with a cold wet rag.

"Susanna and I have three tubs of dye ready."

"But. . ." The tenacity in Mattie's eyes numbed Elizabeth.

"*Cume onn*, girl. Susanna has to leave shortly, and I don't have all day. I must get this done so I can get ready to visit Jonathan this afternoon."

Leah looked stricken, apparently sensing Elizabeth's distress. "Mattie, I'll help Elizabeth with her dresses."

"Nonsense! Susanna's delighted to help me bring those repulsive garments to a respectable color, and I trust her judgment." Mattie smiled, but it looked more like a subdued sneer. "Susanna figured out what dye would work best to cover that light-green thing." She waved her hand. "And the light-blue one." Her eyes glittered. "I can't wait to get my hands on that disdainful pink!"

Elizabeth's heart pounded. "You. . .were in my room looking through my clothes?"

"Don't be ridiculous!" Mattie spread her right hand across her chest. "When you were so busy in the summer kitchen saying good-bye to Elam, I merely went upstairs to check on Priscilla to make sure she was all right. I just happened to see your dresses hanging there." She twisted her face, apparently attempting to look hurt. "And I've spent all morning, doing my best to make sure you look presentable when you're introduced to the ladies in our district."

Elizabeth handed the baby to Leah and slowly made her way up the stairs. In her bedroom, she took her pink dress off the hanger, folded it, and then her eyes darted frantically around the room. If Mattie couldn't find the dress, she wouldn't be able to ruin it. Crossing the room, she gripped the top corner of the mattress, intending to lift it far enough to slip the dress under.

"I'll take them down for you."

Elizabeth whirled. Had Mattie guessed her intention?

The woman grasped the pink material.

"Wait."

"Susanna and I don't have time to dawdle." She jerked the other two dresses off of their hangers and flung them over her arm. "It's time for Leah to help Mama Miller get dressed, so you'd better take care of baby Priscilla and keep an eye on that mischievous boy."

A flash of pink, probably the last view of her lovely new dress, was all Elizabeth saw as Mattie scurried from the room. Her lips tightened. How did Leah put up with that woman? Closing her eyes, she prayed for patience and the ability to show Mattie kindness. Then, drawing a long breath, she descended the stairs. Putting up with Mattie was only a temporary arrangement. After she and Elam were married, Mattie would no longer be able to control her life.

Curiosity drew Elizabeth toward the door of the summer kitchen, but dread kept her from pushing it open. The acrid scent of vinegar assailed her nostrils. Evidently the women were using it to set the dye in the fabric. Maybe her dresses would be all right. Susanna's dark colors were pretty.

Susanna helped Mattie hang the dresses on the clothesline to dry. Elizabeth didn't round the house to look. There would be plenty of time, later, to assess the damage.

Susanna seemed more bubbly than usual when she said her good-byes. "I must hurry home to help Mama with the noon meal." She flashed deep dimples at Elizabeth. "I'm glad I could assist Mattie with your dresses. I hope you adore the new colors." In a flare of waves and good wishes, she was gone.

After dinner, a hired car came to take Mattie to the hospital. Elizabeth put Priscilla down for a nap and went to the porch. Summoning courage, she rounded the house, stared at the unfamiliar garments on the line, and fought despair. The light-green dress was now a dismal, dark reddish-brown. *Like an old scab*, Elizabeth thought with an uncontrolled shudder. Her light-blue dress had been dyed a dull navy, and her beautiful new pink dress was now a drab deep-plum.

"I know how you must feel, Elizabeth," Leah said softly, putting an arm around her shoulders. "That woman makes me so angry, I'm afraid God will punish me."

"God is just, Leah. Mattie isn't." She coughed to excuse the lump in her throat and forced herself to be calm. "I thought Susanna would be able to convince Mattie to be less drastic!"

"I thought so, too." Compassion shimmered in Leah's eyes. "Elam will make this up to you, Elizabeth." She hugged her. "Last night, he told me the two of you were going to be married. I'm so delighted to be getting a sister-in-law I can love and trust." She smiled. "Who could be better than my best old friend's sister?"

Elizabeth studied the girl's face. "I thought you liked Susanna."

"Oh, I do!" She laughed softly. "Elam likes her, too, but he loves you, and that's what counts."

"*Ja*. Jesse Mark and I get along fabulously, but Daniel is so . . . *vell*, he's so distant."

"The boys are close to Susanna. Jesse Mark is innocent, ready to love and trust. It's more difficult to gain Daniel's confidence. He felt so deserted when Mary died, and he hasn't fully trusted any woman since — except members of the family — and especially Susanna."

Elizabeth vowed to win the boy's love and trust. She glanced back at her dresses. They were only coverings, and it was the deeper things in life on which she must concentrate on. She had the joy of knowing Elam loved her. Her relationship with Jesse Mark was growing nicely, and she prayed Daniel would learn to love her, too. Other than serving God with all her heart, soul, and mind, Elam and his boys were the most important.

Daniel returned from school with his first papers. He rushed into the living room. Barely glancing at Elizabeth, he proudly showed them to Leah.

Elizabeth renewed her determination to win the boy's affection. "I must make a trip to the back of the lot, Leah. Will you listen for Priscilla."

"*Ja.*"

Part way across the lawn, Elizabeth's footsteps faltered. She'd used the outhouse last night after dark. It hadn't been as bad as she'd expected, but she didn't like having to retrogress. During the night, she'd used the chamber pot under her bed. This morning, she'd used it again to keep from using the outhouse. "This is ridiculous," she whispered.

Slowly she approached, turned the knob and went in. Her fingers fumbled as she clasped the hook. She wrinkled her nose. Maybe she was becoming too prissy. Would God be displeased?

She turned to peer at the bench of holes. There were three graduated sizes. The one her parents had used when she was a child had had round covers to fit the holes. These each had a hinged lid. She looked at the sales catalogue on the floor. Was it to read or use? She sighed with relief when she noticed the roll of tissue.

She lifted the center lid and turned. That was when she saw it. It was hunched in the corner as though it were making ready to leap on her. Screaming, she hurled herself against the outhouse door, her terror canceling the knowledge that the portal had to be unhooked. A splinter pierced the soft flesh of her palm as she grappled to unfasten the catch. When the door flew open, she hurled herself through space, missed the step, and nearly sprawled on the path. Regaining her balance, she raced toward the house, her throat constricting around another scream.

11

Leah sat on the bench, a book in her lap and a little boy on each side. "Daniel stood among the hungry lions," she read, "but he wasn't afraid, for he loved and trusted God. The lions couldn't harm Daniel, for God had closed their mouths."

Jesse Mark's eyes were large blue spheres. "They were hungry, but they didn't eat him?"

"*Ja!*" Daniel grinned. "Papa says the king threw Daniel into the lion's den because he worshiped God. God loved Daniel, so he protected him."

A scream rent the air. Jesse Mark's eyes widened even farther. "Is the lions gittin' somebody?"

Slapping the book shut, Leah leaped to her feet. What was the matter with Elizabeth? Picturing a mad dog or rabid raccoon, she headed for the kitchen door, the boys on her heels.

"Stay inside!" she commanded, frantically searching for a weapon.

Elizabeth clambered to the porch, jerked open the screen, and stumbled into the kitchen. Leah yanked out a chair. Elizabeth slumped onto it and hid her face in her hands.

Leah put an arm around her. "What happened?"

"A. . .a. . .spi-der."

Leah laughed, then reading the fright in Elizabeth's pale face, she sobered.. "Where is it?"

"In. . .the outhouse!"

Daniel laughed, but covered his mouth and turned away

when Leah looked sternly at him.

Jesse Mark rested a hand on Elizabeth's knee as he studied her face. "Was he a big one?"

"Oh . . . *Ja*!"

Leah pictured a furry creature the size of one of the kittens, wondering where it could've come from. She searched for a club, but settled for the broom. Armed, she opened the screen and stepped onto the porch. "You boys stay with Elizabeth."

The outhouse door was wide open. Leah approached gingerly, the broom slung over her right shoulder. She frowned. Would the spider bite? Was the thing poisonous? Pausing at the doorway, she peered in. Seeing nothing, she leaned farther through the opening. After searching the entire tiny building, even peering down the holes, and still finding nothing, she sighed. The spider must have been frightened away by Elizabeth's screams.

A spider the size of a quarter scurried across the floor. She stepped on it, then swept the remains out the door. The men said spiders ate insects, but she still squashed them on sight. After another thorough search, she closed the door and headed for the house.

Elizabeth sat on a kitchen chair. Jesse Mark stood by her side, patting her shoulder. Lifting the little boy, she sat him in her lap. Hugging him, she kissed his golden curls. Daniel stood at a window, trying to catch a fly that buzzed against the glass.

Elizabeth glanced at Leah. "Did you see it?"

"No." She propped the broom in a corner. "The only thing in the outhouse was a spider the size of a quarter."

"Then you did see it! Did you kill it!"

Leah laughed. "You mean that small spider was the one that frightened you?" Noticing Elizabeth's hurt expression, she felt ashamed. "*Es spied mich*."

"Oh, Leah, it's silly to be frightened of such a little thing." She massaged her temples. "I've prayed about it, but God hasn't taken the fear away, yet."

"I've heard of people being afraid of spiders. It's called

arachnephobia." She poured hot water into a small pot, made tea, and served Elizabeth a cup.

"*Danka dich.*" She sipped the brew.

"I'll use insect spray in the outhouse."

Elizabeth shivered. "I'm determined to conquer this. Living on a farm and being afraid of spiders, I'm constantly on guard." She sighed. "It's ridiculous."

Jesse Mark grinned. "Daniel isn't even afraid of hungry lions, 'cause he trusts God."

Elizabeth turned to the child in her lap, her soft lips parting.

Leah laughed softly. "I was reading them the story of Daniel in the lion's den."

"Oh." Elizabeth smiled at Jesse Mark. "Daniel was a man of God. I must pray to have faith like he did."

"*Ja*! I bet he wasn't scared of nothin'."

"There's no need to have fear if we trust Jesus."

Jesse Mark's grin broadened. "Then you won't be scared no more, *Ja*?"

"I'm going to try to be brave."

Leah marveled at the way the little boy had grasped the meaning of the story. It deepened her sense of responsibility, and she vowed not to miss a day's reading time. She fished a pan from the bottom of the cabinet near the stove. "I'd better start heating the soup for dinner."

"What can I do to help?"

"You may set the table."

"Eat your stew, Susanna," Anna Mary Yoder urged.

"I'm not hungry."

"Eat it anyway, dear. You need your strength."

Susanna pictured Elizabeth with Elam and her jaw tightened. If she was going to do something to snuff out their budding romance, she'd better act posthaste.

"Dear?" Anna Mary looked worried. "Is something bothering you?"

Susanna fabricated a grin that deepened her dimples, knowing it helped to quell her mother's concern. "I just have things on my mind, Mama."

"Are you going to see Leah this afternoon?"

"No! I don't live at Millers!"

Anna Mary straightened, her brows lifting severely.

Susanna realized the brusqueness behind her statement had been fueled by unfulfilled desire. "*Es spied mich*, Mama," she said quietly, trying to camouflage her distress.

"My sweet Susanna," Anna Mary crooned, "I know you didn't mean to be cross."

"I think I'll go for a walk." Flashing a brilliant smile, she left the house, intending to plan her strategy where no one could translate her expression. She thought about how she'd dumped more dye in the three tubs of water when Mattie had briefly left the summer kitchen. Making Elizabeth's dresses frumpy had made her feel giddy. She would have dyed them black if she could have gotten away with it. A grin curved her mouth. Would Elam be as turned on by his sweetheart now that she had nothing to wear but unsightly dresses?

She went to the apple tree on the other side of the spring house. Boosting herself to the hip-high branch, she leaned against the trunk and frowned. She'd enjoyed her visits with Leah. Now, she dreaded witnessing Elizabeth's satisfied smile. If only Elizabeth weren't so pretty. She was virtuous as well, which made matters worse.

Susanna pursed her lips. *I'd make Elam a good wife. What's the matter with him?* Other men adored her. She had dozens of admirers. "Ach!" The others were mere males. Elam was a man!

"His sons!" Maybe she could get through to Elizabeth by way of Daniel and Jesse Mark. They trusted her. She cared deeply for them, too, especially Jesse Mark.

"He's like my own little boy." Susanna's jaw tightened as she pictured him on Elizabeth's lap. The child could switch his allegiance! She couldn't let that happen. Maybe she should visit

Miller's this afternoon and take the boys for a walk. Her determination ardent, she hurried to the house to tell her mother she might be late for supper.

Elam's stomach growled. He listened to the clop-clop of his horse's shoes against the pavement as his buggy rumbled homeward. Leah had said that Elizabeth was making the meat loaf. He could almost smell it. He closed his eyes. An image of Elizabeth formed before him, making his heartbeat quicken. The soft alluring essence of her soap seemed to tickle his nostrils. He inhaled deeply. The scent of mowed hay mingled with the smell of drying corn and the neighbor's freshly plowed field. He would have to cut corn this evening. He must begin plowing for the winter wheat soon, since Jonathan wouldn't be helping this year. First, he would have to spread the manure from the cattle shed.

When he rounded the bend in the lane, he noticed Elizabeth on the swing with Jesse Mark. The boy dangled a string in front of the black-and-white kitten. Ruffy and Tumbles were always together. Where was the gray-tiger kitten?

Elizabeth glanced up, recognized the buggy, and a smile illuminated her lovely face. He waved and all thought of the truant kitten vanished from his mind.

He stopped the horse at the front gate. Elizabeth grasped Jesse Mark's hand, and they headed down the flagstone path to meet him. His heart swelled to capacity, but the absence of Daniel kept it from bursting. Why wasn't his older son with Elizabeth and Jesse Mark? Why did the boy seem resistant?

Jesse Mark's grin broadened. "*Vea-gaits*, Papa."

Elam smiled as he swept through the gate. Reaching down, he swung the little boy into his arms. Then, he pulled Elizabeth against his side and kissed her cheek. The smoothness of her skin sent rivulets of pleasure surging through him, and he stifled a moan that would display his delight.

Jesse Mark giggled. "I like her, too, Papa."

Elam's arm tightened around the boy. "I'm glad."

Delicious aromas of meat loaf and freshly baked bread drifted from the kitchen as they climbed the steps to the porch. Leah pushed open the door, Priscilla cradled in one arm. The baby reached toward Elam. Taking the squirming baby in the arm he'd had around Elizabeth, he chuckled. "I should have three arms."

Jesse Mark poked Elam's chest with a chubby finger. "You need an arm for Daniel, too, Papa."

Elam laughed. "*Vell*, I guess Elizabeth and I together have all the arms we need."

Daniel strode from the living room, stopped, and watched. His brown-green eyes seemed to hold a haunted look that disturbed Elam. Some hidden fear seemed to be festering in his mind, but so far the boy had refused to discuss it.

Jesse Mark reached out to pat Priscilla's hand. "Aunt Susanna brought us yummy cookies today. Prissy-cilla had one."

"That's nice." Elam glanced at his younger sister. "Was she here long?"

Leah took the lid off of a boiling pot to stir the lima beans. "She and Daniel took a long walk."

"Oh?" Elam looked at his oldest son. "Did you have a good time?"

He shrugged one shoulder. "*Ja.*"

"What'd you and your Aunt Susanna do, Son?"

"We . . . looked at the trees." Whirling, he headed through the living room. "I'm gonna go see Mammi Rachel." The swinging door flapped, signaling his departure.

Elam sighed. "Leah, did Amos Yoder drop in today?"

"No." She replaced the pot lid. "Were you expecting him to?"

"*Ja.*" He frowned. "Did Susanna say anything about his coming over this evening?"

"No."

"He promised to help me cut corn if Samuel didn't return."

Leah shrugged. "If Amos made you a promise, he'll keep

it." She stirred the fudge icing she'd made earlier and began to spread it on a cake. "I expected Samuel back before this."

"Does he know about Jonathan's heart attack?"

"No." Leah sighed. "I don't know how to reach him. He dropped a postcard from Holmes County, Ohio, informing me that instead of coming home, he and his friend were planning to visit someone in Indiana."

Elam scowled. "At twenty-two, you'd think he'd be more responsible."

Leah surrendered her icing knife to Elizabeth, who continued frosting the desert. "Samuel was Mama's baby boy. I think she spoiled him."

Elizabeth laughed softly. "He was a bit spoiled, but delightful. I'm looking forward to seeing him again."

Elam sighed. "After supper, I'll get as much corn cut as I can before dark." He carried Priscilla and Jesse Mark into the living room. Sitting on the couch, he bounced a child on each knee.

Elizabeth followed to the doorway, but stopped to watch, a smile curving her adorable mouth. "I'm going up to my room for a moment."

He nodded. Jesse Mark bent forward to grasp the baby's feet. Squealing, she seized a handful of his blond curls. Elizabeth's light tread resounded on the stair steps as Elam endeavored to balance the two and untangle the little girl's tiny fingers from the golden strands of his son's locks. As he fumbled with her right hand, she seized another curl with her left.

Elizabeth screamed. Elam leaped to his feet. Twisting, he put Priscilla on the couch. "Watch her, Jesse Mark. Don't let her roll onto the floor." He raced from the room, through the kitchen, and climbed the stairs two at a time. Entering Elizabeth's room, he saw her pasted against the far wall. Staring wide-eyed at the bed, her complexion livid, she pointed.

He moved closer to the bed. The quilt had been thrown back to reveal an open match box. It looked similar to the one he'd given Daniel to play with. A spider the size of a dime crawled out of the box and across the mattress. Brushing it to the floor, he stepped on it. Then, noticing a small one on her pillow, he killed it.

"There are . . . two more!"

Perceiving her fright, but not understanding it, he searched the room. He found one spider on the wallpaper and the other one on the floor under the chair by the bed. "Where'd they come from, Beth?"

"They . . . were in the box." Her hand went to her pale face. "It was under the quilt. When I tossed the cover aside to see what was making the bump, the spiders crawled out!" A shiver seemed to travel her full length.

Elam stared at the box. Was it the one he'd given Daniel?

"Are you sure you got them all, Elam?"

Jerking the quilt from the bed, he shook it, then did the same with her pillow. "There aren't any in your bed." He turned and saw tears pooling in her eyes. "Beth." Two quick strides took him near enough to take her in his arms.

"Oh Elam, who would do such a horrid thing to me?"

"I don't know." He intended to find out. Drawn by her need for him, he kissed her long and slow. His heart raced, sending blood surging through his veins in torrents. He hoped time would pass quickly and she would soon be his wife. Pulling slightly away, he gazed into her upturned face. Her velvety-brown eyes shimmered with desire that mirrored his own. Forcing control, he smiled. "Wash your pretty face. Supper's almost ready."

"*Ja.*" She grinned. "And Mattie will be home. If she finds you in my bedroom, she's liable to have a spasm."

He chuckled. "At least that!"

Leah was strolling around the kitchen with Priscilla as Elam descended the stairs. She glanced at him. "I came up, but it looked like you had the situation under control."

Jesse Mark ran to meet him. "What was the matter with, Liz-beth Papa?"

"She had a little scare, but she's all right."

His blue eyes shimmered with innocent wonder. "Aunt Leah killed the ole spider in the toilet that scared 'er this afternoon."

Leah quickly explained Elizabeth's arachnephobia.

Elam understood, and wondered who else knew about her fear. Who could have instigated such a demented joke? He watched Elizabeth gracefully descend the stairs as though nothing had happened. His heart throbbed with love for her.

Mattie came in, peered at the set table, glanced at the stove, then looked at Leah. "Is supper ready, yet?"

"*Ja.*" She handed the baby to Elam. "I just have to lift up. Elizabeth made her special meat loaf."

Mattie's dark eyes flashed at Elizabeth. "*Vell*, if it tastes as good as it smells, I'll ask for your recipe." Her lips curved into a half smile, which was a lot for Mattie. As she untied her brown bonnet, she studied the dyed dresses that now hung in the corner of the kitchen to finish drying. "*Vell*, Elizabeth, your dresses turned out lovely."

Elizabeth supposed the woman was waiting to be thanked, but . . . She prayed to love Mattie, and hoped her smile didn't appear as false as it felt.

"Under the circumstances, it was the least I could do," Mattie said as though she'd received appreciation. "Of course, sweet Susanna assisted me." Clutching her bonnet, she swept into the downstairs bedroom, her ugly dark reddish-brown skirt swishing.

Elam watched her, then turned to stare at the sorry-colored garments that hung in the corner. "Those are yours?"

Elizabeth struggled to control the tremor in her voice. "Mattie said they were too. . ." She cleared her throat and tried again. "She thought the darker colors would be better for this district."

"*Vell*. . .*ja*, but. . ."

Leah set a bowl of baked potatoes on the table, then stepping closer to Elam, she lowered her voice. "Mattie said

Elizabeth's pretty pink dress made her look like a harlot."

Elam's lips parted. "The ladies in this district are forbidden to use brightly-colored material, but. . ." His eyes roamed back to the sad-looking dresses. "That's a bit drastic, isn't it?"

Leah shrugged. "You know Mattie."

Elam frowned, then facing Elizabeth, a slow smile formed on his mouth. "You'll be making a medium-blue dress for our wedding." His smile broadened into a generous grin. "In the privacy of our own home, you can wear whatever color you wish."

Mattie stepped into the kitchen in time to hear Elam's last words. She sniffed. "If you want your own private hussy, that's up to you, Elam Miller!"

He threw back his head and laughed.

During the meal, Elam studied his oldest son. The boy seemed extra quiet, but he cleaned his plate, including the green beans he didn't like. Elam intended to take him for a walk to ask him if he knew about the spiders in the match box, but Amos came to help cut corn.

Elam hitched three draft horses to the binder, drove the animals to the field, and began cutting the first row of corn. Amos followed with a second binder. The machines cut the stalks and tied them together in bunches, then spit them out behind the binder. Later, they would stand them in shocks of eight to ten bunches. The task took little concentration, so he was able to ponder Elizabeth's problem. What could have prompted someone to frighten her?

Darkness forced the men to quit. Elam was tired, sweaty, and would have to get up early in the morning for work. He didn't like to discuss serious topics with his sons when he felt irritable, but a confrontation concerning Elizabeth's scare couldn't be put off.

He took the boys home, washed them up and got them ready for bed. Daniel said a hasty good night and headed for his room.

"Wait," Elam called.

The boy turned to face his father. "*Ja?*"

Elam sat on his dark-green bench and patted the place beside him. "*Cume* sit with me."

Daniel obeyed. Jesse Mark bounced on a chair across the room and watched as though he figured something interesting was about to happen.

Drawing a long slow breath, Elam faced his oldest son. "What did you do with the match box I gave you last week?"

"I played with it."

"Where is it, now?"

The boy squirmed. "I. . .don't know."

"Where'd you put it, Daniel?"

"*Vell*. . .I kept it with me for awhile."

"Did you catch grasshoppers and put them in it like you said you wanted to?"

"*Ja.*" He looked at the floor and tapped the braided rug with one toe.

"Did you capture any other insects?"

Red hue crept across Daniel's face. "*Vell*. . .*ja.*"

"What were they?"

Bowing his head, he remained silent.

"Daniel," Elam kept his words under control, but his tone had sharpened. "Did you catch any spiders?"

"*Ja.*" Daniel's voice was low.

"Did you know Elizabeth was frightened of them?"

"*Ja.*" His voice lowered another degree.

Elam drew a long breath. "Did you put them in her bed?"

Chewing his bottom lip, he slowly nodded.

"Daniel, why would you deliberately try to frighten her?"

Leaping to his feet, the boy stared defiantly at his father. "I wanted to scare her away!" Whirling, he headed for his room.

"Daniel."

He increased his pace.

Elam stood quickly, but forced calmness. "Daniel!"

Pausing, the boy turned slowly.

"I demand an explanation!"

"She's not my Mama!" Sudden tears brimmed in his eyes, then streamed down his face. "I want her to get scared and go away! Far away, and leave us alone!"

Elam felt as though a barn beam had rammed his stomach. "*Ferwass* (why), Son? *Ferwass?*

12

Racing across the room, Daniel flung himself facedown in the dark-green chair and sobbed. Dumbstruck, Elam stood on a multi-colored braided rug, his arms limp by his sides.

Jesse Mark slid from his chair, crossed the room to stand beside his brother, and blinked his long blond lashes. "Why don't you want Liz-beth to be our Mama?"

"She's mean and horrid!" Daniel's shoulders shook. "I hate her!"

Elam stood in the soft glow of the oil lamp, staring at his sons. Mean and horrid? Elizabeth? Moving to Daniel, he scooped him into his arms, sat in the chair, and held him close.

"Make her go away, Papa." He clutched the front of Elam's shirt. "I want her to take her baby and go away!"

So that was it! Daniel must feel threatened over the baby's presence. "I will never love you and Jesse Mark less, just because there's another baby to love. Most Amish families have many *kinder*."

"That's different."

Jesse Mark climbed into the chair and wriggled between Elam and the arm. Reaching out one chubby hand, he patted his older brother's knee. "Why don't you like Prissy-cilla?"

"She'd be all right if her Mama went away."

Jesse Mark looked puzzled. "I like Liz-beth."

"That's 'cause you're still a baby." Daniel turned his head enough to look at him. "You don't know what she's tryin' to do!"

Elam's brain had seemed scrambled, and his heart ached. The boy's last remark puzzled him more. "Daniel, what do you think Elizabeth is trying to do?"

The boy looked up with red, swollen eyes. "She's gonna take you away when she goes home. We'll never see you again."

Elam's mouth gaped. Finally he found his voice. "I would never leave you boys."

"But you did! And Elizabeth made you stay longer. If Uncle Jonathan hadn't gotten sick, you'd still be away!"

He *had* remained at Emma's longer than he had planned, and it *was* because he'd needed more time with Elizabeth, but . . .

Daniel wrapped his arms around Elam's neck. "Please don't leave us, Papa."

"I won't leave you." He kissed the top of the boy's head. "What makes you think Elizabeth would want to take me away?"

"You said you loved her."

"I do. Very much. I want her to come here to live with us."

"But she won't! So she'll take you away."

"Why do you think that, Daniel?"

"Aunt Susanna said Elizabeth would take you from us and we'd never see you again."

Elam gasped. "Susanna said that?"

"*Ja.* She helped me catch the spiders, and told me how to fix them under Elizabeth's quilt."

"Susanna's wrong! And what she did was wrong. Elizabeth wants to live here and be your Mama." Anger welled up within Elam. He'd warned Elizabeth that because of Susanna's fixation to become his wife, the woman might do almost anything, but he'd never dreamed she would poison one of his son's minds.

"Are you sure about Elizabeth, Papa?" Daniel asked, drawing a jagged breath.

"*Ja.* She loves you boys already."

Jesse Mark bounced, his blue eyes wide. "Then, can we call her Mama, now?"

"That is up to you and Elizabeth."

"*Vell...*" the older boy drawled. "She's nice. If she wants to stay here and be our Mama, I guess it's all right." He sat straight and sniffed. "Can I take her a present?"

"*Ja.* What do you have in mind?"

Daniel pursed his lips. "I don't know, yet."

Elam hugged his sons, and a relieved chuckle vibrated his throat.

Morning came softly. Elizabeth stared at her dresses, wondering which one to put on. "They're all dismal," she whispered, her heart sinking as she looked at the dark-purplish-plum dress that had been her pretty new pink one.

Donning the dark-blue one, she slipped downstairs to help with breakfast, confident that Elam would love her in ugly colors the same as he would in pastels.

Leah had the cooking well in hand, so Elizabeth went to the porch to sit and wait for Elam. The chain squeaked as she moved the swing back-and-forth. Chirping, a blue bird fluttered to the flower garden and scratched among the few fallen September leaves in search of scattered seeds. She peered in the direction of Elam's house, but from the porch, the tall corn cut off her view. She smiled when she glimpsed Cavalier's nose, then Elam's approaching buggy. Strolling to the front gate, she opened it, enjoying the sun that caressed her back. Jesse Mark waved frantically the moment he saw her. Elam smiled.

When the carriage stopped, Daniel jumped from the seat, a bunch of vivid flowers clutched in one fist. Scurrying through the open gate, he held them up. "I picked these for you this morning."

She accepted the bouquet, and bending, she hugged the boy. Her embrace tightened when he began to cry. "Daniel, what's wrong?"

"*Es spied mich,*" he gasped. "*Es spied mich.*"

"Sorry for what?"

"The spiders." He gazed up at her, his brown-green eyes filled with remorse. "I won't ever do it again."

She kissed his tear moistened cheek. "Then all is forgiven." Still grasping his hand, she stood. Elam had remained at the buggy, clinging to Jesse Mark's arm, evidently giving his oldest son time to apologize. As he strode forward, the little boy broke free and ran, getting to Elizabeth before Elam. She hunkered to hug him.

"I wanted to bring you posies, too. Papa said to wait till tomorrow."

"Tomorrow will be fine." She kissed his chubby pink cheek.

His eyes were big blue spheres as he gazed up at her. "He said we can call you Mama."

"I'd like that." She fought tears of happiness as her eyes met Elam's.

"After breakfast I'm gonna hunt spiders," Daniel said.

Elam's lips parted. "I think you've done enough of that."

He shook his head adamantly. "I'm gonna find all I can and squish 'em, so they won't scare our new mama."

Elizabeth laughed.

Elam's head jerked sideways. "What was that?" Bending, he squinted, trying to see under the porch.

Elizabeth stooped to peer under as well, but saw nothing.

Jesse Mark giggled. "That was Ruffy."

Elam straightened, his brows lifted. "Ruffy? That thing was red! *Vell*, partly red."

Daniel backed toward the house, his expression betraying guilt.

Elam propped a hand on his hip. "What happened to that kitten?"

Another giggle bubbled from Jesse Mark. "We painted 'im, Papa."

"You. . .painted. . ." He looked bewildered.

Elizabeth smothered a laugh. "Ruffy's all right, Elam." Interpreting Daniel's relief, she figured she'd secured a friend forever.

"What's going on out there?" Mattie's voice, like a cracking whip, prodded them into action.

"We're coming." Elizabeth was thankful she'd met Elam and the boys in the yard. She hoped to keep the identity of the perpetrator of the spider scare from Mattie. She was also glad the woman hadn't heard Elam's question concerning the red-striped Ruffy.

During breakfast, Elizabeth noticed Daniel frequently eyeing her. When she caught him looking, he grinned. She winked at him. His grin broadened.

Mattie left for the hospital. Daniel set his lunch box and book on the bench inside the kitchen door and stared down the lane for a glimpse of the freckle-faced second grader who accompanied him across two fields to the school.

"Joas won't be here for thirty minutes," Elizabeth said. "Let's go to the living room and read a story while we wait."

Settled on the couch, a boy on each side, she opened the book. "This story's about David, the little shepherd boy." As she read, both boys asked numerous questions.

"Wow!" Jesse Mark bounced. "He even killed an old bear!"

"And a lion, too," Daniel said. "That's because he didn't want 'em to hurt his lambs."

Elizabeth smiled. "God protects us that way, because he loves us."

"*Ja*!" Jesse Mark grinned. "Papa says we're Jesus' lambs."

"Your Papa's right." She hugged both boys.

"Joas is here, Daniel," Leah called.

Jumping from the couch, he raced to the door and grabbed his belongings. "See ya," he called over his shoulder as the screen door slammed.

Before noon, while Priscilla slept, Elizabeth sat on the living room floor helping Jesse Mark build a barn out of the wooden blocks Elam had made the boys. A car stopped in front of the house.

Jesse Mark raced to the front door and stopped with a jolt. "It's Aunt Susanna!"

Elizabeth opened the door.

Susanna swept into the room. "*Vea-gaits.*" Her light-navy skirt seemed bright compared to Elizabeth's dismal frock. The woman's smile was warm, her manner charming. "John Zimmerman is on his way to Prospect to drive a family to New Castle. He said he'll be passing Moraine State Park. He offered to drop me and some of my friends off for a picnic." She grasped Elizabeth's hands. "We haven't had a chance to get to know each other. It would be delightful if you rode along so we could chat."

"*Vell. . .*" Elizabeth wondered if John had rented a room from Elam and stayed in the area more because of the taxi work he'd managed to secure — or because of his apparent attraction to Susanna.

Leah stood in the doorway to the kitchen. "Go ahead, Elizabeth. I'll watch the *kinder.*"

Elizabeth glanced at her drab skirt, but knew she had nothing prettier.

"Your dress is fine." Susanna's dimples deepened. The sparkle in her bright blue eyes encouraged Elizabeth. "*Cume onn.* John's waiting."

"It's. . .nearly noon."

Susanna beamed. "Mama packed us a lunch."

Elizabeth accompanied Susanna to the van, greeted John, and climbed into the middle seat beside the woman. If Leah sanctioned the outing, it must be all right.

The entire way, Susanna chatted cordially. Elizabeth saw no reason to distrust her. Actually, she was quite likable. She couldn't blame Susanna for caring for Elam. What woman wouldn't?

"Amos and a friend went to the park earlier," Susanna said.

Elizabeth smiled. "Elam mentioned someone named Amos Yoder. Is he a relative?"

"My big brother. He's the same age as Samuel, Elam's

youngest brother." She giggled. "Sam's adorable! He has honey-colored curls and sparkling turquoise eyes. He isn't as tall or muscular as Elam, but he's a lot of fun."

John swung the vehicle off of the main road and wound through the park.

Susanna pointed. "That's Lake Arthur." She smiled. "Let's eat at a table near the water."

Not knowing how to swim made a chill travel down Elizabeth's spine.

John stopped the van and got out. The sun shimmered on his sandy hair as he opened the back. Donning his straw hat, he gripped the handle of the picnic basket and grinned at Susanna. "I'll carry this to the table for you."

She rested a hand on his arm. "Will you join us for dinner?"

His green eyes became lustrous. "I'd love to, Susanna, but..." He consulted his watch. "I mentioned the Amish family I'm driving from Prospect to New Castle, and I haven't much time. In New Castle, I'm to pick up a man and drive him to a construction sight near New Wilmington where he works." He strolled across the grass to set the basket on a table near the water. "Will you ladies be all right for about three hours?"

"*Ja.*" Susanna opened the lid of the basket and proffered John a chocolate chip cookie. "This will stave off starvation until dinner."

Chuckling, he bit into the treat. "Um. No wonder Elam's boys love you."

Laughing prettily, she lowered her long blond lashes.

"You're sure you'll be all right?" John's brow furrowed.

Susanna pointed to two men in an aluminum rowboat several feet from shore. "There's my brother and his friend."

"Good." John matched her grin. "It makes me feel better to leave you in capable company." With a wave, he turned and strolled to his van.

Susanna clasped her hands as she faced Elizabeth. "I'm so delighted that you'll get a chance to meet Amos."

"Will he and his friend be having dinner with us?"

"I hope so. Mama packed enough for a dozen people." She laughed. "She always makes more than plenty."

Elizabeth listened to chirping birds and breathed deeply of the fresh air. The sound of splashing drew her attention. She turned to watch the men maneuver the rowboat toward the dock. The dark-haired man with a thin mustache rowed. Elizabeth noticed his broad shoulders and powerful arms. He wore a T-shirt splashed with brilliant colors. The other man wore a straw hat. Honey-colored curls dangled on his collar. When he stepped from the craft, she could see that he wore broadfalls.

"Is the blond one Amos?"

"*Ja.* The other one is Clyde. He's an *Englischer.*" She turned to wave to the men.

Amos waved back, then said something to his companion. As the two approached, Elizabeth studied Amos. He was the tallest of the two, but wasn't as muscular. As he strolled closer, she noticed his sparkling turquoise eyes. His dimples, much like his sister's, gave him a boyish air without diminishing his masculinity.

Susanna made the introductions, then turned toward her brother's friend. "You'll eat with us, won't you Clyde?"

"You bet." He chuckled. "Especially if I get one of your chocolate chip cookies for dessert."

"Hum." Susanna looked reflective. "I'll give you two if you take us out in your boat."

"I'd like to, but I have to leave right after lunch, pick my sister up at her school, and drive her to her orthodontist."

Amos took a place beside Elizabeth. "Let's eat. I'm famished."

"You're in a constant state of starvation, brother." Susanna took a place across from him and motioned for Clyde to join her.

After grace, then Susanna dished up sandwiches, potato salad, and baked beans. She seemed to be unnecessarily touching Clyde's fingers as she passed the food to him. "If you can't take Elizabeth and me out in the boat, can we take it ourselves?"

He frowned. "Well . . ."

"Don't you dare refuse me, Clyde." Her voice took on a melodious tone. "We'll stay near shore." She flashed him a seductive smile, then blinked. "I'll give you all the cookies that are left."

He looked pensive, but seemed to be softening. Elizabeth hoped he would refuse Susanna. The calm lake mirrored the sky, but no matter how placid it looked, not knowing how to swim made her apprehensive.

"Do you know how to handle a rowboat?" Clyde asked.

"*Ja.*" Susanna's smile seemed infectious. "Amos taught me last summer."

Clyde seemed a bit pensive, but said. "If you promise to stay near the shore, you may take the boat."

"Thank you. You're a true friend."

Concern shadowed Amos's handsome features as he surveyed his sister. He turned to Elizabeth. "Do you swim?"

"No."

He frowned. "Then it probably wouldn't be wise to. . ."

"Don't be silly, Amos." Laughing softly, Susanna crumpled her napkin into a ball and threw it at him. "A rowboat has a flat bottom! We couldn't upset it if we tried!"

"She's right," Clyde said. "Gwendolyn is as sea-worthy as a rowboat can get. They'll be as safe as they would be in an exercise gym."

Elizabeth peered at the boat and her mind whirled. Could she decline Susanna's invitation to go out on the lake without appearing rude or prudish?

Clyde gently touched the back of Susanna's hand, his smile appealing. "Thanks for lunch."

Dimpling, she grabbed the plastic bag containing the seven leftover cookies and proffered them.

"Ah! Thanks." He glanced at Amos. "You ready, pal?"

Amos seemed hesitant, but left the table and accompanied Clyde to his car.

Too soon, they were gone. At some distance, two teenage boys played catch with a soft ball, and a young girl ran along the shoreline with a brown retriever. Farther back in the park, two women played with several children. Worrying about the coming venture, Elizabeth methodically collected the paper plates and discarded them in the garbage can.

Susanna took a small paper bag from the basket and set it aside. "I only brought two cupcakes, so I didn't serve them." She grasped containers and leftover sandwiches and tossed them into the picnic basket, laughing when Elizabeth strove to bring some semblance of order to the items. Grasping the tablecloth, Susanna gave it a flip, folded it haphazardly, and rammed it into the basket. "Let's go." Taking the paper bag, she headed for the lake.

Elizabeth slowly followed. She stopped at the edge of the dock, drew a deep breath, and shivered.

"What's wrong?" Susanna seemed concerned. "Are you as frightened of water as you are of spiders?"

"No, but. . ."

"I'll row, Elizabeth. That way you can enjoy the scenery." Smiling, she waved a hand toward the boat. "Get in and sit in the back.

"Susanna, I can't swim."

"You won't drown in three or four feet of water, and that's as deep as it gets near shore."

Not wishing to be rude, Elizabeth complied. She surveyed the two floatation pillows and forced calmness. Clyde was right. What could happen in a rowboat?

Susanna stepped into the boat, placed the paper bag that contained the cupcakes behind her seat, then untied the rope, freeing the craft. Sitting, she grasped the oars. "Here we go!"

After being on the water for fifteen minutes, Elizabeth gazed at the blue sky, then at the clouds mirrored on the calm surface of the lake. Drawing a long slow breath, she watched a bird dip and soar. Elizabeth faced the far side of the lake, paying no heed to the shoreline behind her.

"I'm glad . . . Clyde let us borrow . . . his boat."

"You seem to be getting a little winded, Susanna. Need you row so feverishly?"

"I . . . suppose not, but . . . It's fun."

"I'd change places and take a turn at rowing, but if I stood, I'd probably fall overboard."

Susanna laughed. She paused to take a deep breath, then continued to row at a more leisurely pace. Her blue eyes, apparently mirroring a reflection, shimmered with a greenish hue.

Several minutes passed. Elizabeth peered over the edge of the boat. Unable to see bottom, she shivered, then glanced over her shoulder. "Susanna!"

"Is something wrong?"

"You said we'd stay near shore! We must be two hundred feet out! How deep is this water?"

Susanna shrugged.

"Please go back."

Dropping her hands in her lap, Susanna sighed. "I'm tired." She smiled. "Would you like to try rowing?"

Elizabeth's heart lurched, then beat more rapidly.

"If we're careful, we can change places." Standing, Susanna peered tentatively at Elizabeth.

Lowering her eyes, Elizabeth studied Susanna's bare feet. *Why had the woman removed her shoes? And when? Why'd I agree to this excursion?* She drew a long breath. The thought of standing made her weak. "I . . . can't!"

Susanna resumed her seat. "We'll just rest a bit." She reached to the floor behind her seat and retrieved the small paper bag. "Let's eat our cupcakes. It's so peaceful on the water." She opened the bag slowly, peered in, then retrieved a cup cake and handed it to Elizabeth. Taking her own, she dropped the paper bag on the bottom of the boat. "We can throw our cupcake papers in the bag when we finish eating."

Somewhere in the distance a child squealed in delight. A startled duck quacked, birds fluttered along the shoreline, and water slapped gently against the aluminum sides of the rowboat. A pleasant breeze toyed with the blond curl that had escaped from under Susanna's cap. All seemed serene, yet . . .

What Elam had said about Susanna replayed through Elizabeth's gyrating mind. Why had she disregarded his concern? Apprehension stole her appetite, and she only nibbled her sugary treat. Gripping the side of the boat, she looked toward shore. No one was near. Susanna's foot struck the paper bag, making it crinkle. Elizabeth reached for it, intending to drop her unfinished cupcake inside. As she touched the paper, a hairy spider the size of a nickel scurried across her hand. Screaming, she jerked back. The eight-legged creature landed on the bottom of the boat at her feet. She jumped up. "Kill it!"

"Kill what?" Susanna peered toward shore, looking confused.

The spider crawled toward Elizabeth. Gasping, she leaped to the seat, rocking the boat.

"Elizabeth, sit down!"

"Kill it! Please!"

Susanna continued to peer at Elizabeth's face. "Sit! You'll fall!"

The hairy menace raced up the side of Elizabeth's seat. She flailed her arms, struggling to maintain her balance. Susanna grasped the oars. The boat rocked. Elizabeth screamed as she toppled. Her cry died as she splashed into the water and plunged beneath the surface. As the coolness closed around her, a new terror gripped her heart. She kicked feverishly, but her feet tangled in her long skirt. She plowed with her arms, but water filled her shoes, weighing her down. *God help me! I'm going to drown*!

13

"Please hurry, John," Elam pleaded.

"I'm already traveling over the speed limit!" John gripped the wheel as he maneuvered around a curve.

When John had returned one of the construction workers who worked with Elam, he'd casually mentioned that he'd taken Susanna and Elizabeth to Moraine State Park. Picturing Lake Arthur, Elam had felt an icy chill travel down his spine. He'd left work early to have John rush him to the lake. He prayed his fear had false roots, but his anxiety persisted. Why had Elizabeth trusted Susanna?

Elizabeth splashed to the surface. Susanna sat staring at her. A sudden revelation stunned Elizabeth. *She brought me out on the lake to drown me!*

Her lungs burned for air, but the water closed around her again. Thoughts flashed through her mind. She was ready to meet the Lord, but the thought of leaving her precious baby behind gripped her heart. Tightening her lips, she battled not to breathe.

God help me! Please forgive Susanna and help her to see the wrong she's doing.

Lights seemed to explode in Elizabeth's head. Without oxygen, she had only seconds of consciousness left. Again she cried out to God. Her foot touched something hard. Was she at the bottom of the lake? Scrambling, she endeavored to gain a foothold. Was her struggle taking her closer to the surface, or making her sink faster?

Lights flashed behind her eyes. After one more desperate lunge for the top, her water-logged clothes and shoes pulled her down. Her energy spent, she stopped kicking. However, her arms kept trying to lift her body. She discovered she was standing, apparently one toe on a rock.

Air struck her face. Gasping, she choked. God had miraculously placed her foot on a tall rock or submerged log, but she couldn't maintain her balance for long.

Susanna stood in the boat, the color draining from her lovely features. Seizing a flotation pillow, she tossed it to Elizabeth.

Flailing and splashing, she grappled with the pillow. Her fingers closed on the edge, then slipped. The pillow floated out of reach. Susanna hurled the second one at her. On the way under, Elizabeth clutched wildly. Her right hand managed to grab an attached cord. She yanked it toward her, grappling with her other hand. At the last moment, she managed to seize the pillow.

"Hang on!" Susanna cried. "Dear God, please hang on!" She knelt in the bottom of the boat, tears trailing down her face. "I killed the spider."

Elizabeth gasped, choked, and thanked God. What now? The boat was several feet away, and no one was in sight.

Susanna gripped the oars. "I'll try to maneuver the boat to where you can get ahold of it." Sweat dotted her forehead as she struggled with the awkward craft.

Finally, she managed to get it close enough to touch the flotation pillow. In water to her neck, Elizabeth was too terrified to release her grip to grasp the back edge of the boat. Susanna looked frustrated. She crawled to the back of the craft, leaned over, seized the pillow, and yanked. It jerked Elizabeth off of the pinnacle her foot rested on. The nothingness beneath her sent another lightening bolt of horror through her, jangling her fingers and toes.

A deep furrow creased Susanna's otherwise smooth brow. She lunged, grasped Elizabeth's wrist and pulled. The action tore Elizabeth's fingers from her means of remaining afloat. She gasped. Bracing herself, Susanna tugged until Elizabeth's hand rested at the edge of the boat. "Grab it!"

In desperation, Elizabeth obeyed. Bending, Susanna clutched the pillow and tugged it over the side of the craft until Elizabeth's other hand could grip the metal rim.

Tears coursed down Susanna's face. "I don't have enough strength to haul you into the boat!"

Elizabeth knew that was true. She clung to the boat, her knuckles white. The muscles in her arms cramped, but when she relaxed them, even slightly, her sodden skirts and water-filled shoes dragged her beneath the surface. Calling on strength she no longer had in reserve, she strained to keep her face out of the water. Each time she bobbed, she gasped, wondering how long she could hold on.

"Can you kick off your shoes?"

Elizabeth shook her head. She'd tried, but the ties were too tight. She struggled to keep kicking, for every time she stopped, her weight seemed to tug her under the boat.

"Hang on! I'm going to row for shore." Susanna took her seat, seized the oars, and rowed feverishly. Her jaw tensed, her face turned red, and her features twisted from exertion. Her eyes had a frenzied look. Elizabeth wondered if her assumption had been wrong. If Susanna wanted her dead, why was she trying so desperately to save her? Everyone would have believed it had been an accident — except Elam.

As the last ounce of strength drained from her limbs, her legs drifted downward and her toes touched bottom. *Praise you, God!* She began to believe the incident had been her own fault. She must pray more diligently to get over her fear of spiders.

Apparently, Susanna interpreted relief on Elizabeth's face, for she stopped rowing to gasp for breath. "Can you . . . touch bottom?"

"*Ja*. But, I'm so weak. I can't stand."

"Hey!" a tall, slender teen age boy called from shore. "You ladies need help?"

Too weak to respond, Elizabeth stared at him. Another boy, slightly younger, shorter, and more stocky, joined the first. Jerking off their shirts, they kicked off their shoes and splashed into the water. Elizabeth hoped they would reach her quickly.

"God help me." Grasping the oars, Susanna's pretty face twisted in anguish. She continued to row until Elizabeth was in waist-deep water.

The first young man splashed nearer. "You ladies okay?"

If Susanna hadn't rowed so feverishly, Elizabeth figured she would be gone by now. The boys would have tried to save her, but by the time they had reached the place where she'd gone under, it would have been too late. Grasping her arm, the tall slender young man supported her as she sloshed toward shallow water. The short, square-shouldered one gripped the bow of the rowboat and tugged it to the dock. Reaching a hand to Susanna, he aided her climb from the craft. When Elizabeth reached the grass, she collapsed.

Susanna hurried to her, knelt, and threw her arms around her dripping body. "*Es spied mich*! Oh, *es spied mich*!"

Elizabeth detested making a spectacle. Smiling weakly, she glanced at the two boys. "Thank you. We're all right, now."

They looked unsure, but collecting their cast-off T-shirts, shoes, and a basketball, they trotted across the park, their jeans dripping. Susanna sat on the grass, tears running down her sweat streaked cheeks. She looked at her hands, cringed, and closed her eyes. Elizabeth gripped the woman's wrists to examine her palms. Blisters had formed and broken. Bowing her head, Susanna began to sob.

Elizabeth patted the younger woman's arm. "It's all over, now."

"You don't know what I almost did!" Her words were difficult to understand because of her crying. But the next statement was shockingly clear. "I almost. . .let you drown."

Elizabeth shivered. Even in the warm sun, her wet clothing

gave her a chill, but it couldn't compare to the icy realization of what Susanna was saying.

"Oh, God, forgive me!" Susanna gasped, her voice tremulous. She turned her tear-filled eyes to Elizabeth. "I might have been able to stop you from falling overboard. I didn't try!" A new fit of sobs racked her slender body.

Elizabeth brushed a truant wet curl from her face. "What happened wasn't your fault."

"It might as well have been." She sniffed and gulped. "I saw that spider about the same time you did. I knew of your fright and I should have killed it."

Elizabeth shuddered. "I shouldn't let my fear get out of control. I pray God helps me get over it, soon."

"At first, I didn't even toss you the float cushion! Oh, Elizabeth!" Susanna wailed. "Will you ever be able to forgive me?"

"You could have let me drown. In the end, you saved my life." She took the younger woman in her arms. Susanna seemed lost and needed understanding.

When her sobbing ceased, she straightened. "I permitted my desire to become Elam's wife to tempt me to almost permit something evil to happen."

"Is this the second time?"

Susanna's red-rimmed eyes widened. "What?"

"Elam said. . .you were jealous of Mary and you could have pushed. . ."

"No! Oh, no!" Distress furrowed her brow. "I was jealous, but that day in the barn, I tripped over an uneven board. As I fell, I grabbed for the nearest thing. It happened to be my sister. She lost her balance and nearly tumbled into the bull pen." Shuddering, she continued. "I was jealous over her being Elam's wife, but. . ." Sniffing, she swallowed. "I never would've harmed Mary. Besides, at the time, she was pregnant with Jesse Mark!"

"From what you say, today wasn't entirely an accident, Susanna." Elizabeth kept her voice low, but felt it necessary to discuss the episode.

"Oh, Elizabeth, how could I have let my faith slip so far? I've failed God! I've failed you as a friend. I've failed Elam. And I've disgraced my family."

"If you're sorry and repentant, God has forgiven you." Reaching out, Elizabeth touched the back of Susanna's blistered hand. "And neither do I condemn you."

Susanna swiped at a persistent tear. "You're wonderful. Elam's blessed to have you. So are his sons." She took a deep breath. "It's past time that I abandon my obsession to get Elam and get on with my life." She studied Elizabeth's face. "I pray that someday we can be good friends."

Elizabeth looked across the lake, thanking God for saving her life, and for cleansing Susanna's heart. "What happened out there today is in the past, Susanna."

"I don't deserve your forgiveness, and my actions don't warrant your friendship."

"All have sinned and come short of the glory of God, and no one deserves His forgiveness. He loves us even when we do wrong and He pardons all our sinful acts when we ask Him. He wants us to love each other the way he loves us." Elizabeth smiled. "Dry your tears. Tomorrow is a new day."

A light pink hue began to creep back into Susanna's pale face. "From now on, with God's help, I'm going to trust and serve Him with all my heart."

"Then what happened today was worthwhile." A familiar scripture verse replayed itself through Elizabeth's mind. *And we know that all things work together for good to them that love God, to them who are the called according to his purpose.*

"God, don't let me be too late," Elam prayed, his heart throbbing in his temples.

The van skidded as John Zimmerman turned into the park drive. Gripping the wheel, he twisted his hand to point with one finger. "I took them to that table."

A picnic basket sat there, but no one was near. Elam's heart constricted. Unfastening his seat belt, his eyes frantically searched the area. "Drive on!"

John slowed the car when a basketball rolled across the road in front of them. Elam gripped the dash as though his will could push the car faster. "There they are!" He opened the door before the vehicle came to a full stop, leaped out, and raced toward the lake.

"Elizabeth!" he called. "Elizabeth!" She turned. Her face was pale, but she smiled. Instead of jumping up and coming to meet him, she remained sitting on the grass. He gasped when he got near enough to tell that her clothing was soaked. Dropping to his knees, he took her in his arms and pressed his face against the wet prayer cap that covered her sodden hair. "Thank God you're all right. I was so afraid."

"God was merciful, Elam."

He surveyed Susanna's stricken expression. "What happened?"

"I. . .We. . .I. . ."

"There was a spider in the boat, Elam," Elizabeth said, resting her head against his chest. "I jumped up, lost my balance, and fell into the water."

He eyed Susanna. "How far out were you?"

"We. . .went farther than we planned to."

"How far?" He didn't try to control the brusqueness in his tone.

Elizabeth's arms encircled his neck. "The water was over my head, but Susanna threw me a flotation pillow, then helped me to get a grip on the back of the boat." She shivered.

"I've got to get you home and into dry clothing."

John had raced back to his van. Smiling, he strode forward, a quilt slung over his arm. "I carry a blanket in case of an emergency." Unfolding it, he draped it around Elizabeth.

"Let's go home, darling." Elam helped her to her feet, praising God that she hadn't been taken from him.

John stepped to Susanna, proffered his hand, and drew her to her feet. "Your skirt is a bit wet. You've been through a lot too."

Shivering, she gasped. "Thank God it turned out as it did."

As they settled in the car, Elam in the back seat with Elizabeth, Susanna in front with John, Elam wondered about his sister-in-law. Evidently she and Elizabeth had resolved any differences. He suspected that Susanna had been responsible for the mishap. Apparently she had had a change of heart. His embrace tightened. His heart repeated, *Danka Got. Oh, danka Got.*

Elizabeth's eyes roamed the countryside all the way home, when she could tear her gaze from Elam's. The apostle Paul had said that to die and be with Christ was gain, and she believed it; however, she wasn't ready to leave her baby, Elam, or his little boys. She knew God had spared her life for a purpose. She'd always sought His will and tried to be obedient, but since her near escape from death, her perspective had broadened and deepened.

Mattie stood on the porch, scowling. Elizabeth's jaw tightened as she thought about what the woman had done to her dresses. Then, as rapidly as the thought had come, she squelched it. *How quickly one is tempted to forget God's mercy,* she mused.

The older woman drew her lips into a tight line, but held her tongue until John drove away with Susanna. She glared at Elizabeth's wet dress. "Where have you been?"

Thankful for life, Elizabeth laughed. "In the lake."

Mattie's eyes widened, but before she could retort, Daniel and Jesse Mark thrust open the screen, raced across the porch, and down the steps, letting the door bang. Mattie jumped.

Elam knelt to hug his sons. They returned his greeting, but two sets of eyes peered curiously at Elizabeth.

Daniel grinned. "Did you fall in?"

"*Ja.*"

Dimples deepened in Jesse Mark's cheeks. "Was it fun, Mama?"

"*Vell*...not very." She clutched the now damp quilt and shivered.

"Humph." Mattie turned to open the screen. "What's the world coming to? Even some Amish are going crazy."

Laughing, Elam hugged his beloved.

Inside, Elizabeth changed quickly into her plumb-colored dress. Its ugliness no longer mattered. She could hardly wait to get her hands on Priscilla. Holding her baby again was a miracle. She gazed down into the tiny face that was haloed with golden curls.

The baby blinked long blond lashes, looked adoringly at Elizabeth, and grinned. "Ma-ma."

Elam stepped closer and tickled the baby.

She giggled and gripped his finger. "Pa-pa."

The two sweet syllables showered her with joy, erasing the horror of the afternoon, and filling her heart with grateful praise to God.

The next morning, Elam ate a hurried breakfast. He was in danger of being late for work. After kissing Elizabeth, he hugged the children, strode to his buggy, climbed in, and slapped Cavalier's flank with the reins, encouraging the horse to trot down the lane. The horse ran faster than usual, but Elam let him go. Turning onto the highway, Elam held the reins loosely in his hands and sang a hymn in German.

At the brow of the first small hill, Elam stared ahead and gasped. A van coming toward him was passing another vehicle where there was a solid yellow line. He yanked on the reins, but the horse had already swerved to the right. The driver of the oncoming van slammed on his brakes. Tires screeched as the vehicle careened toward Elam's buggy.

"God help . . ."

A siren wailed in the distance. Elizabeth gripped the back of a kitchen chair, and frowned.

Leah paused by a window, her head cocked to one side.

"That doesn't sound like a police chase."

Elizabeth's heartbeat quickened. "Fires and accidents make me anxious." She hurried to the porch, a hasty prayer for the victims on her lips. She scanned the horizon for a plume of dark smoke that would designate a barn or house fire. Hardly breathing, she listened for the peal of a bell that would signal the whereabouts of the disaster. No toll sounded, and the clear blue sky was dotted with fleecy clouds.

Frowning, Leah grasped a porch roof support. "The siren sounds like it's coming closer!"

"I don't see any smoke toward the west." Elizabeth hurried into the yard, so she could see the sky on the far side of the house. "There's no sign of a fire."

"It's probably a car accident." Leah peered toward the highway. "I don't know why *Englischers* don't leave home in time to get to work without speeding."

"*Ja.*" Elizabeth bit her lip. "Elam left later than usual this morning. He was hurrying."

"That's unusual for him."

Sitting on the top porch step, Elizabeth gazed in the direction Elam had gone. Her stomach knotted. Surely he hadn't done something careless to make up lost time. She thought back over a few narrow escapes her brother had had because he loved driving fast. Elam was mature enough to be more cautious.

The siren slowed, then came to a stop just over the brow of the hill. Elizabeth stared at the trees that screened the main highway, her pulse throbbing in her temples. "Watch Priscilla and don't let the boys follow me." Opening the gate, she ran toward the sound of traffic.

"Elizabeth!" Leah hurried across the lawn. "Ladies shouldn't race off alone."

The turmoil in her stomach increasing, Elizabeth ran faster.

Leah gripped the top of the gate. "Elizabeth! *Cume* back!"

Her jaw set, she ran on. She wouldn't return to the house

until she could be assured of Elam's safety.

As she rounded the bend in the lane, she saw that the highway traffic was piling up. Not pausing at the end of the lane, she headed up the hill. Holding her head up, she ran along the berm. Passengers peered out their windows, curiosity on their faces. Disregarding possible ridicule, she raced on. A man whistled. She set her jaw.

A woman rolled down her window and stuck her head out. The wind fluffed her frizzy red hair. "Hey, Amish lady! What's the holdup?"

Not deeming it necessary to answer, Elizabeth ran on.

"Hey! I asked you a question, stupid girl!"

A young man jumped out of a car into her path. "Oh! I'm sorry." Whirling, he raced toward the accident, his long legs allowing him more speed than Elizabeth's long skirts permitted her.

At the top of the crest, she stopped to stare, and her cry of horror rent the air.

14

Elizabeth clutched her face with trembling fingers. The blood in her veins felt like icy rivulets; nausea washed over her, and her throat constricted. "Elam! Oh, Elam," she cried, yet no sound came.

She forced her numb legs to propel her forward. Pieces of Elam's demolished buggy lay scattered on the highway; his horse lay unmoving at the side of the road, it's neck twisted to an odd angle. The remains of the buggy was a jumbled heap of splintered wood and twisted orange-brown canvas. A burgundy van set sideways across the highway, the crumpled metal merging with the mangled carriage. A silver station wagon had plowed into the far side of the van, further damaging it as well as compounding the snarled remains of the buggy. Elizabeth's eyes darted frantically as she searched for Elam.

"Stay back, ma'am," a short, dark-haired man told her in a kind voice.

She disregarded him. He gripped her arm, apparently endeavoring to physically keep her away. Jerking free, she rushed to the wreckage. Her heart nearly stopped when she saw Elam's hand protruding from under the canvas. "He's buried in the rubble!" she cried, her heart throbbing wildly. She ripped at the debris, disregarding the splintering ends of wood that scratched her flesh.

"Stop!" A squat, balding man grasped her wrist.

Jerking free, she seized the canvas and tugged. A section

tore away, revealing Elam's ashen face. Blood trickled from a gash on the side of his head and soaked into his hair. The blood on his shirt and broadfalls made it difficult to tell the location of his wounds or assess his injuries. "Elam!"

He lay motionless, his eyes closed. His left arm looked broken. She rested her hand on his chest. Thank God he was breathing.

"Get him out!" she cried, anguishing over how his legs remained pinned under debris. Grasping a crushed buggy wheel, she wrestled to pry it loose.

A tall, muscular blond man grasped her arms. "Wait." His voice was kind but firm.

She turned to face him, strengthened by the compassion in his blue eyes. "We have to get him out!"

"The way he's wedged in the wreckage, we would kill him if we tried to pry him loose." His tone was soft, but firm.

A smaller hand grasped her fingers and tugged gently. "Come with me, dear."

Elizabeth faced an older woman with gentle gray eyes. "I can't leave him!" She glanced over her shoulder at a second police car as it jerked to a stop.

"Come on," the kind woman urged. "The ambulance is here and the paramedics are going to get your man out."

Her heart pounding, Elizabeth stepped aside long enough to let the men through, but refused to be led away. Clasping her trembling fingers, she prayed. Tears streamed down her face.

"I can't get his legs out," one of the medics said.

Breathless, Elizabeth watched, dots of cold sweat moistening her forehead. Minutes seemed like hours.

"Get a surgeon out here," a medic told his female attendant.

She hurried to the radio, her brow deeply furrowed. The medics had worried expressions as they conversed in whispers. Creeping closer, Elizabeth strained to hear what they were saying.

"The surgeon will have to amputate his legs to get him out," the first medic said.

"No!" To maintain her balance, Elizabeth gripped a spoke of the crushed buggy wheel. "You can't mangle him!"

The medic glanced up, surprise on his face. "I'm sorry. We're doing all we can."

A muscular blond man stepped forward. "There's a machinist on the next farm. He'll know how to cut that metal and free Elam."

"He could be right," the second medic said, glancing at the nearest man. "Get that machinist and make it quick! The way his circulation is affected, he may lose more than his legs."

Elizabeth moaned and prayed for God to strengthen her faith.

A young sandy-haired woman with soft-green eyes handed Elizabeth a cup of steaming liquid. "I had a thermos of coffee in my car. A cup may help you."

"Thank you." Elizabeth sipped the aromatic brew without taking her eyes from Elam. She had to believe he would be all right. Had he moved? She pressed closer. "Elam?"

His lips moved and his eyelids fluttered, then his features twisted as though he were in agony.

She pressed the coffee mug into the girl's hand. "I'm here, Elam. You're going to be all right."

"Beth." He looked at her with glazed eyes. "Take . . . care of . . . my boys."

"*Ja*, Elam."

"I . . . love you." His lashes lowered.

She touched his shoulder. "Elam?"

"He's unconscious, again, Ma'am. Please step back."

A man rushed past the waiting line of cars and stopped at the buggy. "I'm Dr. Oaks." Spotting Elam, he knelt to examine him. His frown deepened. "His legs may have to be sacrificed to save him."

"No!" Elizabeth cried. "I can't let you! I won't!"

"I don't have the authority, Ma'am, but a surgeon may have to amputate."

"I won't permit it."

"Are you his wife?"

"No."

"Are you next of kin?"

"No, but—"

"Then you'll have nothing to say about it." He turned back to Elam.

Elizabeth seized his sleeve. "I won't let you cripple him!"

"Lady, the surgeon will do all he can, but the way his legs are pinned, we may not be able to get him out any other way."

Arguing to save Elam's legs might cost him his life, yet she felt she had to do all she could to keep them from unnecessarily mutilating him. Anguished, she wrestled to try to figure out what he would want. She must fight for him, until he could speak for himself. "You'll have to wait."

The doctor scowled. "That man could die if you stand in the way."

Elizabeth choked on a sob, but firmly stood her ground. She looked at Elam. Was the doctor right? Was she killing the man she loved by interfering? Somehow, she felt God telling her to prevent the amputation. As long as she had breath, she intended to do what she thought was right.

A red pick-up roared as it bounced across the nearby field. Elizabeth prayed the driver was the machinist the tall blond man had mentioned.

The vehicle jerked to a stop beside the highway. Leaping out, the driver, a small but wiry man, grasped some tools from the bed of his truck. "Bring those containers of water and the fire extinguisher," he called to some nearby men as he rushed to the pile of rubble entrapping Elam.

The muscular blond came around the end of the buggy and hurried to aid the new stranger. "Can you help?"

Inspecting the situation, he frowned, then nodded. "Everyone please stand back." He fastened a chain to the twisted metal pinning Elam and handed the end to the huge man. "When I say pull, do it. He adjusted a mask over his face. Lighting a torch, he began.

Elizabeth gasped. "You'll burn his legs!"

"Stay back!" The machinist turned to a stocky bystander wearing jeans and a green plaid shirt. "If his broadfalls ignite, douse the flames."

"Dear God, please . . ." Covering her face, Elizabeth turned away, then looked back. She couldn't stand to watch, yet she couldn't bear not to. An obese woman crowded in front of her, obstructing her line of vision. The torch hissed. A woman sucked in her breath.

"Pull!" the machinist yelled. "Pull!"

Metal scraped against metal.

"Harder!" the man handling the torch cried.

"Please excuse me." Pulling frantically on the huge woman's sleeve, Elizabeth convinced her to step aside.

With the wreckage situated the way it was, the chain was too short to get a vehicle close enough to attach it. The links dug into the blond's thick arm and his face reddened as he strained. Voices mingled in the chaos. Horns blasted, and men shouted above the din. In the distance, another siren wailed.

The smell of charred wood stung Elizabeth's nose. Imagining how seared Elam's legs would be, tears ran down her face. She clenched her fists until her fingernails cut into the palms of her hands.

Smoke curled upward in a small spiral. A young girl gasped. "It's on fire! The canvas is burning!"

"He'll be burned alive!" another woman cried.

The stocky man had used all the water. The man controlling the fire extinguisher trained the spray on Elam, then aimed it at the spreading flames.

Disregarding danger to herself, Elizabeth leaped forward to seize the canvas near Elam's face. A spider raced across the material near her fingers. Ignoring it, she jerked feverishly on the fabric. It would not rip. A tall, broad-shouldered man waved a hunting knife. Striding forward, he reached above her head and grasped the canvas. He hacked with his knife and helped Elizabeth yank at the smoldering material. Part of it tore away, but flames were spreading quickly to other sections of the buggy.

"Pull!" the welder yelled to the husky man with the chain. "Pull!"

The wreckage groaned. Metal scraped and bent. Wood snapped and splintered. The rubble shifted.

"He's free!" the welder shouted above the din. "Get him out!"

Two medics rushed forward, lifted Elam's limp form, and laid him on a stretcher. Firemen, finally able to get the fire truck into position, began to spray water on the wreckage. Elizabeth followed as the medics wheeled Elam to the waiting ambulance. A female attendant opened the back of the vehicle. When Elam was safely inside, she jumped in and slammed the door.

Another fire truck approached, it's siren wailing. The moment it stopped, the firemen leaped into action and spread hoses. The ambulance roared away, its siren screaming. Elizabeth stood in the middle of the highway staring after it. An emptiness yawned within her. She watched until it vanished over the crest.

"Get back!" a fireman shouted. "These cars could blow."

Elizabeth looked at the snapping crackling fire that engulfed the buggy. Had Elam still been trapped, there would be no hope.

"Thank you, God, for sparing Elam's life," she said, clasping her scraped and bruised hands and moving to a safe distance.

The machinist climbed into his pick-up, turned the vehicle around, and left. Elizabeth hadn't thanked the man. Assuming he was a neighbor, she figured she could show him her appreciation later. She asked several people who lived nearby for the man's name. She discovered the machinist hadn't been home, and no one knew the welder who had freed Elam. She searched for the huge, muscular blond. He, too, was gone. No one had any idea who he was, either. Picturing them, and remembering the illumination on their faces, Elizabeth's heart warmed. *Did my Savior King send angels to rescue Elam?*

She eyed the motionless carriage horse, then turned to a skinny young man in a denim jacket. "The. . .animal?"

"He never knew what hit him." He shoved an unruly lock of brown hair from his forehead, unknowingly smearing soot on his freckled cheek.

Elizabeth was sorry about Cavalier, but was glad the horse hadn't suffered.

A warm hand rested on her arm. She turned to peer into the kind gray-green eyes of a pretty Amish girl about Leah's age.

"*Vea-gaits.*" The girl handed Elizabeth a dark-brown bonnet that was a shade darker than the dresses they wore. "I assume in your rush you forgot your bonnet. A woman shouldn't go out without one."

"*Danka dich.*" Grateful to the lovely stranger, Elizabeth donned the bonnet.

"I'm Elsie Miller, Elam's cousin from the next farm up the lane. My father's the machinist the attendants sent for. I'm so sorry he wasn't home. Thank God for the skillful stranger." She smiled. "I suppose you're Elizabeth?"

"*Ja.*"

"Leah has spoken often of you and your sister Sarah." She glanced at the chaos, the noisy crowd, and the smoldering rubble. "You can't do any more here. God saved Elam, and He can completely restore him." She linked an arm in Elizabeth's. "*Cume onn*, I'll walk you back to the house."

Leah sat on the porch swing with Jesse Mark, grateful to her parents for volunteering to watch Priscilla. *Danka Got Daniel's in school.* Reading to Jesse Mark was difficult, for she couldn't help worrying about the accident. Since Elizabeth hadn't returned, Leah assumed Elam had been injured. How she longed to race to the scene to find out, but she must stay calm for the sake of her brother's son.

Jesse Mark's usual grin had been replaced with a somber expression. "Are you sad, Aunt Leah?"

"I'm just wondering who could've been hurt in the accident."

His frown deepened. "When's Mama Liz-beth comin' back?"

"Soon, I hope." She opened the book. "Let's read about baby Moses."

"Nah." The little boy slid from the swing and strolled the length of the porch. "I wanna go see the wreck."

Leah sighed. "Get your ball and play with Tim."

At the sound of his name, the collie bounded to the porch, his tail wagging. Leah glanced across the barnyard and saw Elizabeth coming with Elsie Miller. Their somber expressions signaled trouble.

"You wait right here." A stern glance at the little boy emphasized her command.

She raced down the lane toward the women. Elizabeth's pale face and furrowed brow caused her worry to grow. Out of breath, she rested a hand on Elizabeth's arm. "Elam?"

"The ambulance took him to the hospital," Elsie said quietly.

"Is he. . ."

"He's alive." Tears coursed down Elizabeth's face. "But, he's been hurt."

Leah felt sick. "What hospital?"

Elizabeth touched her face with trembling fingers. "I don't know."

"They mentioned Jameson Memorial," Elsie said.

Leah chewed her lower lip as she thought. Then she looked at Elsie. "Please watch the *kinder*. John Zimmerman was going to visit Amos Yoder this morning. I'll go for him." She glanced at Elizabeth. "You change your dress and get ready to go to the hospital." Whirling, she headed for the barn. She'd intended to take the buggy, but if she took time to hitch it to Bonny, she might miss John at Yoders'. Seizing a bridle, she put it on Bonny, led her out of the building, leaped to her back, and slapped her with the reins.

Elizabeth turned to see Leah's horse galloping down the lane. Jesse Mark giggled. "Where's Aunt Leah goin'?"

Elsie put an arm around him. "She's going to visit Amos. You come and play ball with me."

Elizabeth decided to let Leah tell Rachel and Jonah about Elam's accident. Hurrying to the summer kitchen, she put bath water on to heat, then went upstairs to her room for a change of clothing. Her blood seemed to course through her veins in icy rivulets. All her life she'd been protected in an Amish community. The thought of going alone to the hospital made her short of breath. What was she to do first? How could she find Elam? Who would explain his condition to her? Since she wasn't his wife or the next of kin, would anyone tell her anything? If he was in intensive care, would they permit her to see him?

She donned her clean drab-plum dress, not even remembering its original lovely light-pink color. She fumbled with the straight pins as she closed the garment. In her haste, she jabbed her finger, jerked the pin, and had to refasten the material.

Leah appeared at the door of the summer kitchen. "John's here."

Elizabeth's heart lurched. "Will you go with me?"

"I would, but I have to stay with Jesse Mark and Priscilla."

"Oh, *ja*." Her hands fluttered. "It's just that I won't know what to do first!"

"Susanna's with John. She offered to accompany you."

Elizabeth's first impulse was to tell the woman to go home. However, she was thankful she wouldn't have to face the nurses alone. Going outside, she thought about Susanna. Wasn't the woman afraid of anything?

John slid open the side door of his van for Elizabeth. "*Vea-gaits*, Susanna," Elizabeth said joining the woman on the center seat. This was the first time Elizabeth had seen her since the boating incident. Susanna seemed older and more serious. Her blue eyes were bright with apprehension, and her usually smooth brow furrowed.

"Tell me about Elam," she said in a quiet but tremulous voice.

On the way to the hospital, Elizabeth described the accident. Assuming Susanna would want to know the details, she held nothing back. When the girl's face paled, she wondered if being honest had been a mistake.

"What if he . . . What if he . . ." Susanna swallowed. She gasped as though she needed oxygen, then blurted, "What if he died on the way to the hospital?"

"I pray not," Elizabeth choked.

"We couldn't be contacted by phone." Tears glistened in Susanna's eyes. "We won't know until we get there."

Elizabeth swallowed hard. Her near drowning flashed through her mind. What if her life had been spared only to have to live with the anguish of losing Elam?

Her heart raced as John pulled his van into the hospital parking lot. Her first impulse was to leap from the vehicle and run into the building, but gripping the door handle, she froze.

John glanced over his shoulder. "I'll go in with you ladies, if you want me to."

"Oh, *ja*," Susanna said, looking relieved.

He led the way to the emergency room, then approached the nurse at the desk. Susanna and Elizabeth hung back. Only a few minutes passed, but it seemed like forever.

John rejoined them. "Elam's in surgery."

Susanna clutched his arm. "That means he's alive!"

The room seemed to sway. Elizabeth braced herherself with her hand against the wall. Elam wasn't out of danger, yet. "What's his chance for full recovery?"

"The nurse can't tell us that." John gently grasped her arm. "Come and sit. I'll get you ladies a cup of coffee."

"I can't just sit!" Susanna cried. "I have to know about Elam."

"We'll have to wait." John guided her to a chair. "The doctor will come to explain when he's out of surgery."

Sitting, Elizabeth closed her eyes, took a deep breath, and prayed.

Three tedious hours ticked by before a doctor approached.

"Is the family of Elam Miller present?"

Elizabeth leaped to her feet, staggered, then stepped quickly forward. "Is he all right?"

The doctor was short with a slight frame. His thinning gray hair swept away from his round, boyish face. "Are you Mr. Miller's wife?"

She opened her mouth to say yes, but the lie stuck in her throat. She tightened her jaw. Was it going to be like this everywhere?

Susanna appeared at her side. "I'm Elam's sister-in-law."

The doctor hesitated. "Is his wife present?"

"Elizabeth is," dropping her voice, she added, "almost."

"I'm Dr. Peters. Mr. Miller came through surgery as good as can be expected."

"His legs?" Elizabeth choked, reliving the argument at the accident scene. Dr. Peters hesitated. Her anxiety exploded.

"I was able to save his limbs, but I can't promise a full recovery."

Susanna gasped. "You mean he won't be able to walk?"

"It's too early to tell the extent of nerve damage." He sighed. "His burns will heal, although there will probably be some scarring."

"*Danka Got,* he's alive," Elizabeth whispered. "When can I see him?"

"He's in recovery." Dr. Peters smiled. "I suggest you get some lunch. A nurse will tell you when you can see him."

"Dr. Peters," the intercom summoned. "Dr. Peters."

"I'll keep you informed as to Mr. Miller's prognosis." Turning, he strode quickly away.

The next two hours seemed like an eternity. Finally a nurse said they could see Elam for a few minutes. John accompanied Susanna. Elizabeth followed them to intensive care, her heart drumming and her legs hardly able to support her.

A tiny, redheaded nurse met them at the door. The cordiality in her smile softened the strictness in her brown eyes. She barely came up to Elizabeth's shoulder, but she stood like a fortress. "One visitor, please."

Elizabeth assumed Susanna would rush ahead. She felt like seizing her skirt to yank her back.

Susanna turned, a faint smile on her lips. "He'll want to see you, Elizabeth."

"*Danka dich.*" The nurse led her through swinging doors and into intensive care. When she stopped, Elizabeth looked through the glass at the man on the bed, and her eyes widened.

15

Gripping the end of Elam's bed, Elizabeth stared at him. The nurse grasped her arm. "Are you going to be all right?"

Praying for strength, she nodded. Both Elam's legs were in traction. A cast bent his left arm. Intravenous tubes connected inverted bottles of solution to needles stuck in his right arm, and in a vein in his neck. An oxygen tube extended from his nostrils.

"He's. . .so pale." Elizabeth stared at the bandage on the left side of his head.

"He suffered shock from the accident and he's been through traumatic surgery."

Moving to his side, Elizabeth rested a hand on his shoulder. "Elam?" He didn't respond.

The nurse stepped closer. "Just talk softly to him. Even in an unconscious state, it can encourage the patient."

Elizabeth drew an uneven breath. "The boys send their love." Her mind whirled. What should she talk about? She pictured the Amish girl who had offered her a bonnet. "I met Elsie Miller. She says she's a cousin of yours. I like her. She reminds me of Liz Lapp." With gentle fingers, she stroked his forehead. "John Zimmerman drove me to the hospital." Should she tell him that Susanna was here? Since he mistrusted the woman, would her presence worry him? It would be better to explain the situation, she supposed. When Susanna visited Elam, he might leap to the wrong conclusion.

The nurse smiled. Just keep talking softly, Mrs Miller."

Elizabeth intended to explain her position in Elam's life, but wondering if the nurse would make her leave, she looked back at the man she loved. "I was a little scared of coming here alone, Elam." She took a breath and prayed for wisdom. "Susanna offered to accompany me. She's been a dear. John is in the waiting room keeping her company. She told me to visit you first." Bending, she kissed his cheek. "I love you."

She continued to speak softly and stroke his arm.

The nurse had stepped away, now she was back, hovering at the end of the bed. "Your time is up, Mrs. Miller."

"But, I just got here."

Sympathetic but stern brown eyes surveyed her. "Your husband is in critical condition. We can only allow you thirty minutes every two hours."

Had a half hour passed so quickly? "What if he regains consciousness, and I'm not here?"

"I'll inform you immediately if there's any change." She patted Elizabeth's arm. "You can sit in the waiting room with your friends."

Walking away from Elam's bedside was anguishing. She longed to remain near him. *Thirty minutes every two hours*, ricochetted through her mind. Susanna would demand the next turn. It would be four hours before she would get another few minutes with Elam. If she were his wife, she could insist on seeing him every visiting period. *How selfish of me*! What had happened to her charitable spirit? Fighting tears, she paused at the waiting room door. The beige tones of the hospital walls and drapes echoed her mood, and she prayed for God to soothe her jangled nerves.

Susanna hurried to grasp her hands. "How is he?"

Slumping to an orange chair, Elizabeth sighed. "He's unconscious. "They'll only let us see him every two hours, and you'll want to go in the next time."

"*Ja*, I want to." She smiled weakly. "But I won't. He needs you, Elizabeth. I'll remain here to keep you company, but it's up to you to cheer Elam."

"*Danka dich*, Susanna." The woman really had changed!

"You ladies should eat," John said. "It's well after noon, and neither of you have had lunch."

Susanna stood. "Where will we eat?"

"The cafeteria's closed until supper, but there's a snack shop handy."

She stepped to John's side. "Lead the way." She glanced back at Elizabeth. "*Cume onn.*"

"I can't eat when Elam's so. . ." She blinked to ward off tears.

"You must keep up your strength."

Elizabeth shook her head. "The nurse said she'd let me know if there was any change. I can't leave."

"That's all right." John smiled. "We'll bring you a sandwich. Do you prefer beef, ham, or turkey?"

Her head ached. The mere thought of food made her stomach protest. "Just a cup of black coffee, please." She wondered how she could drink anything, let alone coffee.

She watched the couple stroll down the corridor. John smiled at Susanna with more than a little interest. What if she fell for him? He was Beachy Amish, she was Old Order. If she became involved with John, she would suffer Meidung (shunning). Had Susanna only climbed out of one emotional fiasco to tumble headlong into another?

Strolling aimlessly around the room, Elizabeth peered at the pictures of birds on the wall, then perched on the edge of a chair, she picked up a magazine and flipped unseeingly through the pages. The only image she could muster was Elam's still form. Gripping the arm of the chair, she prayed.

In little more than a half hour, Susanna returned with John. He carried a paper plate, Susanna a cup.

John placed the plate on the small table beside Elizabeth. "We brought you a ham and turkey club on toast. The dessert is tropical fruit-flavored Jell-o with peaches."

Prying the top off of the cup, Susanna proffered it. "I

brought you fruit juice. John will get you coffee if you still want it."

"Juice sounds better." After eating, Elizabeth felt stronger and more under control. Her friends were right. If she were to keep the vigil she intended to, she would have to take nourishment.

During the second day, Susanna's enthusiasm seemed to wane. Elizabeth surveyed her. "I'm grateful to you for accompanying me to the hospital and remaining with me through the night, but you don't have to stay today, too."

"I won't desert you." Susanna smiled through a sigh. "But, would you mind if I went out for a bit of fresh air with John?"

"I think you should. If you pass the snack shop, will you bring me another cup of juice?"

"*Ja.* Would you like anything else?"

"Not until supper." She watched the couple until they turned a corner, then she looked at the magazine in her lap, trying not to worry about Elam. A "huff" drew her attention to the doorway of the waiting room. Mattie, wearing a dark-brown dress, stood, her feet apart, her fists on her plump hips. Her thick brows, accentuated by a scowl, shadowed her dark eyes, making her look more austere than ever.

"You've been here for two days, and you haven't put forth the effort to visit Jonathan."

Elizabeth straightened, but forced her tongue into submission. When she could trust it to speak, she said, "I must stay close in case Elam regains consciousness."

"Nonsense! The nurses are with him. Besides, Jonathan's room is on this floor. I'll take you to see him."

"I should wait to tell Susanna and John where I've gone.,"

The woman took a challenging step forward. "Where you go and what you do is none of their business."

Elizabeth wished Susanna hadn't left. She sighed. *When I'm Elam's wife, even though we have our own home, I'll have to handle Mattie.* Standing, she glanced at the clock. "I'll be glad to visit Jonathan, for I have thirty-five minutes before I can get in to see Elam."

Mattie's lips drew taut. "You see Elam every two hours. His condition hasn't changed, so it won't hurt to miss one visit."

Elizabeth straightened her shoulders. She maintained a low tone, but spoke with firmness. "I will leave Jonathan's room in time to see Elam at the top of the next hour, Mattie."

The woman looked taken aback. She blinked as though no one had ever opposed her.

Elizabeth smiled. "Let's go."

Mattie silently led the way. There were two men in Jonathan's room. Striding to the far side of the second bed, Mattie peered at her husband's closed eyes.

Pausing across the bed from the woman, Elizabeth studied Jonathan. He was as tall as Elam, but not as broad-shouldered. His straight light-brown hair fell in disarray across his pillow. Above his beard, his complexion was ruddy, yet his eyelids looked ashen. His handsome features resembled Elam's, although his forehead and nose had more breadth. He'd changed little in the eight years since she'd seen him.

"Jonathan," Mattie said.

His light-brown lashes fluttered, then lifted. He trained dulled indigo eyes on his wife. Sighing, he lowered his lashes.

"Jonathan Miller, don't you dare pretend you're sleeping. I came to visit you."

"*Ja*, Mattie."

"I take time out of my busy day to travel in here. The least you can do is talk to me."

"*Ja*, Mattie."

She sniffed. "I brought Elam's future wife in to visit."

He opened his eyes, glanced around, and focused on Elizabeth. A slight smile curved his full mouth. "*Vea-gaits*. It's been a long time."

"*Ja*." She clasped his proffered hand and returned his smile. "It's good to see you. I hope you'll be home soon."

His arm dropped back to the mattress. "How's Elam?"

"I've told you there's been no change." Mattie sounded irritated.

"*Ja,* but . . ." He frowned as he faced Elizabeth. "I'm concerned about harvesting the corn."

Mattie sniffed. "It would be done, if Elam had cared enough to stay home to help with the work!"

Jonathan eyed her. "He has a responsible job."

"*Ach*! It wasn't his job that kept him in Lancaster when he should've been cutting corn."

"I'm sure we'll get the grain cut, Mattie," Elizabeth said, hoping to quell Jonathan's anxiety.

"The corn's only one task." Mattie's nose twitched. "The manure needs forked from the shed, and someone has to plow the fields or we won't have a winter wheat crop. That along with the regular chores! It's a good thing we don't have as many cows as before."

Elizabeth frowned. Couldn't Mattie see how she was upsetting her husband? No wonder he'd had a heart attack. The woman's critical attitude was probably keeping Jonathan from recuperating as quickly as the doctors had expected. What was keeping him from suffering a relapse?

"Leah could do more if it weren't for Elam's naughty boys," Mattie continued.

"They're just little boys," Elizabeth said softly.

"They're going to be spoiled when they grow up, just like Samuel the prodigal."

"Now Mattie." Jonathan sighed.

Elizabeth patted Jonathan's arm. "Don't worry about the farm work. I'll see that everything gets done."

Mattie cackled. "You can start with dunging out the cattle shed and spreading the manure on the fields so it can be plowed under."

Jonathan's brow furrowed and he rubbed his chest.

"Do you have pain?" Elizabeth asked.

"*Ja.* A little."

Eyeing Mattie, Elizabeth wondered if God was urging her

to set the woman straight or if it was her own desire. Mattie's tongue should be harnessed. Jonathan's life could depend on it.

A nurse entered with Jonathan's medication. Elizabeth promised to stop in again soon, and left. As she hurried down the corridor toward the elevator, she could hear Mattie prattling about the unreliability of doctors. *God, please help Jonathan to get well, and please enlighten and somehow soften that shrew,* Elizabeth prayed.

Another day dragged by. Elam's condition remained unchanged. John had left during the second night, but Susanna had stayed with Elizabeth. John returned the morning of the third day carrying two paper bags. Leah had sent Elizabeth a change of clothing, and Anna Mary Yoder had sent Susanna a clean outfit.

Retreating to a restroom, Elizabeth washed and changed into her medium-blue dress and returned to the waiting room. Feeling refreshed, she watched the clock. At nine sharp, she went to intensive care. Her meek knock was answered by a short, plump nurse with black hair and a round cheerful face.

"May I see Elam Miller?"

Nodding, the girl stepped away from the entrance. By now, the way to Elam's bedside was like a well-worn path. Elizabeth had been to visit Jonathan twice, the second time during Mattie's absence, so she would have lots to talk to Elam about. She frowned, vowing to repeat none of Mattie's critical comments.

Stopping beside Elam's bed, Elizabeth peered lovingly at him. She ran her fingers through his wavy light-brown hair to comb it into place. Glancing over her shoulder to make sure no one watched, she kissed his forehead, then his pale cheek just above his beard. "I love you, Elam Miller." Bending, she brushed his closed eyelids then, his mouth with her lips. Overcome with yearning, she kissed him fervently, thrilling at the way he seemed to return her kiss. When she drew away slightly, she looked into his brown eyes and gasped. "Elam!"

He blinked as though he were trying to focus. "*Vea-gaits,* Beth." His voice was low, but his words clear. A slight smile curved his sensuous lips. "Things are backwards, aren't they?"

"Backwards?"

"I thought the prince was to wake the princess with a kiss."

She laughed softly. "Elam Miller, have you been reading questionable literature?"

"When I was little, Emma told me stories an *Englischer* friend had told her. I think that one was *Sleeping Beauty.*" He glanced around, his brow furrowing. "Where am I?"

"In the hospital."

"Oh, *ja.* The accident." He stared at his sheet-draped legs as though they belonged to someone else. "How's Cavalier?"

Elizabeth didn't want to upset him, but she couldn't lie. "Your horse didn't suffer, Elam."

He continued to stare at his legs. "Are those mine?"

A chill froze her spine. She swallowed. "You've had surgery, but I'm sure you'll be as good as new in time."

His frown deepened. "Why can't I feel my feet?" Alarm flashed across his face. "What's wrong with my legs?" He began to struggle.

Elizabeth held his shoulders against the mattress.

Two nurses hurriedly approached. "Please relax, Mr. Miller," the first one said softly. "You're going to be fine."

"Where's my doctor?" Elam stared at one nurse, then at the other. "I can't feel my legs! I want to see my doctor!"

"If you'll rest quietly, I'll get him."

Elam promised, the crease in his forehead growing deeper. Elizabeth smiled to hide her apprehension. The redheaded nurse ushered her from the room. "Why can't I stay to hear what the doctor has to say?"

"Dr. Peters will be with you after he examines the patient. Please wait in the waiting room, Mrs. Miller."

Elizabeth felt a twinge of guilt for not admitting her marital status, but not wanting to lose the privilege of visiting Elam, she retreated quietly. Several strangers stared curiously at her as she entered the waiting room. Most times, she paid no heed, but today it bothered her. Choosing a chair by the window, she sat stiffly. Lowering her lashes, she prayed.

Susanna sat in the front seat of John's van. Sipping a Pepsi, she eyed him over the rim of the styrofoam cup. Sighing, she set the container on the dash. "I shouldn't lounge out here and leave Elizabeth to fend for herself."

Tossing his straw hat behind his seat, John surveyed her with laughing green eyes. "She's shy, but she's a capable lady."

"That's true, but . . ." Because of the contemptuous way she'd treated Elizabeth, she wanted to make it up to her. Thinking of the growing friendship between herself and Elizabeth, she rested her left hand on the seat. John's fingers closed around hers. A strange pleasant sensation showered her. She returned his generous smile, but knew she must stop his advances. He was a Beachy! She was Old Order.

"Susanna." His voice was soft, his syllables caressing. Reaching out, he gently touched her cheek. "I love your dimples."

His eyes became lustrous, reminding her of the emerald she'd seen one of the receptionists wearing. Grasping her shoulders, he drew her closer. Lured, she leaned forward. His lips touched hers, gently, tenderly caressing. She closed her eyes as her arms found their way around his neck. Her heart raced, making her temples throb and her blood surge. It was her very first kiss, and it awakened feelings deep within her. She wanted it to go on forever.

John pulled away slightly, his eyes dancing with silver highlights. The spark of yearning within Susanna ignited into flames. If this was what kissing was like, no wonder people loved it! A sandy-colored curl dangled on John's forehead like a sensuous lure. Reaching up, she put it back into place. The fire she felt in her heart seemed to be reflected in his eyes. His head lowered until his mouth covered hers, sending her twirling in the fury of another emotional whirlwind.

"Susanna, we have to stop!" Pulling away, he leaned back against his seat and closed his eyes.

She paused to permit her eyes to caress his handsome profile. "John, I'm. . .Old Order Amish."

"I. . .know." His gold-tipped sandy lashes lifted, revealing troubled eyes. "Have you joined the church?"

"*Ja.*"

His brow furrowed and he grasped the steering wheel, gripping it until his knuckles turned white. Taking a deep breath, he reached between the seats to seize his straw hat, then opened his door. "We'd better get back to Elizabeth."

She was reluctant to leave the warm emotional cocoon of John's van, but sighing, she accompanied him into the hospital.

He walked her to an elevator. "You go on up. I'll get Elizabeth some juice."

When Susanna stepped into the waiting room and saw Elizabeth crying, her throat constricted. Hurrying across the room, she knelt beside Elizabeth's chair. "What's happened?"

"Elam's. . . Elam's. . ."

Assuming the worst, remorse plagued her. "*Es spied mich.* Oh, Elizabeth, *es spied mich!*"

Drawing a shattered breath, Elizabeth crushed a tissue in her fist.

"I never dreamed he'd take a turn for the worse, or I wouldn't have left you alone. When did it happen?"

"Dr. Peters was just here." She peered at Susanna with red-rimmed eyes. "He explained Elam's prognosis."

"Oh. Then, he's still alive?"

"*Ja*, but . . ."

She gripped Elizabeth's hand, her heart racing. "But what?"

16

Elizabeth read anxiety in Susanna's eyes. "Dr. Peters said that Elam could be. . .paralyzed."

Still kneeling, Susanna gripped the arm of Elizabeth's chair. The pink hue faded from her cheeks, giving her face an alabaster gleam. "Permanently?"

"Some nerves in his back have been damaged."

"Won't they heal?"

"Dr. Peters seems a bit skeptical."

Getting to her feet, Susanna slowly moved to the chair beside Elizabeth and sat mechanically. "Does Elam know?"

"*Ja*. He could give up hope, and a positive attitude could be crucial to his recovery."

"We must pray for him, Elizabeth."

Elizabeth had been praying, but fear, an evil thing, lurked in the corner, trying to suffocate her faith. "Elam's strong. With God's help, he'll be able to accept his condition and adjust to it."

Susanna gripped Elizabeth's hand. "*Ja*, but what about his job with the construction company? What about the farm work . . . and the boys?"

"We must take this one day at a time. God will give us wisdom and courage."

"*Ja*." Susanna's smile seemed hesitant.

Elizabeth took a deep breath. "The power of the Holy Spirit sustained me after Moses's death. He'll do it again. Thank God Elam's still alive. He and I, with God's help, will adjust to whatever circumstances we're asked to face."

Susanna hugged her. "Let's refuse to believe that Elam will never walk. We must encourage him to believe or he may give up without trying."

Susanna's light-blue eyes shimmered as John entered the room, her expression telling Elizabeth that the girl could have more heartache in store. He handed Elizabeth a glass of orange juice. Grateful, she sipped it. Fifteen more minutes would pass quickly, and she must be ready to encourage Elam.

Elam tightened his lips to stifle a moan. His head ached, his cracked ribs hurt, and pain throbbed under the cast on his left arm. A strap held an air-hose to his nostrils. He longed to change his position, but the weight of the cast and being connected to intravenous tubes made movement difficult, not to mention being in traction.

He stared at his numb legs. Wishing for more pain seemed sadistic, yet the uselessness of his limbs tortured his spirit. He felt like half a man. What if the sensation never returned?

A plump, dark-haired nurse set a tray on the stand beside his bed. The dimpled creases at her wrists, reminded him of Jesse Mark's chubby baby hands. She'd told him her name was Gloria. It was appropriate, for she smiled a lot.

"We have chicken broth, Mr. Miller. Dessert is cherry gelatin."

Pain and worry had stolen his appetite. "I'm not hungry."

As though she hadn't heard him, she dipped a spoon into the warm liquid and held it to his lips. Compassion shimmered in her amber eyes. He opened his mouth, more to please her than to receive nourishment. After a few swallows, he turned his head. The pain in the upper half of his body nauseated him. Calculating the cost of the time he was spending in the hospital created mental spasms. He wanted to go home, but he abhorred having to depend on his family to take care of him. Closing his eyes, he pictured Elizabeth, longing for the gentleness in her touch. Suffering through two hours to spend thirty minutes with her racked his senses.

"Elam."

He blinked. She stood beside the bed, her face radiant. He yearned to leap out of bed to embrace and kiss her. The inability to do so created a lump in his throat that restricted his speech.

"You didn't finish your broth." She dipped the spoon into the bowl of liquid, then held it to his lips.

He accepted a few more swallows of weak soup, but the tasteless red gelatin felt like rubber in his mouth. "That's enough."

"You aren't going to get stronger if you don't eat."

She held the spoon in place. Was she waiting for him to say something so she could tip the broth into his mouth? He wasn't a child, and he resented being treated like one. His physical misery and emotional torment was burden enough. Had he no say in what he did? Was this what recuperating was going to be like? What if he didn't fully recover? Indignation curled his fingers into fists.

As though she understood, she removed the spoon and placed the bowl on the tray. "Jonathan is improving. He may be released from the hospital in a few days."

Elam frowned. "If Mattie keeps up her usual antics, he may suffer another attack." He figured the woman would give Jonathan a difficult time, heart problem or not. It was Mattie's shrewish nature, although she'd seemed affable at the time his brother had married her. She'd seemed to have a measure of virtue as well. What had happened to sour her?

He sighed. "Even if Jonathan goes home, he won't be able to do the farm work for awhile." Concern stoked the pain that racked his body. "Samuel is off somewhere, and now, I can't harvest the corn or do the fall plowing."

"Don't worry about the work. Leah and I will see that it gets done."

Sardonic laughter echoed in his brain, but he refused to let it escape. He wanted to shout, *How*? knowing it would be nearly impossible for her to manage all the farm work, but her wonderful smile partly soothed his frustration. Her gentle caresses alleviated some of his misery.

Smiling, she touched his cheek with a finger. "When you're out of intensive care, I'll be able to visit you as much as I like."

"You look tired. I want you to go home and get a good night's rest."

"I don't want to leave you."

"I'm being taken care of." He endeavored to get a full breath. A band of pain cramped his chest. Alarm flashed across Elizabeth's face, encouraging him to quickly add, "I'm all right." He forced a smile. "My ribs hurt when I breathe."

"Oh, Elam." Bending, she rested her face against his.

His lips burned for her kiss, but his concern for her needs outweighed his desire. "Is John still available to drive you home?"

"*Ja.* He plans to stay in Mercer County for awhile. He'd like to continue renting a bedroom at your place."

"He's welcome to stay there as long as he likes." He glared at his numb legs. "I won't be using my house for awhile."

"Is there anything you want me to bring you when I come in tomorrow?"

"Stay home tomorrow with the *kinder.* Priscilla won't understand your being away so long." A weak but genuine smile curved his mouth. "Daniel and Jesse Mark need you, too."

"Leah can take care of the *kinder.* I want to be with you."

Worry that he battled to control tormented him. "You'll have to find someone to help with the farm work. Amos Yoder may assist with the harvest, but he'll need help."

She kissed his cheek. "You relax and get well. I'll take care of the farm."

He wanted to tell her not to make promises she couldn't keep, but the sincerity in her gaze halted his words. "I love you, Beth," he whispered.

Gloria appeared at the bottom of his bed. "We want you to let your husband rest, now, Mrs. Miller."

Elam's heart lurched. He met Elizabeth's shimmering

velvety-brown eyes. She smiled vibrantly. Warmth engulfed him. In spite of his effort to appear taken aback, he grinned. He watched her retreat until she vanished from view. Alone, his pain became more acute, and he looked forward to the injection that would send him into oblivion for a time.

A loud knock resounded on Elizabeth's bedroom door. Startled awake, she blinked. Morning sunlight streamed across her bed. Before she could answer the summons, her door swung inward.

Mattie strode to the center of the room, her fists on her hips. "You plan to sleep all day?" She wore her drab deep-plum dress. None of her hair was visible, for she'd yanked it back severely before donning her prayer cap.

Elizabeth wanted to flop back to the mattress and cover her head with a pillow. Not wanting to be rudely awakened, she hadn't set her alarm, but it's nerve-wracking jangle wouldn't have been as bad as being shocked awake by Mattie.

"Leah came up for Priscilla an hour ago."

Elizabeth flipped back the quilt, swung her legs over the edge of her bed, and shoved her feet into her slippers. "I'll be down shortly." Standing, she turned away and made a production out of fluffing her pillow, continuing to do so until she heard Mattie leave. She reached for a dress, then stopped with a jolt. Her eyes widened. The pink dress that Susanna had turned to a horrid dark-plum was now a pretty shade of deep-burgundy. The dark-blue one was much lighter. Even the drab-brown looked fresh and more alive. Bewildered, she donned it and hurried down the stairs.

Leah stood at the sink, giving Priscilla a drink from a glass. Turning, she smiled.

"Did something happen to my dresses, or is Elam's being alive making things look brighter?"

"I bleached them, then used a prettier dye. The material will probably wear out sooner, now, but I think they're more presentable."

"*Danka dich.*" Elizabeth kissed the girl's cheek, then took Priscilla as the baby reached for her. "Where are the boys?"

"Daniel left for school, and Jesse Mark's with Mammy Rachel. She's been reading him Bible stories." Leah's turquoise eyes sparkled. "He likes to be elsewhere when Mattie's home."

Elizabeth glanced around. "Where is she?"

"She went to feed her chickens and gather the eggs."

"Hum. Maybe we should consider getting her a few hundred more hens."

Leah laughed. "Daniel suggested that. He said we should get her enough to keep her out of the house all morning." Sobering, she glanced into the living room, apparently making sure Jesse Mark hadn't returned, then she faced Elizabeth. "Mattie reported on Elam's condition, but I want to hear about his prognosis from you."

The wooden rocker in the corner of the kitchen creaked as Elizabeth rocked and described his condition; then she drew a laborious breath. "They can't promise . . ." She set her jaw, forbidding tears.

"That he'll completely recover?"

"*Ja.*"

Leah slumped to a kitchen chair. "I refuse to believe that."

Elizabeth's throat tightened. "He needs our prayers." She blinked. A tear rolled down her cheek and dropped into Priscilla's golden ringlets.

Leah swept across the room to peer out the window, apparently making sure her sister-in-law hadn't returned to the porch. "Mattie's been huffing about someone cutting the corn."

"There are fields to plow, too, as well as the regular barn work."

"Amos Yoder has been taking care of the milking, but that's about all he has time to help us with. Mattie refuses to do anything except take care of the hens." She turned back to Elizabeth. "I guess it's up to us."

"Yesterday, Mattie said I could start with dunging out the cattle shed."

Leah laughed, then sobered. "It desperately needs doing. It has to be spread on the fields before the plowing." She frowned. "I've never pitched manure."

Elizabeth pursed her lips. "I've done almost everything except that."

Leah shrugged. "If we can't get anyone to assist us, we'll have to do it." The furrows in her brow deepened. "Our neighbors are very busy with their own work this time of year, and with the recent medical expenses, we don't have the finances to hire help."

"Then we'll do it." Elizabeth got up to put the sleeping baby in the crib. "I'm hungry."

Mattie opened the door and stepped into the room in time to hear. "It's no wonder. It's nearly dinnertime."

Leah propped a fist on her slender hip. "It's only nine o'clock."

The older woman scowled at Elizabeth. "Are you planning to go to the hospital today?"

"*Ja.*"

"Don't forget your promise to Jonathan to get the farm work caught up." She huffed. "I suppose you made promises to Elam, too."

"I'll do what I can."

"You'd better start this morning. Jonathan's coming home in a few days, and I don't want him worrying about undone tasks."

Leah tightened her lips. "You can stay home today, too, Mattie. We intend to dung out the cattle shed, and we could use your help."

The older woman's heavy dark brows lifted. "Such impertinence!"

Leah propped her hands on her slender hips. "If Elizabeth and I tackle the job, why can't you help us?"

"That doesn't deserve an answer." Clucking, she took the eggs into the summer kitchen.

Leah waited for the door to close. "I'm not leaving Jesse

Mark to suffer her indignation, and Mammy Rachel isn't up to watching him for very long."

"We'll think of something."

Mattie's ride arrived. Donning her black bonnet, she scuttled to the car and climbed into the back seat. Leah paced, then decided to ride to Yoder's to see if Amos could help clean out the cattle shed. Elizabeth played games with Jesse Mark while she waited for Leah to return with Amos. She came back alone.

"Amos wasn't home." Leaning against the door frame, Leah chewed her lower lip. "I asked three other neighbors, but they're too busy to help this week."

"Was Susanna home?"

"No."

Suspicion wrapped its tentacles around Elizabeth. "Did she go to the hospital?"

"Anna Mary didn't say."

Elizabeth battled anger. She had to fork manure while Susanna entertained Elam. How could she have thought Susanna meant to be her friend? Had the woman just waited her chance to take advantage? "I'll change into my soiled dress, Leah. You'd better dress Jesse Mark in his oldest clothes. We'll have to take him with us."

"What about Priscilla?"

"Rachel can entertain her in the crib."

When Elizabeth came downstairs and saw a young man looking out the screen, his back to her, she sighed. His ill-fitting clothing mattered little. Help had come after all. The man turned. "Leah!"

"You should see your face." Leah laughed. "I borrowed a pair of Samuel's broadfalls and a shirt. They're too big, but they can't be any worse to work in than a long skirt." She crunched her brother's straw hat onto her head, nearly hiding her eyes.

Elizabeth laughed. "We'll be fine, unless the ladies of the church drive by and see us on the manure wagon."

On the way across the barnyard, Leah moaned. "I can't

believe we're doing this."

Jesse Mark giggled. "I never got to play in the manure before."

Leah's lips drew taut. "You're going to sit and watch, young man."

Jesse Mark grinned at Elizabeth. "She dresses like Papa, but she's soundin' like Aunt Maddie."

"This isn't a party." Turning, Leah peered down the lane. "Someone's coming." She pulled the straw hat lower, covering more of her face. "There isn't time for me to hide, so you do the talking."

Elizabeth listened to the approaching buggy. "Maybe we'll have help in the shed."

A horse trotted into view. Leah moaned. "It's Susanna."

Elizabeth remained unmoving until the buggy stopped beside them.

Susanna smiled, flashing deep dimples. "*Vea-gaits.* Leah told Mama you have a smelly task this morning." She glanced at Leah and laughed prettily. "It's nice you found a lad to help."

Leah tightened her lips. "This isn't funny."

Susanna sobered. "*Es spied mich.*"

"We don't have time to visit," Leah said.

"I came to watch the *kinder.* I knew you couldn't take Priscilla to the shed, and I assumed you would rather leave Jesse Mark at the house."

"*Danka dich*, Susanna."

Suspicion still lingered inside Elizabeth. "I thought you might be going to the hospital."

Susanna's face brightened. "I might. John said he'd drop by this afternoon. You'll be free to go by then, too, so he can take us both."

Shame swelled within Elizabeth. "I hope I can go, but there's a lot to do."

"I'm going to call on Elsie Miller. Do you mind if Jesse Mark accompanies me?"

He grinned. "I can't. I'm gonna help shovel poop."

"Jesse Mark!" Leah looked exasperated. "You get into the buggy and go with your Aunt Susanna."

"Aw, do I have to?"

"*Ja.*"

Dejected, he obeyed. When Susanna's carriage vanished around the bend, Leah and Elizabeth headed for the barn.

Three hours later, the spreader was full for the second time and the three horses hitched to it were anxious to go. Both women stood in the shed, perspiration making ribbons through the grime on their faces, and their feet caked with cattle dung.

"You drive this time, Elizabeth, I'll—"

"What's the matter?" At that moment, she heard an approaching buggy.

"That's probably Susanna, but I'd better check." Leah peered out the barn door, then leaped back. The color drained from her face. Her mouth moved, but no sound came.

Wondering what ailed her, Elizabeth headed for the door.

"Wait!" Leah said in a choked whisper, grasping Elizabeth's arm to prevent her from stepping through the opening. "It's several ladies from our district. They probably heard of Elam's accident, and are coming to call." She brushed a trickle of sweat from her face, unknowingly smearing dirt, or something worse, across her cheek. "They've been promising to come to meet you. Oh, Elizabeth, we can't let them see us like this."

"Susanna isn't back yet. Will Rachel tell them we aren't available?"

"I pray so, but Mama's so honest. She might tell them we're out here." Slipping to the corner of the barn, she peered through a crack between two boards to watch. "They're coming out of the house." She moaned. "It's Kate's quilting circle. The other ladies would be all right, but Kate's another Mattie."

"When they leave, we'll wait a few minutes, then spread our wagon load of—"

"Shh." Leah turned, her eyes wide. "Kate's leading them this way!"

17

Elizabeth's heart raced. "How many ladies are with Kate?"

"Four." Leah cringed.

Glancing at the stains on her skirt, Elizabeth pictured her disheveled appearance, knowing she smelled even worse than she looked. *The ladies of the church!* reverberated through her brain. "Why couldn't they have waited until Sunday to meet me?" she whispered. "I'm ruined!"

"So am I, once those biddies get a glimpse of me wearing Sam's broadfalls!"

Elizabeth stepped one way, then the other. "We can't just stand here and wait to get caught."

"*Cume onn.*" Leah nearly fell as she stomped through the manure to the inside shed door.

Following her through the opening, Elizabeth shoved the door shut. Tim whined and scratched on the other side. She knew if she let the dog trail them, the ladies might discover where they were.

Leah scrambled into a calf pen, leaned over the manger, and peered at the fodder room doorway. "They'll probably go to the shed, but they might come into the entry first. We don't have time to get upstairs."

"We have to." Elizabeth gave her a shove. "Go."

Clambering over the manger, they hurried to the back of the barn and scrambled up the stairway. As the ladies entered the fodder room, Leah and Elizabeth stepped onto the second floor. Yipping, Tim scampered back the length of the barn and bounded up the stairs.

"Go away!" Leah whispered, trying unsuccessfully to shoo the animal.

"Leah!"

"That's Kate." Leah caught her lower lip between her teeth, as her eyes darted around the barn floor.

The women's voices grew nearer as they trailed the dog's path. Elizabeth's heart throbbed in her throat. Leah held a finger to her lips, but Elizabeth didn't need encouragement to remain silent. Praying Tim would give up and go away, she motioned for Leah to follow. Tiptoeing across the barn floor, she vaulted over a three-foot partition and into the hay mow. The swoosh of the dried hay seemed loud, but Leah swung herself over, landing beside Elizabeth.

Loose hay formed a mountain at one end of the mow, but there were small bales piled to their left. Pushing and shoving at the scratchy surfaces, Leah squeezed in behind a stack of bales and vanished. Elizabeth pressed after her as far as she could, worrying that some part of her clothing might remain visible. She wished she could silence Tim, but he continued to pace and whine.

The ladies' shoes clacked on the upper barn floor. It was too late for Elizabeth to shove the bales or to crunch farther without making noise. Sweat formed on her brow and trickled down. The rank smell of their clothing intensified in the cramped space. Her pulse throbbed. This was ridiculous. How could grown women hide in the hay like recalcitrant children?

"Leah!" A high-pitched voice summoned.

Something touched Elizabeth's hand. Envisioning a spider, she stifled a scream, then discovered it was Leah's fingers. Grasping hands, they squeezed in companionable silence. Elizabeth remembered the hairy menace that had threatened to race over her fingers as she had yanked on the burning canvas of Elam's buggy. She had ignored it — for Elam's sake. A slight smile curved her mouth. God was strengthening her to overcome her fear.

"Rachel said they were out here," one of the women said.

"She must have been mistaken," a younger voice piped.

"Leah never leaves that old woman by herself for very long," Kate said. "Besides, there's a baby in the crib."

"She probably belongs to that woman Elam's after," the first woman said.

"It's a cute little baby."

An older woman sniffed. "If what Mattie says about Elam is true, Elizabeth will probably head back to Lancaster County as fast as she can."

The young one giggled. "Oh, Mama, she'll probably wait to make sure he can't walk before she runs."

The old biddies, Elizabeth thought. Their comments were more offensive than the dung in the shed.

"Let's go," Kate huffed. "We'll take a look downstairs. It isn't like Leah to vanish."

The sound of voices faded as the ladies departed. Leah tugged Elizabeth's hand. They looked at each other and Elizabeth had to bite her tongue to keep from laughing. Leah began to shake with silent, but uncontrolled mirth. If she kept it up, Elizabeth knew she would burst out, giving away their location.

Moments passed slowly. "I think they're leaving." Leah made her way to the outside wall and pressed her face against the rough wood to peer through a crack between the boards. She watched until the rumble of the visitors' buggy faded in the distance. Laughing, she waved her arm. "Let's get back to work. We have a lot to do before supper."

"What if they return?"

"They won't." Leah headed for the stairs, Tim romping by her side. "Kate was convinced that we were hiding in the barn. They won't be able to wait to visit elsewhere to gossip." Leah giggled. "Nothing they could think up could be worse than they would have discovered if they'd seen us."

Back in the shed, they continued their task.

Hours later, Leah eyed Elizabeth's skirt and wrinkled her nose. "We'd better go to the summer kitchen first and clean up."

As they approached the side of the house, Elizabeth noticed a tub of water setting just outside the door. "Susanna must have filled the rinse tub for our foul smelling clothing."

In the summer kitchen, they found kettles of hot water on the stove, ready to add to the cold water in both of the oval bath tubs.

Leah sighed. "Bless Susanna."

Stripping, they wrapped themselves in towels. Leah grinned as she fumbled in a lower cabinet behind the laundry soap and produced a bottle of bubble bath she'd hidden from Mattie. With a flourish, she dumped a liberal amount into each tub. Elizabeth climbed into the first one, sank into the bubbles, and moaned with pleasure. This was a far cry from the tub and shower she had in her bathroom near Bird-in-Hand, but she was grateful. Her muscles ached and her palms smarted from the blisters she'd acquired.

Later, dressed in fresh clothing and scented by the essence of the strawberry bubble bath, they joined Susanna and the children in the living room.

Remaining on the floor beside the checker board, Susanna smiled. "I found a pot roast in the refrigerator, so I started supper."

"*Danka dich* for the bath water, too." Leah slumped to the sofa beside Elizabeth.

Waving a chubby hand that held a checker, Jesse Mark bounced. "Look, Mama Liz-beth, Prissy-cilla is sittin' up."

A gasp of delight caught in Elizabeth's throat. Her little girl sat in the center of the room, grinning at them. Susanna had placed a pillow behind her for safety, but the baby wasn't touching it.

Susanna looked pleased. "John stopped by an hour ago to see when we would be ready to go to the hospital. I figured if we left about seven, you could visit Elam two or three times before ten o'clock."

"That sounds good." She yawned. "I've never forked so much!"

Susanna's pretty brow furrowed. "I've cleaned behind the horses and laid new straw, but not very often."

"Thanks for watching the *kinder*." Leah slumped into a chair. "This task is the first of many to come. With two of my brother's incapacitated and the third one away, I should have been a boy."

"That might have helped — unless you enjoyed an extra long *Rumspringa* like Samuel." A giggle bubbled up from deep within her. "You could marry Harry Smith. He adores you. I admit he's a little short on brains and looks, but he works hard."

Leah rolled her turquoise eyes. "I'd rather pitch manure!"

Susanna laughed. "I'd better get home and get supper for Mama." Standing, she glanced at Elizabeth. "John and I will be here for you about seven." With a smile and a flutter of skirts, she was gone.

Massaging her back, Leah sighed. "Let's put the finishing touches on supper before Mattie gets home."

"*Ja*!" Jesse Mark grinned, his deep dimples seeming to dance on his pink cheeks. "Aunt Maddie's always hungry. She's called Maddie, 'cause she's always yellin'."

Elizabeth laughed.

Susanna remained in the van with John. Elizabeth swept through the main door of the hospital. As she passed the snack shop, the scent of brewed coffee drifted to her. It was a pleasant change from the smell of antiseptic and laundered sheets. The clock was at the top of the hour. Her heart racing, she hurried to intensive care and made her way to Elam's bed. He lay relaxed in slumber, the creases of pain gone from his face. Not wishing to wake him, she stood silently, holding her emotions in check. How she longed to kiss him.

Nurse Gloria paused at the foot of the bed, a tray of medications in her hand. Her round chubby cheeks seemed to glow. "He's been looking forward to your visit all day." She looked at the sleeping man. "You're good for him."

"Does he sleep a lot?"

"Only when he's medicated."

"How long will he be miserable?"

Gloria tucked a black curl back behind her ear. "The pain in his ribs and left arm are already diminishing some." She frowned. "His legs . . ." Seemingly pensive, she answered slowly. "When the feeling returns, he'll have pain." She moved away, one of her white shoes squeaking softly.

Elizabeth prayed Elam would soon regain feeling in his legs. Then, realizing he would be in a great deal of pain, should her prayer be answered, she frowned. Regaining his sensitivity would bring misery as well as joy, but continued numbness would increase his despair. *You know what's best, Lord. Bless Elam with your healing power.*

Elam stirred. His brow furrowed. His lashes lifted and his clear brown eyes met hers. "How long have you been here?"

"About ten minutes." Bending, she kissed his cheek, then smoothed a hand across his brow.

His frown deepened. "Let me see your hand."

She didn't want Elam to discover her blisters or worry about how she'd acquired them. Grinning, she shrugged. "You can hold my hand, later." His right arm was held straight for the intravenous, the left bent at the elbow by a cast, so he couldn't reach for her.

"Beth, give me your hand."

She resisted, but when frustration showed on his face, she gingerly touched the back of his hand with her fingers.

He turned his arm enough to grip her hand. His fingers moved slightly over her palm. "Elizabeth, I want to see your hands."

"They're a bit rough, but I'm all right."

"What have you been doing?"

She kissed his mouth, hoping to distract him. His warm lips responded, but when the kiss ended, he peered sternly at her.

"Leave the farm work to what Amos can do or manage to get another man to help him with."

"He's doing the milking and caring for the animals."

"Your hands are blistered." His eyes shimmered with pleading. "Promise me you won't overdo."

"Leah is doing as much as I am."

"Is Mattie helping?"

Elizabeth laughed softly. "She takes care of the chickens."

He sighed. "No one's telling me anything about the accident. Was anyone else hurt?"

"No. The driver of the van had been drinking. The accident was his fault."

"Why haven't the police questioned me?"

"They want to, but Dr. Peters says they'll have to wait until you improve. A lawyer's been trying to get in here to visit you, but the nurses won't let him. He stopped by the house yesterday."

"*Ferwass?*"

"He wants you to sue."

"Didn't Leah tell him we Amish don't believe in that?"

"*Ja*, but he wants to talk to you."

"Tell him to seek business elsewhere."

"Leah did, but he's persistent."

"I don't want to ask you to leave, Mrs. Miller," Gloria said, "but Dr. Peters wants to examine your husband."

"The supervisor has been very lenient, but I've been here for over a half hour." Bending, Elizabeth kissed Elam.

He responded, but seemed troubled. "Don't stay at the hospital any longer tonight. Please go home and go to bed."

The suggestion encouraged a yawn. She clenched her teeth to fight opening her mouth, but she knew her expression betrayed her fatigue. She was reluctant to tell Elam she and Leah had forked three wagon loads of manure, for he had enough to worry about without her adding to it. Picturing the way she'd scrambled through the barn to hide from the visiting ladies, she smiled. "I'll stay long enough to visit you one more time. I might not make it in tomorrow."

"I'll be fine. You spend tomorrow with the kinder."

Having no intention of confessing that she and Leah planned to cut corn in the morning, she lovingly touched his face, and left.

"*Danka dich*, Amos." Elizabeth climbed to the seat of the binder, grateful to Amos for hitching the three horses to the piece of machinery. She'd often handled a team of draft horses, but managing three would be a new experience.

Amos appeared concerned. "You want me to accompany you the first round?"

"You're already running late. I'll do fine." She smiled to convince him, wishing she were more confident. She signaled to the animals. As they pulled the binder down the first row, she prayed they wouldn't detect her uncertainty. Amos stood watching, making her nervous. She hoped he would leave soon. If the horses misunderstood one of her commands, she could halt them.

By the time Elizabeth got to the end of the field, she felt out of breath, sweat dotted her forehead, and her hands were cramped from clutching the reins. "Relax," she told herself. These beasts were used to obedience, and they seemed to want to cooperate. The horses stopped at the end of the row. She chewed her lower lip. How did three horses turn a corner? Was it the same as a two animal team? She started them into a turn. They knew what to do, and the maneuver went smoothly. She wiped the excess moisture from her face when they were on their way down another row.

The sun seemed merciless, even though it was September. Sweat formed on her forehead, ran into her eyes, and smarted. The blisters on her hands broke. The smell of horse sweat mingled with the scent of the cut corn stocks. The sound of the animal's clomping heavy feet, the creaking of the machine, and the thwack of the cutter bar competed to drown the chirping of birds.

All morning, Elizabeth worked. By noon, she was ready to collapse. There was no time to rest. After dinner, she went back to the cornfield. Leah took a turn the latter part of the afternoon. Elizabeth watched the children while preparing supper. Mattie came home, irritable as usual. She complained about her difficult day, grumbled at the boys, and criticized the way the corn had been cut. When she wrinkled her nose over supper, it was the last straw.

Elizabeth got up, took the woman's plate to the porch, and scraped the food into Tim's dish. The collie wagged his tail in appreciation. Striding back into the kitchen, she clattered the plate on the counter, and returned to the table with an apple pie. She cut it into several pieces, serving everyone except Mattie. Smiling, Elizabeth said quietly, "You probably wouldn't like my pie either. I don't want you to feel you have to eat a piece." Picking up her fork, she cut through the flaky crust and took a big bite, savoring the taste of juicy apples that had been baked in brown sugar and cinnamon.

Mattie blinked.

Leah's face turned red as though she were fighting a giggle. The little boys looked at each other and grinned, but remained silent. Rachel, seemingly pensive, pretended to be unaware of Elizabeth's action. Jonah cleared his throat and dug into his pie for a hefty bite.

Mattie tightened her lips, but said nothing as she left the table and stomped to her room. Jesse Mark giggled, and Daniel pressed his hand over his own mouth. Jonah glanced at Mattie's retreating back, shook his head, then continued to eat. Elizabeth wondered whether she'd taught Mattie a lesson or only infuriated her. She would save Mattie's piece. How long would it take the woman to sneak into the kitchen for it after the family had gone to bed?

When the day was finally over, Elizabeth slumped onto her bed, too fatigued to sleep. If she and Leah cut corn all day tomorrow, the task would be finished. She sighed. The bound corn would have to be stood in shocks of eight to ten bunches.

That could wait another day.

Mid-morning, Elizabeth walked with John to the waiting room near intensive care. Susanna hadn't been able to come today, but Jameson Memorial hospital no longer seemed frightening.

John smiled. "I'll be back for you in four hours."

She nodded in agreement. Instead of going into the waiting room to wait, she strolled the length of the corridor. Nurses bustled to-and-fro at the station around the corner. The new shift was coming on, the old leaving. Elizabeth hesitated. Not wishing to get caught in the hubbub, she turned to go back the way she'd come. Then, a statement halted her steps.

"It was his heart," one of the nurses said. "The doctors think it was a blood clot from his accident. There'll probably be an autopsy."

"The family thought he was improving. Where are they?"

"We can't reach them by phone."

"Is his wife coming in today?"

"We hope so. He died three hours ago."

Elizabeth waited, but the conversation shifted to new admissions. Thinking about the family of the deceased man, compassion filled her heart. She glanced at the clock. It was time to visit Elam.

A strange blond nurse seemed engrossed with a patient's chart as Elizabeth entered intensive care. She paused, but accustomed to hurrying directly to Elam, she strode to where she could see his bed. She gasped, and her eyes widened. It was empty!

As the nurse's conversation replayed through her mind, she felt the color drain from her face. The blond nurse who had been at the entrance bustled up to her.

"Mrs. Miller?"

Turning toward the woman, the questions she meant to ask seemed to crash into each other, mixing up her words and phrases. Her throat constricted. "Elam?"

"I'm so sorry, Mrs. Miller. We wanted to contact you, but you have no phone."

Elizabeth's bones seemed to turn to liquid, yet she stood statuesque, staring at the woman. Her vision blurred and she blinked. *He's gone. Elam's . . . gone!* shot through her reeling brain. "The police. . .could have. . .informed us."

"We assumed you'd be in today."

Staggering, Elizabeth gripped the end of the bed. "Where. . .is he?"

18

"Follow me, Mrs. Miller."

The tall blond nurse had taken several steps before Elizabeth could get her legs to move. Viewing Elam's body would cause reality to crash in upon her. Numb, she placed one foot ahead of the other until they reached a room at the end of the corridor. The nurse pushed on the door, then stepped aside.

Elizabeth moved mechanically into the room, then stopped to stare. Elam looked so peaceful. His body, including his legs, lay flat under a perfectly draped sheet. His right arm rested by his side, the cast bent his left across his chest. The tubes that had been connected to him were gone. His pale complexion contrasted sharply with his light-brown beard and hair.

Wanting to caress him, she took a step forward. Then, the thought of his cold flesh seared her heart. Her hand hovered inches from him, then withdrew. She turned to derive comfort from the nurse, but the woman had gone, apparently assuming the patient's wife would desire to be alone with the body. A vast emptiness opened up within Elizabeth, creating cold numbness.

She peered at Elam through blurred vision, a sob catching in her throat. Kneeling, she pressed her face against the mattress by his side. How could she go on without him? How would she tell the boys? Waves of shock continued to roll over her, stripping her spirit to the bone. Reality dawned; devastation gripped her; tears came.

A hand caressed her head. "Beth, what's wrong?"

She leaped to her feet, her eyes wide.

Elam surveyed her. "Has something terrible happened?"

"*Ja*! You died. I mean I thought you had."

"*Ferwass?*"

She quickly explained what she'd overheard and what the blond nurse had said. "She brought me here to your room. You looked . . . dead. Besides, you're . . . disconnected."

He smiled crookedly. "Dr. Peters decided to take me out of traction." A frown shadowed his face. "I don't know if it's because he has hope for my recovery or if he's given up."

"How do you feel?"

"Fair, except for the pain."

"In your legs?"

"No."

Bending she gently put her arms around him and kissed his full, warm mouth. "I thought I'd lost you."

Irritation flickered across his features. "The nurses were careless to talk where they could be overheard. The woman who brought you here should have told you that Dr. Peters had had me moved to a regular room."

"She didn't know what I'd overheard, or that I'd leaped to the wrong conclusion!" She studied him. "Is your pain lessening?"

"Some. My broken arm throbs." He sighed. "I wish my legs would pain me instead of giving me nightmares."

She smiled. "Better or not, Elam Miller, you're getting married this November."

He looked anguished. "If I don't get my legs back, there'll be no wedding."

"Don't say that."

"I want you to be prepared."

"I love you. Whether you can walk or not doesn't matter."

"*Ja*, it does." He covered her hand with his. "We won't talk any more about it for now."

A chill had showered her. It felt as though a wet, cold cloak draped her shoulders. Elam didn't mean he intended to throw away their future together if he couldn't use his legs, did he? She refused to harbor the devastating thought. Her heart was too full of joy over discovering her mistake. Elam's warm body soothed away her torment.

"How's the patient?"

Elizabeth glanced over her shoulder at Dr. Peters. His graying hair was thinning, and light from the hall shimmered through the top strands. What the doctor lacked in height, he made up for by being jovial. Moving to the bed, he studied Elam's chart.

She stepped nearer. "How soon can we expect Elam to regain feeling in his legs?"

"We must be patient, Mrs. Miller."

"I'm not. . .Elam's wife — yet."

"Oh?" His gray-blue eyes peered at her over the top of his wire-frame trifocals.

She swallowed. Attempts to quell her contrition failed and heat bathed her cheeks. "The nurses assumed Elam and I were married. I didn't enlighten them for I wanted to visit Elam."

Instead of a reprimand, Dr. Peters chuckled. Moving to the foot of the bed, he squeezed Elam's toes. "Any sensation?"

"No."

"Concentrate. Try to wiggle your toes."

Elam closed his eyes. His brow furrowed. Several tense moments passed. "Anything?"

"Not yet, Mr. Miller." He smiled, apparently striving to encourage him. "Several times a day, try to concentrate on moving your toes. One of these days it could happen."

Elam seemed to brighten. "Is that a promise?"

Dr. Peters hesitated. "Let's wait and see. Nerve regeneration takes longer than the healing of cuts and bruises." He listened to Elam's heart, felt his pulse, checked the chart, then whistled softly as he retreated.

Elam watched him go. "He doesn't act like there's much hope."

"There's always hope—when we can pray." She kissed him. "The corn is cut. Leah and I are going to stand it in shocks tomorrow, so I won't be able to come in until evening."

He looked relieved. "Who drove the horses and binder?"

She moved to a window. "The leaves are changing color. Can you see the crimson maple from your bed?"

"*Ja.* Who cut the corn?"

"The gold-and-orange tree next to the maple is gorgeous."

"Elizabeth."

She turned to him, her smile vibrant. "From the back porch of the farm house, the entire horizon seems aflame with brilliant hues. We'll soon have to rake leaves in the yard."

"Beth, who cut the corn?"

"Amos Yoder hitched three horses to the binder. I never worked with more than two."

"Until yesterday?"

She laughed. "Elam Miller, you should be a lawyer."

"The church wouldn't permit it." He eyed her unrelenting. "The corn?"

She rumpled his hair. "Leah helped."

"But you cut the most of it?"

"It was a challenge." She grinned. "Get that scowl off of your face."

He sighed. "You going to tackle the plowing, too?"

"Elsie Miller's papa said he'd start the plowing next week."

"The shed has to be cleaned out first."

"*Vell*. . .that's almost done." Picturing herself and Leah hiding in the haymow, she chuckled.

"What's funny?"

"Someday, darling, I'll tell you."

"Maybe you should tell him now." Mattie, wearing her usual scowl, shadowed the doorway.

Elam peered at the woman. "She'll tell me when she's ready."

"Elizabeth and your sister disgraced the family."

"They have more to do than any two women could

accomplish, Mattie. You're going to have to accept your share of the responsibility."

With a flip of her hand, she strode to the other side of Elam's bed, smugness replacing her scowl. "Some of the ladies from our church district wanted to meet Elizabeth. When they came to call, she and Leah were in the cattle shed forking manure." Bending forward, she whispered in a harsh tone. "They actually hid from the ladies."

Elam looked pensive. Mattie seemed pleased. Elizabeth tightened her lips, but remembered her vow to pray for Mattie and try to reach her through acts of love. The thought of how she'd taken the woman's plate last night and not served her a piece of pie seared through her mind. She'd hoped to encourage Mattie to stop grumbling and criticizing, but the performance had probably aggravated the situation.

Mattie squared her shoulders. "The ladies have been talking plenty!"

Elam sighed. "Ja, I'll bet they have."

Wearing an innocent expression, Elizabeth blinked. "Are the ladies in your district permitted to gossip?"

Mattie looked appalled. "Absolutely not. We wouldn't think of such a thing."

Elam's right brow lifted. "*Ja.* You ladies usually speak before you think."

"Elam Miller, I left the side of my sick husband to come to cheer you up." Mattie huffed. "Apparently, since you're ready to insult visitors, you must be improving. I'll see you in a few days." Her mouth a straight narrow line, she scuttled from the room.

Watching her retreat, Elam frowned, then he leveled his gaze on Elizabeth. "Forking manure?"

"*Vell...*" Thoughts whirled through Elizabeth's mind. She wouldn't lie to Elam, but she'd planned to keep the shed incident from him. Mattie had made that impossible. Taking a deep breath, she began by describing how Leah had dressed in Samuel's broadfalls. Using comic gestures, she embellished the bizarre situation. Elam's frown gradually faded. His eyes twinkled with admiration, then amusement. When she dramatized how she and Leah had fled from the ladies, vaulted over the partition, and squeezed behind the bales of straw, Elam broke into laughter.

"You moved your foot! Elam, you moved your foot!"

"Are you sure?"

"*Ja.*" She uncovered his right leg. "Can you wiggle your toes?"

His forehead furrowed as he concentrated, but his digits remained motionless. He sighed. "I've been thinking about the cost of my being in the hospital."

"You concentrate on getting well."

"There isn't only my expenses, Beth, but Jonathan's. I'd go home, but it would be impossible to cope without a lot of help."

"Leah and I will be there, but we must wait until Dr. Peters feels it's time to discharge you."

"I can't stay here much longer."

She smoothed the hair from his forehead. "We'll do what's best."

A woman brought Elam's lunch tray, and Elizabeth was thankful for the interruption. She talked about the boys and Priscilla as she assisted him with his meal. He ate over half of it, which was a good sign.

"You'd better go for dinner while the cafeteria is still serving." He yawned. "I'll take a nap before my medication wears off."

"Is there anything I can get for you?"

"A new pair of legs."

"Yours will be fine, Elam. You must be patient." She kissed his cheek. "I'll get a sandwich and hurry back."

"Don't rush, Beth."

As Elam fought to surface from a deep sleep, pain racked his body. He sympathized with another man's misery when he heard him groan, then realized the sound came from his own throat. Fully awake, he battled not to cry out. His legs felt as though they were on fire. It seemed like a hot poker had been thrust against his back; his left arm throbbed. He gasped and stabs of lightning shot across his ribs. Against his will, another groan escaped.

Elizabeth rushed to his side. "What's wrong?"

"Pain," he said through clenched teeth.

"Where?"

"All over. Even my legs."

"*Danka Got*! I think. I'll get a nurse!" Whirling, she fled.

My legs, he thought, realizing most of his pain was in his lower extremities. He thanked God for the misery, then prayed for strength to endure it.

Dr. Peters rushed into the room. "This is what we've been waiting and hoping for. After I examine you, we'll give you an injection to reduce your pain."

Reassured that sensation was returning to his lower limbs, Elam smiled through his agony. "I. . .never thought I'd be grateful. . .to suffer."

"I'm pleased, but not for your pain. We'll make you as comfortable as possible."

"How soon can I go home?"

"It's too premature to discuss that."

"This is going to be costly, doctor. I must go home as soon as possible."

"You'll have to stay off of your legs for some time, yet." Dr. Peters seemed pensive. "However, if you have help, I can probably release you in a few days."

Elam wondered who he could hire to assist him. Would Amos Yoder be available some of the time?

Soon after the injection, Elam's pain began to subside; however, drowsiness overtook him, slurring his speech.

"*Vea-gaits*, brother-in-law."

Hearing the cheerful voice, he blinked. Susanna stood beside his bed, John Zimmerman in tow. "*Vea-gaits*."

Susanna smiled, dimpling her pink cheeks. "Elizabeth

just told us about your legs. We're so happy for you."

He read the lustrous new sparkle in her blue eyes and rejoiced over her apparent happiness. "*Danka dich* for coming." Still concerned about leaving the hospital as soon as possible, he asked, "Do you think Amos could find time to assist me when I get home?"

"*Ja*. He's already mentioned it."

"I'll pay him by the hour."

"Elam Miller!" She propped her fists on her slender hips. "How can you suggest such a thing? We're family."

"Every servant is worthy of his hire."

She laughed. "Amos considers himself a brother, not a servant."

John smiled. "Elizabeth asked me if I'd be available to assist you when you get home. I plan to stay in Mercer County for awhile, so I'll be glad to aid you. My renting a bedroom from you makes me handy."

"Good. There'll be no rent." He fought sleep, but his heavy eyelids closed, shutting out Susanna's lovely smile.

"I'm going home with John and Susanna, now," Elizabeth said. "I won't be able to come in tomorrow." Her lips brushed his forehead. "Leah and I will make sure your house is ready for your homecoming."

"Don't...work...too hard." He felt Elizabeth's gentle hand on his arm, then her warm lips on his. His worry eased, the medication had eliminated his pain, and he drifted into peaceful oblivion.

Expecting to work in the fields, Elizabeth put on her brown dress. Sitting at the kitchen table, she spooned oatmeal into Priscilla's mouth. The baby stuck her tiny fingers into the bowl of cereal, and before Elizabeth could grasp her hand, she smeared the creamy substance on her face and into her gold ringlets. Daniel made a face, but Jesse Mark giggled.

Leah had donned a faded dark-blue dress. She set a plate of scrambled eggs on the table. "I plan to help shock corn today."

"I told Elam I wouldn't be in."

Daniel straightened. "There's no school today, so I can help."

"Me, too." Jesse Mark bounced on his chair.

"You boys will stay out of the cornfield." Glaring at them, Mattie took a place at the table.

Elizabeth stifled a brusque retort, said a hasty prayer for patience, and smiled. "Are you intending to help us?"

Her straight back stiffened. "I have other responsibilities."

Leah helped herself to a slice of ham. "Like visiting Jonathan again today?"

The woman looked wounded. "I promised to meet some of the ladies to make quilts for AIDS babies."

How could Elizabeth argue with that? She had to hand it to Mattie. The woman knew how to get out of hard work. Would she actually stitch quilts or just play with her needle while she gleaned the hottest gossip? *Judge not*, ricochetted through her mind. She wanted to blame Mattie for bringing out the worst in her, but it was her own responsibility to control her thoughts.

Daniel remained silent, but his expression betrayed his determination. Evidently, the boy planned to wait until after Mattie's departure to approach the subject of shocking corn. Jesse Mark's grin remained constant. He chewed on a piece of toast, the sparkle in his blue eyes revealing his calculating little mind. Mattie would have to take stronger vitamins to outsmart Elam's sons.

Mattie ate, then went to her room to dress. Leah washed the breakfast dishes while Elizabeth settled Priscilla with Rachel and Jonah. Mattie finally hitched Bonny to the buggy and left.

Leah tied a fraying navy scarf around her head, a'la pirate style, and joined the boys on the porch. "Are you ready to help shock corn?"

Daniel's grin returned. Jesse Mark's broadened. After securing a dark-green scarf around her head, Elizabeth took the smallest boy's hand. Leah grasped Daniel's. Tim trotted with them to the cornfield. All morning they worked. It took eight to ten bound stalks of corn to build a sizable shock.

Elizabeth sighed. "It's noon, and it doesn't seem like we've done much."

Leah wiped a hand across her moist forehead. "The field always seems bigger at harvest time, but I thank God for the abundance of grain."

Jesse Mark struggled to drag another bound bunch of stalks to the nearly-finished shock. "I'm gittin' hungry, Mama Liz-beth."

"So am I. Shall we go to the house for sandwiches and lemonade?"

He nodded, bouncing his straw hat.

Daniel straightened from his bundle. "Listen."

Buggy wheels crunched and horse's hoofs clattered on stones as a conveyance came up the lane. Elizabeth's heart slumped as Mattie's buggy came into view. Her dark eyes rested momentarily on the boys, and her lips tightened.

Daniel sighed. "I think Aunt Mattie's mad again."

Jesse Mark giggled. "*Ja*, but she can't hurt us. Mama Liz-beth won't let her."

Elizabeth smothered a chuckle. If they needed corrected, discipline would be rendered, but not by Mattie Miller.

Leah moaned.

Following her line of vision, Elizabeth saw another buggy coming.

"That's probably the ladies who tried to visit us in the shed. Mattie knew we were in the cornfield and would look disheveled."

"Let's hide behind the corn shocks," Daniel said.

Leah laughed. "Elizabeth and I are too big." She glanced around. "Where's Jesse Mark?"

Grinning, Daniel pointed. "Inside that shock."

"Young man, *cume onn*. We're going to the house to meet those old bid . . . the ladies."

Elizabeth brushed bits of dried leaves from her skirt and checked the tie on the scarf she wore on her head. Did she look as unkempt as she felt?

Five women waited on the porch. All wore dresses of differing tones of dark-blue. A short, plump one sat on the swing, her feet scarcely touching the floor. A tall slender woman gripped a porch post. The other three were of average size. One of them strolled back-and-forth, one stared at the sky, and the youngest one chewed a fingernail. Mattie strode from the carriage shed, looking important.

"The tall skinny one is Kate Miller, a distant cousin," Leah whispered. "Brace yourself for her rebuttal."

As though on cue, Kate's gray-green eyes met Elizabeth's. Disapproval shimmered in their depths. Elizabeth felt Jesse Mark's fingers tighten around hers, providing comfort, yet, Kate's judgmental stare stung, even before the woman spoke.

Elizabeth forced a smile, praying her lack of confidence wouldn't encourage the woman to pounce.

Kate's chin rose a few degrees as her shoulders jerked back. "You're Elizabeth Stoltzfus?"

"*Ja.*" Elizabeth's smile felt frozen on her face. She prayed it appeared cordial. Her heart pounded as she approached the porch.

"I'm Kate Miller," the tall woman said.

Mattie took charge. Waving toward each of the other four women, she introduced them.

Elizabeth nodded to each, remembering only that Ella was the chubby one with the smiling round face. Somehow, she knew the woman would be a friend. The others seemed curious, but affable — except for Kate. Another Mattie?

Measuring each word with care, Elizabeth spoke. "Mattie will show you ladies to the living room. Leah and I will wash up in the summer kitchen, then join you."

All the ladies looked at Kate for approval, then followed Mattie into the house. Leah hurried to the summer kitchen, filled basins with water, and began to scrub Jesse Mark's hands. Elizabeth's mind whirled as she washed Daniel's face.

"You boys play on the porch until dinner," Leah said as she dumped the dirty water from the basin.

Removing her scarf, Elizabeth frowned at the pieces of corn tassel that had attached themselves to it. She quickly washed her face and donned a white prayer cap. "Shall we invite the ladies for dinner?"

"With my parents and Mattie, there's seven of us, not including Priscilla."

"Then five more won't matter."

Leah laughed. "What could we serve them?"

"I could whip up pancakes. You baked a chocolate cake this morning."

"It isn't iced!"

Elizabeth bit her lower lip. "How about sprinkling each piece with confectioner's sugar?"

"*Ja.* There's whipping cream."

"I saw a jar of Maraschino cherries in the pantry. We'll plop one on top of each piece and sprinkle them with chopped nuts."

"After the way Kate looked down her nose at you, you'd serve her cake?"

"It might sweeten her up a bit."

Leah chuckled. "No wonder Elam loves you."

A soft laugh bubbled up into Elizabeth's throat. "*Cume onn*, we'll face our foe together." She moved to the living room doorway. Her spirit shrank back as she met Kate's cool gray-green eyes. Smiling, she straightened her shoulders.

Kate sat stiffly on a ladder-backed chair. Tilting her chin, she opened her mouth, apparently preparing to accost Elizabeth.

19

Elizabeth stepped quickly into the living room. "Leah and I would like you ladies to stay for dinner," she said before Kate had a chance to speak.

The tall, skinny woman blinked in surprise, looked pensive, then nodded her consent. Watching her, the others smiled and agreed. Mattie seemed puzzled.

Pleasure fountained up within Elizabeth, and she knew that she'd done the right thing. In the kitchen, she got out a bowl, measured and sifted flour, and added baking powder. Suppressing a chuckle, she dumped in a little sugar to sweeten Kate. As she added the remaining ingredients, Leah made coffee, put the griddle on the stove to heat, and set the table.

"We can serve cottage cheese."

"There's only half enough," Leah whispered.

"Get a quart of peaches, dice them in a bowl and add the remaining cherries. If you mix the fruit with the cottage cheese, there'll be enough." Elizabeth tested the grill, then spooned batter onto it. "I should go for Priscilla and tell the old folks that dinner's about ready."

"I'll go. You'd have to parade through the center of the living room.

Warmth spread through Elizabeth. Leah was fast becoming another sister.

As they ate, Kate studied Elizabeth, making her uncomfortable. The other ladies waited for Kate's cues before they spoke. They acted like marionettes. Elizabeth wondered what happened when Kate, the puppeteer, dropped the strings and went home. Did the ladies then become animated or drop to the floor like a pile of lifeless sticks? Kate's right brow lifted, the left lowered. Elizabeth found herself keeping score. Which brow would win? She felt as though her acceptance hung in the balance.

"I'll serve the cake." When she stood, her legs felt weak. Determined not to display anxiety, she smiled, straightened her shoulders, and strolled to the counter. Leah rose to help serve. When Elizabeth placed a piece of cake in front of Ella, the chubby little woman's eyes lit up and she gripped her fork. Twirling it in her hand, she looked as though she could hardly wait for everyone to be served before she attacked her dessert. The plump fingers of her left hand played a staccato rhythm on the edge of the table. Smiling, Elizabeth took her place and lifted her fork. Instantly, Ella's utensil dug into the whipped topping and the tip of her tongue flicked across her upper lip in anticipation.

"We're proud of Elizabeth," Jonah said, clattering his cup to its saucer. "With Samuel gone and my other two sons in the hospital, Elizabeth and Leah do the housework and toil in the fields as well."

Elizabeth held her breath and watched Kate's brows. They wiggled, signifying the woman's indecision.

Rachel sipped her tea. "Elam's fortunate to have found Elizabeth."

"*Ja*. Elizabeth and her sweet child are already part of this family," Mattie said, evidently deciding not to be outdone.

Kate's brows lifted, held, then slowly relaxed. A smile curved her mouth for the first time. "We hope you can make it to the quilting next week, Elizabeth."

"*Danka dich*, Kate. I'd love to come, but Elam may be discharged from the hospital. If so, I might be unable to leave."

Swallowing her last bite of cake, Ella grinned. "That's loyalty."

Using her fork, Kate toyed with the cherry from the top of her desert, apparently saving it until last. "Are you ladies trying to shock the corn by yourselves?"

Leah eyed the woman. "We could use help, but—"

"I'll talk to my Jacob about coming to help." Kate looked at each of her friends in turn. "How about you ladies?"

They all agreed that their men would lend a hand. Ella smiled. "Harry can help with some of the plowing."

"How about the cattle shed?" Jonah asked. "It's partly cleaned out, but we could use some help there, too."

Elizabeth's breath caught. Would Jonah's question remind Kate of the day she and her friends hunted in the barn for she and Leah?

The youngest woman looked at Kate. "My husband will help load the spreader, Mama, if someone else will give him a hand."

After discussing the tasks that needed doing, Kate stood. "We'll help with these dishes, then we must be on our way."

Amish women were usually openly accepted into another group, but Kate's circle was different, supposedly because of Kate. Elizabeth had been approved of by the woman, so she would be readily accepted by the others. Taking a deep breath, she thanked God.

Three days passed. Exhaustion plagued Elizabeth when she returned from visiting Elam at the hospital. Trudging to the porch, she climbed the steps and entered the house. The neighboring men had helped with many tasks, but still she'd plowed all afternoon, then visited Elam in the evening. Crossing the kitchen, she paused in the living room doorway. Leah sat in a rocker darning a sock. "Elam's coming home tomorrow."

Plopping the half-finished sock into her sewing basket, Leah leaned back, and rocked. "Can he walk?"

"Not yet." Elizabeth moved to the couch and slumped onto it. "He'll need a downstairs bedroom. He wants to go to his own place, and he insists the boys stay there with him."

"It's natural for him to want to be home. He has four bedrooms upstairs." She chewed her lower lip. "You'll want to be there with him, but you can't stay unless I do. It wouldn't look right. Besides, if the boys are there, you'll need my assistance — until Elam is well."

"John rents one of the bedrooms. Elam has already hired him to help him until he's physically strong enough to take care of himself."

"Mattie said Jonathan is coming home, too. She can care for him and keep an eye on the old folks. If they need me, she can let me know. I'll go back and forth, filling in where I'm most needed."

Elizabeth massaged her temples, then rested her head against the back of the bench. "I wish Elam and I were married. As it is, John must assist him with his personal needs." She sighed. "Is Priscilla sleeping?"

"*Ja.* The boys are in bed, too." Leah yawned. "I made sure the old folks were comfortable. Mattie went to bed an hour ago." She yawned again. "I'm going up to my room, unless you want to talk more."

A yawn stretched Elizabeth's face. "I'm going to bed." She followed Leah up the stairs, but before undressing, she bent over the crib, peering at her little girl and thanking God for her blessings.

Elam sat in a wheelchair, staring out a window of his downstairs bedroom, watching his sons romp with Tim. How long would it be before he could wrestle in the yard with them? He'd been a positive thinking man, but recently he'd worn depression like a cloak. Would that ever change?

Staring at his legs, he sighed. The doctor had encouraged him to participate in therapy. Without medication, the pain was too great. With it, he felt too drugged to care. At times, determination to walk seized him, then doubt robbed his initiative, making him feel like half a man. Having to rely on another man to help him with his personal needs was humiliating. He tried to accept his situation, feeling that his anguish helped him relate more to Christ's suffering. At other times, he asked, *Why? Why!*

He watched Elizabeth cross the yard and approach the boys to offer each a cookie. Elam's heart warmed as his sons grinned up at her. The wind blew her burgundy skirt, making it billow around her legs. She grasped a hand of each of the boys and started down the lane toward his parent's home. Evidently she was taking a turn to check on them. *My wonderful Beth*, he thought, a lump swelling in his throat. *She deserves more than I can give her.*

"Time for your therapy," Leah said, sweeping into his room.

He waved her aside. "I'm too tired."

"That's not a reason, brother, it's an excuse, and I'm not buying it." She gripped the handles of his wheelchair and pushed him to the contraption John had made out of pipes.

"Go away, Leah." He glanced upward at the horizontal pipe she expected him to grasp to pull himself to his feet. He would have to hang on or fall on his face, for his legs refused to entirely support his weight. Since his left arm was still in a cast, he had to grip the pipe with one hand. Just the thought of straining made him yawn.

Leah nudged his arm. "If you won't accept therapy for me or for your own good, do it for Elizabeth."

"I've tried. Nothing changes."

"It takes time, Elam."

He fought an urge to yell at her. How could she know what he was going through? How could anyone with two good legs understand? Using his good hand, he whirled the chair, faced his bed, and grasped a handful of the quilt. Realizing he couldn't even throw himself across his bed, he fought despair. The only thing worse than helplessness was the aid he was forced to accept because of it. Did the doctors encourage therapy, believing it would help him physically, or were they hoping exercise would develop a more positive attitude?

Gripping the handles of his wheelchair, Leah maneuvered it to the beginning of the exercise pipes. "I can't force you, Elam. I just want what's best for you."

The pity evident in Leah's expression irritated him. "Go do your laundry."

"It's finished."

"Then scrub the floor and let me alone."

She hesitated, then left. He felt rotten. Slumping against the back of the chair, he ran the fingers of his right hand through his hair. What had he done to deserve this? He needed to use the bedside toilet, but couldn't manage without help. John wouldn't be back for an hour, and he refused to ask his sister. Gritting his teeth, he clenched his fist, and struck the arm of the wheelchair.

How can I ask Elizabeth to marry me, now? If he didn't improve, he wouldn't be able to go back to his construction job. The responsibility of raising the boys and Priscilla would fall on Elizabeth's shoulders. Gritting his teeth, he fought the urge to seize the oil lamp on his stand and hurl it against the wall. Anguish seared his soul, and his vision blurred as he reinforced the decision he'd reached the night before.

"Elam! You can't mean that." Tears brimmed in Elizabeth's lustrous velvety-brown eyes, then streamed down her lovely face.

He tightened his jaw, forbidding tears. "I'm doing what's best."

"But, if we were married, I could do more for you."

He shook his head. "Go back to Lancaster, Beth."

"I won't leave you."

Unable to witness her distress, he turned his chair and stared unseeingly out a window of his bedroom. "I won't marry you, Elizabeth. Under the circumstances, I can't."

"I believe you'll soon walk, again, Elam, but even if you don't, my love for you will never diminish."

"I reached my decision because of my love for you. I refuse

to tie you to an invalid."

"What if we'd already been married?"

"Then you'd be stuck with your lot."

"Elam, you're being ridiculous!"

He lifted his left arm, but the weight of the cast pulled it back to his lap. Covering his face with his right hand, he gasped for the air that no longer satisfied his lungs. "Don't make this more difficult, Beth. Please go back to Lancaster County and get on with your life."

"You can be stubborn if you like, Elam Miller, but I'm not leaving."

The tremor in her voice gripped his heart, but he strengthened his resolve. He wouldn't force her from his house, but he wouldn't marry her until he was on his feet.

"Elam?"

He refused to look up. Whirling, she fled. He closed his eyelids tightly, but tears forced their way between his lashes and rolled down his face. He prayed for wisdom and strength. A small hand on his knee encouraged him to open his eyes. Jesse Mark stood statuesque by the arm of the wheelchair, his eyes two blue spheres of quizzical innocence. His usual smile was gone, and his dimples were reduced to shadowy indentations.

"Papa, what'd you do to make Mama Liz-beth cry?"

The lump in Elam's throat doubled in size. How could he explain his situation to a three-year-old? He knew his decision would devastate Elizabeth, but he'd failed to realize how it would hurt his sons. A shadow by the door caught his attention, and he turned his head to face Daniel.

The boy's brown-green eyes appeared dulled. "Aunt Leah said you were goin' to send Mama Elizabeth away. Is it true?"

Elam felt caught in a vice. Life was crushing him, and he felt as though he were about to explode from the inside. "Daniel, I wish you could understand."

"Then it really is true." Tears pooled in the little boys eyes, but his lips drew tight as though he were determined not to cry. He spun, raced from the room, and across the kitchen. The screen slammed.

Elam felt the percussion in his heart. Jesse Mark had pressed his face into Elam's lap. Now sobs shook his small frame. Elam rested a hand on the boy's shoulders, feeling the anguish in his own soul.

Jesse Mark straightened, his chubby cheeks tear stained and crystal droplets sparkled on his long blond lashes. "You're hurtin' Prissy-cilla, too. You was gonna be her Papa, now she won't have a Papa, again."

The words pierced Elam's heart, and misery racked his spirit. Could the boy have said anything that could have cut deeper? "I love Elizabeth with all my heart, and I adore Priscilla as though I were her Papa. I wish things could be different. Maybe someday they will be, but for now, Son, I don't know what else I can do."

"Ask Jesus. You said He always helps us."

"*Ja*, but this is different."

"Ferwass?" He blinked, causing a stray tear to roll down his chubby pink cheek.

Elam hugged him. "You keep believing. Jesus will work this out." The words had been meant to encourage the little boy, but a seed of hope sprouted within his own heart, too. His son was right. God would work this out according to His plan. He would wait and accept whatever the Lord willed.

"You go and cheer up Daniel. Tell him Jesus will work things out." Elam watched Jesse Mark scamper from the room. The boy's faith helped his to grow. Still, his circumstances created anguish.

"*Vell*, Elam." Propping a fist on her hip, Leah glared. "What are you going to do about this mess you're creating?"

"There's nothing I can do."

"If you really cared, brother, you'd try physical therapy." She sniffed. "Your stubbornness is ruining your entire dream — not to mention Elizabeth's or the *kinders*. When your life crumbles, don't blame anyone but yourself." Huffing, she left the room.

Elam clenched his fist. How could his sister have turned against him? His adrenalin flowing, he stretched his right arm upward, seized the pipe, and yanked himself to his feet. Pain shot through his legs, but Dr. Peters had told him to expect that. Gritting his teeth, he took a grip farther along the pipe, forced his right leg forward, then dragged the left to match it. Taking a deep breath, he swung his left leg forward, then drew the right one up beside it. After six steps, he found himself at the side of his bed. Letting go, he collapsed across it.

A hearty chuckle drew his attention to the door. Leah stood, her arms folded, a smug expression capturing her features. Crossing the room, she stood near him. "I'm sorry I had to make you mad, but it worked. Now that you know you can do it, I expect you to put forth that effort four times a day."

"Female tyrant," Elam said, grinning at his youngest sister.

Elizabeth lay facedown on the living room bench, her head on her arms. How could her life have fallen apart so completely? Why was Elam being so difficult? "I'll never leave him," she vowed. *Thou wilt keep him in perfect peace whose mind is stayed on thee,* drifted into her mind, revitalizing her spirit. "Because he trusteth in thee," she whispered.

Sitting, she blew her nose and took a deep breath. There was too much to do to spend time crying. She'd prayed her heart out. She must rely completely on God. She straightened. Was Elam laughing? Had the man gone mad? Hurrying to his room, she peered in. He sat on the edge of the bed, grinning at Leah. When he noticed her, the old familiar luster crept into his eyes.

"We're going to make it, Beth."

Crossing the room in swift strides, she flung her arms around his neck. The force of her embrace knocked him flat on the bed. Unwilling to let go, she went down with him.

Leah laughed.

At the sound of little feet, Elizabeth sat up. Reaching a hand to Elam, she helped him to a sitting position. Daniel and Jesse Mark stood wide-eyed in the center of the room.

Elam laughed again, the sound rippling through Elizabeth, buoying her spirit, and swelling her heart with joy.

"You gonna stay, Mama Liz-beth?" Jesse Mark asked.

"Oh, *ja*."

"I'll have to push myself to do a lot of therapy," Elam said, his brow furrowing. "If I hope to get back to work in a couple of months, I must strengthen my legs."

A buggy stopped in front of the house. Leah hurried to greet the visitor. Within minutes she returned with Amos Yoder. He looked as though trouble had accompanied him. Urging the boys from the room, Leah softly closed the door.

Elam smiled, but apprehension toyed with his features. The solemn expression on his brother-in-law's face made a cold chill travel down Elizabeth's spine.

Amos's brow furrowed. "Our construction boss sent me to inform you that. . ."

Watching him fumble with the rim of his straw hat, Elizabeth's stomach cramped. She could smell dismay as pungent as smoke.

Amos drew a long breath. "The boss wants me to explain the company's policy for collecting compensation."

"I wasn't injured on the job."

"He said since you were on your way to work, he'd see to it that you were taken care of."

"That won't be necessary. I'll be back to work before too long."

Amos looked nervous and uncomfortable. "The boss said I should explain that you qualify to collect a Social Security disability pension."

Elam's lips parted. "Didn't you remind him that we Amish don't believe in Social Security?"

"*Ja*, but he said it's the best the company can do."

Elam gripped the bed post. "I can't accept Social Security. You knew I wouldn't, Amos."

Elizabeth moved a straight-backed wooden chair closer to Elam's bed and motioned to Amos.

Seemingly relieved to sit, he slumped onto it. "The boss said you have no other choice, if you plan to support your boys."

"But, I told you I'd be back to work after the first of the year."

Amos's face creased as though he were in pain. "The boss said to tell you, you had no choice." He drew a long breath. "He's not going to permit you to return. Elam, you have no job waiting."

The color drained from Elam's face. He gripped the bed post as though he felt dizzy. "He can't do this."

"I hated to come here, but the boss insisted. He told me to explain that he's responsible for the safety of the men who work for him. After an injury as severe as yours, he says he can't be sure you won't get hurt on the job. Besides, he feels other men would be relying on you."

"You agree with him?"

"No." He made a helpless gesture with his hands. "I'm only repeating what he told me to say." He gripped Elam's good hand. "*Es spied mich.*"

"Being sorry won't feed my family."

"We'll all help, Elam. We won't leave you needy."

Elam's face reddened. "Why should I accept charity when I can work?"

"Take it easy for awhile." Amos sighed. "When you're back on your feet, you can apply for work elsewhere."

Clenching his fingers, Elam struck the bed post. "Jobs are difficult to find. Besides, my training and experience is in building construction."

"I know. This upsets all of us. We'll pray for a solution." Amos looked miserable. "The boss said If you decide to accept a disability pension, just let him know, and he'll help you fill out an application."

The flesh around Elam's mouth turned white. "No job." His voice was a choked whisper. "No job. No income." His voice dropped until Elizabeth could hardly hear. "No income, no marriage."

Her new-found joy drained as though a bottomless pit had

opened in her heart. Her fingers clenched into fists.

Elam's boss had no right to tell him he couldn't return to work. It was too bad that Amish didn't believe in suing. Elam had rights, didn't he?

Elam gritted his teeth. "He can't do this."

"Will you sue?"

"I can't do that, Beth." He sighed, and his shoulders slumped.

I'll do something, she vowed, her lips drawing taut. Recalling her sister's last letter, a shadow of an idea flitted across her mind. What if . . .

Elam studied her. "Beth, what are you thinking?"

20

Trying not to squirm under Elam's scrutiny, Elizabeth smiled, hoping to appear relaxed.

He sat on the edge of his bed, his gaze unwavering. "You're devising some plan, aren't you?"

She waved her hand, feigning nonchalance. With Amos Yoder's green eyes fixed curiously on her, she remained silent. Her idea was in its elementary stages. It could fizzle, and she didn't wish to build Elam's hopes only to have them dashed.

The black flecks in his eyes seemed to intensify. "*Vell?*"

"We must believe that God will guide us, Elam."

Amos stood, straw hat in hand. "I want to visit awhile with Leah, and I promised Susanna I wouldn't be long." He moved to the door, paused, and turned back. "I told Leah I'd help with some of the plowing next week. If I can do anything for you in the meantime, let me know."

Elam sighed. "*Danka dich.*"

Witnessing Elam's torment created a lump in Elizabeth's throat that grew as she thought about the canceled wedding. She would concentrate on bolstering his courage while she struggled with a solution. First, she would write to Sarah and set a time to call when her sister could be at the phone shack near the Beiler farm.

Gripping the receiver, Elizabeth ran her trembling fingers over the rough windowsill of the phone shack near Miller's. She watched Susanna and John through the glass as she counted the rings that reverberated in her ear. Susanna's purple skirt whipped in the breeze. She tugged her navy-blue cape closer about her neck. John stood close to her, peering into her upturned face. Adoration blazed between them. Elizabeth thought about the complications of their relationship and sighed.

"*Vea-gaits.*" Sarah sounded out of breath.

"It's Elizabeth." An image of her blond, blue-eyed younger sister played before her, warming her heart. "How's everyone?"

"Fine, but busy." She laughed. "Joseph picked me up in his carriage. We were talking, and I almost didn't make it here in time for your call."

Elizabeth laughed. "Just talking?"

"*Vell. . .*" There was music in her sister's tone that portrayed her joy. "Are you going to be able to come home for my wedding?"

The word *wedding* ricochetted through Elizabeth, then lodged painfully in her heart. "I hope to, Sarah, but Elam needs me close for awhile."

"How is he?"

"He's improving physically, but. . ."

"I hear anguish in your voice, Elizabeth. What's wrong?"

"Elam lost his job. Unless he can secure employment, there'll be no wedding on this end."

"Oh, no. Is there anything I can do?"

"That's why I called." Trying to keep a tremor from her voice, she continued. "In your letter, you said Aaron King's planning to expand his cabinet making business and that Rebecca mentioned he was going to hire an assistant. Has he found anyone?"

"Rebecca hasn't mentioned finding anyone suitable."

Elizabeth felt her heart lurch, then beat faster. "Do you think Aaron would consider hiring Elam?"

"Oh!" After a brief silence, Sarah's enthusiasm blossomed. "You could come home!"

"Don't get me too excited, Sister. Please talk to Aaron. If there's a possibility of things working out, have him write to Elam."

"I will. Oh I will!"

"Don't say anything to Mama until we're sure, Sarah. I don't want to build up her hope and then disappoint her and the others."

"I'll tell Joseph, though. We don't keep secrets from each other."

"Good girl." Elizabeth smiled. Joy swelled within her as she thanked God for her faithful loving family. "Good-bye, for now."

"Keep the faith, Elizabeth. Your wedding will happen, too."

Elizabeth hung up, encouraged, yet dubious. Would Aaron give Elam a job? If so, her task would be to convince Elam to move to Lancaster County. Was that too much to hope for?

She got into the middle seat of the van. Susanna sat in front with John. On the way back to Miller's, she thought about her house, livestock, and carriage. She'd planned to sell her property after she and Elam were married. Her pulse quickened. Dare she dream of returning home with Elam and his boys? Would he agree to leaving Mercer County until Jonathan was fully recovered? Could he leave his aging parents? Although questions bombarded her brain, her heart rejoiced. *Oh, God*, she prayed, *please bless my hopes and dreams.*

On the way up Miller's lane, she hummed to the tune of the melody in her heart, hardly noticing the admiring glances that electrified the air between Susanna and John. When he parked in front of Elam's house, Elizabeth got out of the vehicle and strode to the white picket gate.

Leah stepped onto the porch, excitement turning her cheeks a rosy pink. Wind whipped her faded dark-blue dress, but she seemed to ignore the chilly October air. Elizabeth clutched at her black cape as she hurried up the walk. Pausing on the top step, she turned to wave to Susanna as John turned his van and headed down the lane.

"Mattie's pregnant," Leah whispered.

Oh no! Elizabeth thought. *That poor little unborn angel.*

Clutching her hand, Leah pulled her inside and closed the door, but didn't stop until they were in the living room.

"Leah, where are the *kinder*?"

"In with Elam. Mattie stopped here on her way home. She's so happy."

"Happy?" Elizabeth echoed, untying the strings of her black bonnet.

"*Ja*! I never dreamed Mattie wanted a baby so badly." She bounced to the bench. "She broke down and cried. She said not being able to conceive had made her bitter and resentful."

Taking off her bonnet and cape, Elizabeth flung them over the end of the bench and sat down. "Is that going to change?"

"It's already starting to perform a miracle in Mattie. She asked me to pray that God would mellow her and make her the best wife and mother in our district. She hugged me and asked me to forgive her for her past nastiness."

"*Danka dich, Got*," Elizabeth whispered, knowing if Mattie really changed it would be easier for Elam to move back to Bird-in-Hand and trust that the woman would do her share to care for his parents. "Does Jonathan know about the baby?"

"Mattie told him this afternoon as soon as she got him home from the hospital. He's ecstatic."

"He'll be grateful for the change in Mattie."

Leah rolled her eyes. "Won't we all?"

Furrow by furrow, the neighbors, along with Elizabeth, finished plowing two fields. Learning how to handle the horses to turn a straight furrow gave Elizabeth callouses, but also increased her confidence. Amos helped Leah sow the winter wheat. Elizabeth noticed the fondness the couple had for each other and wondered.

As November approached, the Millers had a corn-husking party. Elizabeth picked up two red ears, and since a red ear symbolizes fertility, Mattie teased Elam about preparing for a larger family. They all laughed when Mattie got a red ear, too. The many hands soon had the grain in the corn crib.

Amos supervised filling the silo. Elizabeth thought about Aaron King's cabinet business and worried over why he hadn't written to Elam.

"Your move, Daniel." Elizabeth sat in the middle of the living room floor across from him, a Chinese checker board between them. She'd been teaching him the rules and how to play the game. Jesse Mark played nearby with his wooden blocks.

Grinning, Daniel hopped one of his red marbles in a zigzag pattern the entire way across the board.

Elizabeth clapped her hands. "That's good."

"Elizabeth!"

She jumped as Elam's voice reverberated through the house. Jesse Mark's eyes widened, and he dropped a block, demolishing one side of his loosely constructed building. Daniel blinked, his hand hovering in the air above the marbles.

"Elizabeth!"

She leaped to her feet, swishing her warm-brown skirt. Her heart pounded as she raced to Elam's bedroom. She expected to find him on the floor or hung up in the rope contraption Amos had devised to aid Elam's therapy, but he sat in his wheelchair by the window, gripping a sheet of paper.

He flipped the letter until it crinkled. "What's the meaning of this?"

Cautiously, she crossed the room to accept the proffered paper. When she saw the signature at the bottom, she grinned. "It looks like a letter from Aaron King. What's he want?"

"You don't know?"

She shrugged. "I could guess. Sarah wrote to me about Aaron needing to hire an assistant. She said he was extremely choosy, so it made it difficult for him to find a suitable employee."

"And you made a suggestion?"

She shrugged. "I simply mentioned the name of a man who

could be the perfect solution to his dilemma."

Elam laughed. "You are a meddling female, woman, but I love you. Aaron has offered me the job."

She gasped. "Then our problem is solved."

"Not that easily, Beth." He sobered. "We'd have to move to Lancaster County."

"Would that be difficult? I still own the house and some acreage in Bird-in-Hand."

He looked pensive. "My salary would be less than I was making before the accident."

"We could manage."

"Aaron promises a sizeable raise when I'm able to take on more of the responsibility." He sighed. "It wouldn't be easy. My experience is in construction. I'm not a cabinet-maker."

"What's the difference? You've worked with wood. You'd just be constructing smaller things."

He laughed. "You sound like a woman."

"Oh, Elam, won't you give it a try? Aaron is understanding. He'd train you."

Scratching his beard, he withdrew into silence, his brow furrowing.

"Now that Mattie's pregnant, she's changing into a likeable person, Elam. She has already taken on more responsibility."

His frown deepened. "*Ja*, but . . ."

"If you're worried about your parents, we can take them with us. We'll give them the downstairs bedroom and use the upstairs ourselves."

His brows rose. "You're assuming we'll be married?"

"*Ja*."

He grasped her wrist, pulled her forward, and dumped her onto his lap. "Your tenacious determination is one thing I love about you, woman — along with your faith and trust in God."

Smiling, she traced his lower lip with a finger. His eyes became lustrous, his head lowered, and his mouth covered hers in a long ardent kiss.

He drew inches away and grinned crookedly as his gaze

caressed her. "Would three weeks be long enough to prepare for a wedding?"

"That would be perfect, Elam Miller. Sarah and Joseph are being married in three weeks, and I don't want to miss it. Maybe we can have a double wedding."

He hugged her. "We have to make a lot of quick decisions."

"God will guide us." She kissed his warm tender lips. "And, I have a man who knows how to put plans into action."

"I can't walk, yet, Beth."

"No problem. Sarah said that Rebecca told her there's plenty to do that you can manage from a wheelchair. As your legs gain strength, you'll gradually take on more responsibility in the shop."

His right brow quirked. "You didn't read Aaron's letter. How do you know so much about his proposition?"

"*Vell*. . .maybe it was hope. . .or," her voive trailed off.

"Or someone conniving behind my back."

She laughed softly. Her embrace tightened as she caressed his lips with hers. His kiss was gentle, at first, then as his ardor rose, the pressure of his mouth increased.

Several moments later, a noise drew her attention to the doorway. Two little boys watched, wide-eyed. Daniel blinked.

Jesse Mark grinned, deepening his dimples. "Does this mean that Liz-beth is our mama, again?"

Elam's laugh was deep. It's resonance reverberated through Elizabeth, creating a melody of love in her heart. The past two months had been difficult, but her faith had grown and her spirit had gained strength. She marveled at how the power of God had reached through their adversity and blessed them.

"How would you boys like to move to Lancaster County?" Elam asked.

Jesse Mark bounced, making his blond curls bob on his forehead. "When can we go?"

Elizabeth's heart rejoiced, then she noticed Daniel's scowl. Planting his feet, he crossed his arms. "I'm not leavin'."

Elizabeth suddenly realized ripping the boy from his roots

would be the first of many snags before they could hope to reach a workable solution.

A horse and buggy rattled up the lane at top speed. It jerked to a stop, then footsteps resounded on the porch. The kitchen door burst open. "Oh, Leah," Susanna sobbed, "I'm so miserable, I want to die."

Elizabeth hurried to the kitchen. "Susanna."

The woman flung herself into Elizabeth's arms. "The Bishop came to see me this afternoon. He said if I don't stop seeing John he'll take it before the church and I'll be shunned!" Tears streamed down her face, and her slender shoulders shook. "I love John so much. What am I going to do?"

Patting the woman's shoulder, Elizabeth murmured soothing phrases, but knew they could have little affect. She'd seen this coming, but had felt powerless to change the course of Susanna's emotions.

"Come in the room and sit, Susanna," Leah coaxed. "I've made tea."

Sniffing, Susanna moved to the living room and slumped onto the center of the bench. "John said if it came to this, he'd leave. He says he loves me too much to cause me torment." Tears had turned her long lashes to a deeper gold. She blinked, causing another crystal droplet to roll down her ashen cheeks. "What does he think leaving me will do?" She dabbed at her red, swollen eyes with her wet handkerchief.

Sitting beside Susanna, Elizabeth rested a hand on the younger woman's forearm, although she knew the gesture couldn't offer much comfort.

Leah came in, sat on the other side of Susanna and pressed a mug of steaming tea into her free hand. "John loves you. I'm sure the two of you can work this out."

"He said he's leaving in a few days!" Susanna sipped the brew, then handed the mug back to Leah as a new flood of sobs wracked her slender frame.

Daniel and Jesse Mark had been watching from the doorway. They stepped aside as Elam wheeled his chair into the room. Since his broken left arm made maneuvering a manual wheelchair too difficult, he'd been loaned an electric one. Concern shadowed his face.

Susanna looked up. "I'm going to be shunned," she wailed, her fist clenching her sodden handkerchief.

"*Ja, vell* . . ." His brow furrowed. "You'll have to decide what your love is worth and make whatever sacrifice seems most acceptable to you."

"I can't give John up." She looked pale and vulnerable. "But, I can't live through shunning. Amos would have to turn his back on me. Mama would be forbidden to speak to me or eat at the same table!" She gasped as a sob choked her. "I'd lose all my friends and family. Even you."

Elam ran his fingers through his hair. "You knew John was a Beachy before you fell in love with him. Didn't you know you'd have to choose between him and your Amish church?"

"I thought we could just be friends, but our feelings got out of hand."

Compassion washed over Elizabeth. How many times had she heard that refrain? Which ever choice Susanna made, her heart would be broken. If she chose her family, she would yearn for the man she loved. If she married him, the shunning would be irrevocable, and painful.

The next afternoon, Elizabeth wrung out the last of her hand wash, grasped the small basket of wet items, and left the summer kitchen. As she clipped the last garment to the clothesline, Leah's squeal of delight aroused her curiosity. Heading to the front yard, she heard voices and paused to check her medium-blue dress for damp spots or lint. Presentable, she hurried on, but stopped when she caught sight of the visitor.

A slender, clean shaven man about five-foot-ten stood in the center of the yard. He looked to be in his early twenties. His straw hat lay on the grass, allowing the October sun to shimmer on his honey-colored waves. His turquoise eyes sparkled, lighting up his handsome features, and a vibrant smile created slight indentions that threatened to become dimples but didn't quite succeed. He held his arms open for Leah. "*Vea-gaits!*"

Leah raced to greet him.

Samuel, Elizabeth thought, glancing at his black broadfalls and blue cotton shirt.

After a quick hug, Leah poked him playfully. "Where have you been?"

He laughed, the resonance joyous. "Where haven't I been?"

She propped her fists on her hips, but her grin ruined her apparent attempt to appear austere. "You old prodigal!"

"How's everyone?"

"Didn't you stop at the main house yet?"

He shook his head. "I wanted to test the water before I splashed into it."

"That's a new twist for you, Brother."

After a slight hesitation, she said, "Jonathan had a heart attack, but he's improving. Elam's in the house recuperating from a serious accident."

The man sobered. "If I'd known, I would've come home."

Elizabeth strode toward them. The man glanced at her. His brow furrowed, but then a generous smile curved his mouth. "Elizabeth Beiler?"

"I was. And you're Samuel."

"*Ja*. The incurable runaway." Scooping his hat from the grass, he plopped it onto his head. He motioned toward the fields. "Since Jonathan and Elam are laid up, who did all the work?"

Before either woman could answer, Daniel and Jesse Mark shoved the screen door open. "Uncle Samuel!" they cried, racing into the yard.

He scooped a boy into each arm. Whirling in a generous circle, he whooped. Leah glanced at Elizabeth, shrugged, turned her hands palms-up, and grinned.

Leah yawned. The children were asleep and she longed to go to bed, yet Susanna's dilemma gripped her heart. She paused in the living room doorway to watch Elizabeth pacing back-and-forth. "You look exhausted. Why don't you go to bed?"

Sighing, Elizabeth sat in the rocker. "I want Elam to stay with me in my house near Bird-in-Hand so I'll be close if he needs me." She frowned. "That wouldn't look right — until we're married."

"Your in-laws live close. Maybe you could stay with them."

"I'd be welcome, but Moses's brother Abe lives there. Before I came to Mercer County, he asked me to marry him."

Leah hid her surprise behind another yawn. "What about Elam staying at Emma's?"

Elizabeth laughed. "Emma has seven *kinder* with an eighth coming soon. With Elam's sons added to that rambunctious brood, I'm afraid the chaos wouldn't be conducive to Elam's recovery."

"*Ja.*" Leah leaned back against the bench, but suddenly a solution caused her to sit straight. "I've been longing to visit Emma. Samuel's home. He could live here and look after the farm. Now that Mattie is willing to care for my parents, I could go to Bird-in-Hand with you and Elam. If I stay at your house, you can be there, too."

A smile brightened Elizabeth's tired features. "Elam can use the downstairs bedroom. I have three rooms on the second floor. You can use my guest room. I'll sleep in one with Priscilla. We can move my quilting frames and arrange the third room for the boys.

Leah laughed. "I'll be there for Sarah's wedding, and yours."

"*Ja!*" Standing, Elizabeth stretched. "Now that my housing problem is solved, I'm going to bed."

"*Ja,*" Leah said with a sigh. "Now all we have to deal with is Daniel's refusing to leave Mercer County."

Gripping the pipe above his head, Elam slowly made his way across his bedroom, then dropped into a chair by the window. His legs were gaining strength, but still couldn't support his entire weight. Crutches could have helped, if it hadn't been for his broken left arm. He would be forced to use a wheelchair until he was strong enough to manage walking with a cane.

He frowned. The past two days he'd worried about Susanna. She wasn't his responsibility, yet he longed to help her find a solution to her problem. A vehicle stopped in front of the house. Elam watched out the window as John climbed from his van and headed up the walk.

John entered the room, his face downcast. "I've come for the lecture I know I deserve, Elam."

"Marry her."

John's sandy brows lifted, and his green eyes widened. "What?"

"Marry Susanna and take her to Lancaster County. Your church will accept her."

John looked stunned. "She would anguish over losing her family." He sighed. "I've been praying, Elam. I'm considering joining the Old Order Amish church. I'd have to give up my van and find another means of earning a living, but Susanna's worth the sacrifice. Do you think she'd be willing to live in Lancaster County?"

"Ask her."

"I need to work out some details first."

Elizabeth appeared at the open door, her smile brightening the room. "I just received a letter from my sister. I wrote to her concerning Susanna. Sarah thinks a vacation would help her clear her thinking. She offered to share her bedroom. After Sarah and Joseph are married and living at King's farm, Susanna can have Sarah's room to herself."

Elam nodded. "Esther and Isaac would enjoy Susanna's company."

John appeared pleased. "I love Susanna dearly. The thought of leaving without her devastated me, yet I didn't dare hope to take her along." He sobered, then looked pensive. "With Susanna, the two of you, Leah, and the *kinder*, there won't be room in my van for your packed boxes. And what about furniture?"

Elam smiled. "Sam's going to live here. I'm leaving most of my furniture for him. Elizabeth has what we'll need, but I hired a man with a pick-up to take our personal items. We'd like to leave by the end of the week, if you can manage."

Agreeing, John shook Elam's hand and left, a new spring in his steps.

"Oh, Elam." Elizabeth clasped her hands. "Rebecca Wenger said she was searching for her garden of Eden and found it unexpectedly with Aaron King in Eden, Pennsylvania." She smiled. "You'll be working there, and going back to Bird-In-Hand will be like returning to our garden of Eden."

He chuckled. "Living with you, Beth, will be like abiding in Eden."

Elizabeth had most of the dishes, pillows, and quilts packed, and she began to collect the boy's personal items. Daniel entered the room and removed his orange ball from the box.

"I'm stayin' here." His declaration was not as strong as it had been, but the set to his small shoulders remained.

Elizabeth brushed a piece of lint from her blue dress and studied his small face. "I know change is difficult, Daniel. You must feel like I did when I packed to leave Bird-in-Hand."

He searched her face. "You didn't want to come here to live?"

"I didn't want to leave my family and friends, but I loved your father enough to make the sacrifice."

"*Ja.*" He turned the ball over in his hands and stared at it. "I love Papa, too."

Taking the small drawstring bag containing his marbles from his dresser, she dropped them into the corner of the box and sat on a stool near him. "I thought you'd decide you wanted to go when you knew Leah was going with us."

"Vell. . .there's still Tim."

Laughing, she pulled him onto her lap. "Your dog and I had a long talk. When I told him about Lancaster County, he became anxious to go — unless you refused to."

The boy looked expectant. "You mean Tim can *cume* along?"

"*Ja.* Your Aunt Susanna is coming, too."

Sighing, he tossed his ball back into the box.

"I'm not saying it will be easy, Daniel, but Jesus will help you."

His troubled hazel eyes met hers. "Did Jesus help you?"

"*Ja.* You have a lot of good things to look forward to." She smiled. "For one thing, in my district we're permitted to have bathrooms in the house."

His countenance brightened slightly. "Can I take a bath in the tub?"

"*Ja.* Every night if you want to."

He pursed his lips, then slowly nodded. "I guess I can try living in Bird-in-Hand."

"Your Papa and I will make it as easy as we can." She hugged him. "Your cousins are looking forward to playing with you."

"I never saw them."

"Getting to know your Aunt Emma's children is only one blessing. You'll have lots."

"*Ja,* he said slowly. "I guess it won't be so bad." Sliding from her lap, he headed for the door. "I'm gonna tell Jesse Mark."

Elizabeth smiled.

The next day, when John stopped his van in front of Elam's house, the boys ran to get in, both securing a spot in the back seat by a window. John helped Elam to the van while Elizabeth rapidly collected Priscilla's last-minute items. Clutching the baby, she climbed into the vehicle, smoothed her burgundy skirt, and sat on the middle seat next to Elam.

Pale, but smiling, Susanna sat in the front seat with John. She was distraught over leaving her mother, but since John was returning to Lancaster County, she was grateful for the invitation to stay with the Isaac Beilers for a time. John had proposed and told her he planned to join the Old Order Amish church. Her sparkling blue eyes and stolen glances at him portrayed her hope that things would work out. Elizabeth prayed for their happiness.

Both boys had brought a large pillow. Sighing, Leah crammed into the back seat between them.

"Cume onn, Tim!" Daniel called, giggling when the canine scrambled aboard.

"Stay down, Tim!" Leah sounded disgusted as she jerked her head away from the dog's wet kiss.

Reaching, Daniel roughed the collie's head. "Good boy."

As they traveled, Leah played games with the boys, John explained Lancaster Amish customs to Susanna, Elizabeth chatted to Elam about the upcoming weddings, and the first two hours of the trip seemed to pass quickly.

At noon, John pulled the van into a rest stop where they could relax and enjoy the picnic Mattie had packed. After munching a sandwich and guzzling a cup of lemonade, the boys took Tim for a romp, visited the rest room twice, caught bugs, played with a dead bird, threw stones, then crawled back into the van to share the seat with their aunt.

Leah wrinkled her nose. "We're only halfway, and I already need a gas mask!"

Daniel laughed. "Tim doesn't smell that bad."

"I wasn't referring to only the dog." She brushed at a smear of mud on her dark-blue skirt. Retrieving a handkerchief she dabbed her face. "I'll be glad when we get there."

Straining against his seat belt, Jesse Mark bounced. "Me too!" Eagerness sparkling in his blue eyes, he stared out one window, then another.

Jostling the tired cranky baby, Elizabeth sighed.

"Let me cuddle her awhile." Leah reached for the sleepy baby.

The afternoon lagged, but finally they entered Lancaster

County. Elizabeth's heart raced in anticipation. Elam withdrew into silence, apparently pondering his new job. Spying the Bird-in-Hand sign, Elizabeth clasped her hands and struggled to control her eagerness. "Home," she whispered.

Elam put his arm around her.

Her vision blurred with joyous tears as John stopped the van in front of her house. Abe had painted the porch and built a ramp for Elam's wheelchair, although the conveyance was temporary. It was Abe's way of giving his blessing.

As Elizabeth climbed from the van, the October wind swept under her cape, it's frosty fingers threatening. Scattered snowflakes kissed her cheeks, but the warmth in her heart overpowered the chill.

Minerva's tail swept and curled, but she sat regally, a queenly feline, enthroned on a porch chair. Vashti raced from the barn. Yipping, she circled Elizabeth. Tim woofed a welcome.

Elam grasped the edge of the van as he clambered unsteadily to his feet. Gripping the vehicle for support, he reached for Elizabeth's hand.

Their fingers entwined. "We're home," she whispered. "Our return to Eden."

"*Ja, Beth.*" His fingers tightened around hers. "Our own special garden."

The End

DOG JACK, beloved mascot of the 102nd Regiment of the Pennsylvania Volunteers, comes to life again through this historical novel. Written by Florence Biros, the story is told through the eyes of Jed, a runaway slave boy, who identifies with Dog Jack. Thousands have responded to this unique Civil War drama depicting the life of Pittsburgh's canine hero. Wounded in battle three times — once critically — he was actually held prisoner of war for six months until being exchanged for a Confederate soldier. Illustrated with pictures of the 125th Reenactment at Gettysburg. Four-color portrait cover. Trade paper. 0-936369-47-7. **$7.95.**

A visit to her New England roots led Elizabeth Shaffer to extensive research and the writing of **DAUGHTER OF THE DAWN**. Descended from Pilgrims Elizabeth Tilley and John Howland, she has created an intriguing romance. Against the background of the storm-lashed voyage of the Mayflower and the privations of the first year of Plymouth Colony, Elizabeth Tilley battles her love for John Howland who is engaged to her best friend. Photos of Mayflower, Plymouth Plantation replicas, and English ports. Four-color portrait cover. Trade paper. ISBN-0-936369-72-8. **$7.95.**

143 Greenfield Road, New Wilmington, PA 16142
1-800-358-0777